UNIVERSITY OF
WINCHESTER

KA 0031981 3

THE NEW WESSEX EDITION
OF THE STORIES OF THOMAS HARDY
VOLUME THREE

OLD MRS CHUNDLE AND OTHER STORIES

WITHDRAWN FROM
THE LIBRARY
UNIVERSITY OF
WINCHESTER

'Upheld by the rope I floated across to the spot under the opening', an illustration from the periodical publication of 'Our Exploits at West Poley', in The Household, *March 1893*

THE NEW WESSEX EDITION

Old Mrs Chundle and Other Stories

with

The Famous Tragedy of the Queen of Cornwall

THOMAS HARDY

EDITED BY
F. B. Pinion

THE NEW WESSEX EDITION OF THE STORIES OF THOMAS HARDY
VOLUME THREE

Editorial arrangement, introduction and notes
© Macmillan London Ltd 1977
Typography © Macmillan London Ltd 1977

Thomas Hardy's texts © as follows:
'The Famous Tragedy of the Queen of Cornwall'
© Macmillan London Ltd
All other texts included in this volume
© Trustees of the Hardy Estate

'An Indiscretion in the Life of an Heiress' is reproduced
by arrangement with Hutchinson & Co.

ISBN: 0 333 19983 9

All rights reserved. No part of this publication may
be reproduced or transmitted, in any form or by any means,
without permission.

The New Wessex Edition first published 1977 by
MACMILLAN LONDON LTD
London and Basingstoke
Associated companies in New York Dublin
Melbourne Johannesburg & Delhi

Published in the United States by
ST MARTIN'S PRESS INC.
175 Fifth Avenue, New York

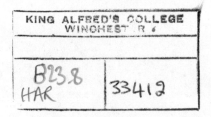

KING ALFRED'S COLLEGE
WINCHESTER

B23.8
HAR   33412

Printed in Great Britain by
WESTERN PRINTING SERVICES LTD
Bristol

Contents

List of Illustrations

Introduction

OF THE two other volumes of Hardy's short stories in the New Wessex Edition, the first contains *Wessex Tales* and *A Group of Noble Dames*, the second *Life's Little Ironies* and *A Changed Man*. This third volume is devoted mainly to short stories which have remained hitherto uncollected. Four of these have never previously been published in Great Britain.

The collection is arranged as follows: stories intended for adult readers; a longer story or novelette adapted from Hardy's first (unpublished) novel, 'The Poor Man and the Lady'; outlines of stories which he never completed; and two stories for young people. Hardy's late poetic drama, *The Famous Tragedy of the Queen of Cornwall*, follows, the text being that of the revised and enlarged edition of 1924. Notes on all sections of the volume are provided at the end.

The earliest of Hardy's completed short stories (the outline of a novelette) suggests that in 1874 he was prepared to write a magazine story more hastily than he appears ever to have done subsequently. By contrast, it gives us some idea of the intensive thought he had devoted to the best of *Far from the Madding Crowd* and his previous novels.

The interest of 'An Indiscretion in the Life of an Heiress' relates principally to its origin, but the circumstances of its composition, after the completion of *The Return of the Native*, make one realize how relatively light was the task of rounding out a romantic story from those portions of 'The Poor Man and the Lady' which had not been used in his early novels. In his old age he rather disparagingly described the story he had salvaged as 'a sort of patchwork of the remains'; he had rejected the more satirical and unreal elements. At the same time he thought it would be amusing to restore the original as far as he could, from memory, from the modifications which were preserved in his published fiction, and from a fragment of the manuscript he still possessed. Clearly he thought better of the plan, for all that remained of the manuscript, after being bound and presented to Florence Hardy on the anniversary of her wedding in February 1917, was destroyed.

The Famous Tragedy of the Queen of Cornwall was written, partly as a tribute to the memory of Hardy's own 'Iseult' (Emma Gifford, who became his first wife), and in fulfilment of a hope which had been deferred for more than half a century. In execution and intention, the play shows commendable originality. Hardy 'tried to avoid turning the rude personages of, say, the fifth century into respectable Victorians', as he felt Tennyson, Swinburne, and Matthew Arnold had done in their several ways. He put into practice a principle which seemed right to him when he saw *Hedda Gabler* in 1891 – that the length of the action represented should coincide with the time of acting – and advocated a 'mumming' performance which would create an 'antique spell', a sense of time-distance, and of the resurrection of 'old, unhappy, far-off things'. His ideas on the staging of the play are sensible and progressive.

For Hardy scholars and readers the interest of this rather miscellaneous volume must be considerable, ranging as it does in effect from his first major work to his latest. It gives evidence of both haste and very careful preparation. Some of Hardy's subjects, completed or merely contemplated, may occasion surprise. He believed that adults require unusual or exciting events to hold their interest, and the two stories he wrote for young people show conclusively that he could have excelled in juvenile fiction. The literary merit of this collection is variable but altogether far from negligible. Even in the least carefully prepared work, fascinating touches and situations are to be found. The stories rarely fail to hold one's attention, and one, 'Old Mrs Chundle', though not highly finished, must rank among Hardy's finest. In close juxtaposition it provides a wider range of responses than any other of his stories; and it is a reflection of the age in which he lived that, as far as is known, he made no effort to publish it.

F. B. PINION

Old Mrs Chundle

THE curate had not been a week in the parish, but the autumn morning proving fine, he thought he would make a little water-colour sketch, showing a distant view of the Corvsgate ruin two miles off, which he had passed on his way hither. The sketch occupied him a longer time than he had anticipated. The luncheon hour drew on, and he felt hungry.

Quite near him was a stone-built old cottage of respectable and substantial build. He entered it, and was received by an old woman.

'Can you give me something to eat, my good woman?' he said.

She held her hand to her ear.

'Can you give me something for lunch?' he shouted. 'Bread and cheese – anything will do.'

A sour look crossed her face, and she shook her head. 'That's unlucky,' murmured he. She reflected and said more urbanely, 'Well, I'm going to have my own bit o' dinner in no such long time hence. 'Tis taters and cabbage, boiled with a scantling o' bacon. Would ye like it? But I suppose 'tis the wrong sort, and that ye would sooner have bread and cheese.'

'No, I'll join you. Call me when it is ready. I'm just out here.'

'Ay, I've seen ye. Drawing the old stones, baint ye?'

'Yes, my good woman.'

'Sure 'tis well some folk have nothing better to do with their time. Very well, I'll call ye, when I've dished up.'

He went out and resumed his painting; till in about seven or ten minutes the old woman appeared at her door and held up her hand. The curate washed his brush, went to the brook, rinsed his hands and proceeded to the house.

'There's yours,' she said, pointing to the table. 'I'll have my bit here.' And she denoted the settle.

'Why not join me?'

'Oh, faith, I don't want to eat with my betters – not I.' And she continued firm in her resolution, and eat apart.

The vegetables had been well cooked over a wood fire – the only way to cook a vegetable properly – and the bacon was well boiled. The curate ate heartily: he thought he had never tasted such potatoes and cabbage in his life, which he probably had not, for they had been just brought in from the garden, so that the very freshness of the morning was still in them. When he had finished he asked her how much he owed for the repast, which he had much enjoyed.

'Oh, I don't want to be paid for that bit of snack 'a b'lieve!'

'But really you must take something. It was an excellent meal.'

' 'Tis all my own growing, that's true. But I don't take money for a bit o' victuals. I've never done such a thing in my life.'

'I should feel much happier if you would.'

She seemed unsettled by his feeling, and added as by compulsion, 'Well, then; I suppose twopence won't hurt ye?'

'Twopence?'

'Yes. Twopence.'

'Why my good woman, that's no charge at all. I am sure it is worth this, at least.' And he laid down a shilling.

'I tell 'ee 'tis *twopence*, and no more!' she said primly. 'Why, bless the man, it didn't cost me more than three halfpence, and that leaves me a fair quarter profit. The bacon is the heaviest item; that may perhaps be a penny. The taters I've got plenty of, and the cabbage is going to waste.'

He thereupon argued no further, paid the limited sum demanded, and went to the door. 'And where does that road lead?' he asked, by way of engaging her in a little friendly conversation before parting, and pointing to a white lane which branched from the direct highway near her door.

'They tell me that it leads to Enckworth.'

'And how far is Enckworth?'

'Three miles, they say. But God knows if 'tis true.'

'You haven't lived here long, then?'

'Five-and-thirty year come Martinmas.'

'And yet you have never been to Enckworth?'

'Not I. Why should I ever have been to Enckworth? I never had any business there – a great mansion of a place, holding people that I've no more doings with than with the people of the moon. No, there's on'y

two places I ever go to from year's end to year's end: that's once a fort-
night to Anglebury, to do my bit o' marketing, and once a week to my
parish church.'

'Which is that?'

'Why, Kingscreech.'

'Oh – then you are in my parish?'

'Maybe. Just on the outskirts.'

'I didn't know the parish extended so far. I'm a newcomer. Well, I
hope we may meet again. Good afternoon to you.'

When the curate was next talking to his rector he casually observed:
'By the way, that's a curious old soul who lives out towards Corvsgate –
old Mrs – I don't know her name – A deaf old woman.'

'You mean old Mrs Chundle, I suppose.'

'She tells me she's lived there five-and-thirty years, and has never
been to Enckworth, three miles off. She goes to two places only, from
year's end to year's end – to the market town, and to church on Sundays.'

'To church on Sundays. H'm. She rather exaggerates her travels, to
my thinking. I've been rector here thirteen years, and I have certainly
never seen her at church in my time.'

'A wicked old woman. What can she think of herself for such decep-
tion!'

'She didn't know you belonged here when she said it, and could find
out the untruth of her story. I warrant she wouldn't have said it to me!'
And the rector chuckled.

On reflection the curate felt that this was decidedly a case for his
ministrations, and on the first spare morning he strode across to the
cottage beyond the ruin. He found its occupant of course at home.

'Drawing picters again?' she asked, looking up from the hearth, where
she was scouring the fire-dogs.

'No, I come on a more important matter, Mrs Chundle. I am the new
curate of this parish.'

'You said you was last time. And after you had told me and went away
I said to myself, he'll be here again sure enough, hang me if I didn't.
And here you be.'

'Yes. I hope you don't mind?'

'Oh, no. You find us a roughish lot, I make no doubt?'

'Well, I won't go into that. But I think it was a very culpable – unkind
thing of you to tell me you came to church every Sunday, when I find
you've not been seen there for years.'

'Oh, did I tell 'ee that?'

'You certainly did.'

'Now I wonder what I did that for?'

'I wonder too.'

'Well, you could ha' guessed, after all, that I didn't come to any service. Lord, what's the good o' my lumpering all the way to church and back again, when I'm as deaf as a plock? Your own commonsense ought to have told 'ee that 'twas but a figure o' speech, seeing you was a pa'son.'

'Don't you think you could hear the service if you were to sit close to the reading-desk and pulpit?'

'I'm sure I couldn't. Oh no – not a word. Why I couldn't hear anything even at that time when Isaac Coggs used to cry the Amens out loud beyond anything that's done nowadays, and they had the barrel-organ for the tunes – years and years agone, when I was stronger in my narves than now.'

'H'm – I'm sorry. There's one thing I could do, which I would with pleasure, if you'll use it. I could get you an ear-trumpet. Will you use it?'

'Ay, sure. That I woll. I don't care what I use – 'tis all the same to me.'

'And you'll come?'

'Yes. I may as well go there as bide here, I suppose.'

The ear-trumpet was purchased by the zealous young man, and the next Sunday, to the great surprise of the parishioners when they arrived, Mrs Chundle was discovered in the front seat of the nave of Kingscreech Church, facing the rest of the congregation with an unmoved countenance.

She was the centre of observation through the whole morning service. The trumpet, elevated at a high angle, shone and flashed in the sitters' eyes as the chief object in the sacred edifice.

The curate could not speak to her that morning, and called the next day to inquire the result of the experiment. As soon as she saw him in the distance she began shaking her head.

'No, no,' she said decisively as he approached. 'I knowed 'twas all nonsense.'

'What?'

' 'Twasn't a mossel o' good, and so I could have told 'ee before. A wasting your money in jimcracks upon a' old 'ooman like me.'

'You couldn't hear? Dear me – how disappointing.'

'You might as well have been mouthing at me from the top o' Creech Barrow.'

'That's unfortunate.'

'I shall never come no more – never – to be made such a fool of as that again.'

The curate mused. 'I'll tell you what, Mrs Chundle. There's one thing more to try, and only one. If that fails I suppose we shall have to give it up. It is a plan I have heard of, though I have never myself tried it; it's having a sound tube fixed, with its lower mouth in the seat immediately below the pulpit, where you would sit, the tube running up inside the pulpit with its upper end opening in a bell-mouth just beside the book-board. The voice of the preacher enters the bell-mouth, and is carried down directly to the listener's ear. Do you understand?'

'Exactly.'

'And you'll come, if I put it up at my own expense?'

'Ay, I suppose. I'll try it, e'en though I said I wouldn't. I may as well do that as do nothing, I reckon.'

The kind-hearted curate, at great trouble to himself, obtained the tube and had it fixed vertically as described, the upper mouth being immediately under the face of whoever should preach, and on the following Sunday morning it was to be tried. As soon as he came from the vestry the curate perceived to his satisfaction Mrs Chundle in the seat beneath, erect and at attention, her head close to the lower orifice of the sound-pipe, and a look of great complacency that her soul required a special machinery to save it, while other people's could be saved in a commonplace way. The rector read the prayers from the desk on the opposite side, which part of the service Mrs Chundle could follow easily enough by the help of the prayer-book; and in due course the curate mounted the eight steps into the wooden octagon, gave out his text, and began to deliver his discourse.

It was a fine frosty morning in early winter, and he had not got far with his sermon when he became conscious of a steam rising from the bell-mouth of the tube, obviously caused by Mrs Chundle's breathing at the lower end, and it was accompanied by a suggestion of onion-stew. However, he preached on awhile, hoping it would cease, holding in his left hand his finest cambric handkerchief kept especially for Sunday morning services. At length, no longer able to endure the odour, he lightly dropped the handkerchief into the bell of the tube, without stopping for a moment the eloquent flow of his words; and he had the satisfaction of feeling himself in comparatively pure air.

He heard a fidgeting below; and presently there arose to him over the pulpit-edge a hoarse whisper: 'The pipe's chokt!'

'Now, as you will perceive, my brethren,' continued the curate, unheeding the interruption; 'by applying this test to ourselves, our discernment of—'

'The pipe's chokt!' came up in a whisper yet louder and hoarser.

'Our discernment of actions as morally good or indifferent will be much quickened, and we shall be materially helped in our—'

Suddenly came a violent puff of warm wind, and he beheld his handkerchief rising from the bell of the tube and floating to the pulpit floor. The little boys in the gallery laughed, thinking it a miracle. Mrs Chundle had, in fact, applied her mouth to the bottom end, blown with all her might, and cleared the tube. In a few seconds the atmosphere of the pulpit became as before, to the curate's great discomfiture. Yet stop the orifice again he dared not, lest the old woman should make a still greater disturbance and draw the attention of the congregation to this unseemly situation.

'If you carefully analyze the passage I have quoted,' he continued in somewhat uncomfortable accents, 'you will perceive that it naturally suggests three points for consideration—'

('It's not onions: it's peppermint,' he said to himself.)

'Namely, mankind in its unregenerate state—'

('And cider.')

'The incidence of the law, and loving-kindness or grace, which we will now severally consider—'

('And pickled cabbage. What a terrible supper she must have made!')

'Under the twofold aspect of external and internal consciousness.'

Thus the reverend gentleman continued strenuously for perhaps five minutes longer; then he could stand it no more. Desperately thrusting his thumb into the hole, he drew the threads of his distracted discourse together, the while hearing her blow vigorously to dislodge the plug. But he stuck to the hole, and brought his sermon to a premature close.

He did not call on Mrs Chundle the next week, a slight cooling of his zeal for her spiritual welfare being manifest; but he encountered her at the house of another cottager whom he was visiting; and she immediately addressed him as a partner in the same enterprize.

'I could hear beautiful!' she said. 'Yes; every word! Never did I know such a wonderful machine as that there pipe. But you forgot what you was doing once or twice, and put your handkerchief on the top o' en, and stopped the sound a bit. Please not to do that again, for it makes me lose a lot. Howsomever, I shall come every Sunday morning reg'lar now, please God.'

The curate quivered internally.

'And will ye come to my house once in a while and read to me?'

'Of course.'

Surely enough the next Sunday the ordeal was repeated for him. In the evening he told his trouble to the rector. The rector chuckled.

'You've brought it upon yourself,' he said. 'You don't know this parish so well as I. You should have left the old woman alone.'

'I suppose I should!'

'Thank Heaven, she thinks nothing of my sermons, and doesn't come when I preach. Ha, ha!'

'Well,' said the curate somewhat ruffled, 'I must do something. I cannot stand this. I shall tell her not to come.'

'You can hardly do that.'

'And I've half-promised to go and read to her. But – I shan't go.'

'She's probably forgotten by this time that you promised.'

A vision of his next Sunday in the pulpit loomed horridly before the young man, and at length he determined to escape the experience. The pipe should be taken down. The next morning he gave directions, and the removal was carried out.

A day or two later a message arrived from her, saying that she wished to see him. Anticipating a terrific attack from the irate old woman, he put off going to her for a day, and when he trudged out towards her house on the following afternoon it was in a vexed mood. Delicately nurtured man as he was, he had determined not to re-erect the tube, and hoped he might hit on some new *modus vivendi*, even if at any inconvenience to Mrs Chundle, in a situation that had become intolerable as it was last week.

'Thank Heaven, the tube is gone,' he said to himself as he walked; 'and nothing will make me put it up again!'

On coming near he saw to his surprise that the calico curtains of the cottage windows were all drawn. He went up to the door, which was ajar; and a little girl peeped through the opening.

'How is Mrs Chundle?' he asked blandly.

'She's dead, sir,' said the girl in a whisper.

'Dead?... Mrs Chundle dead?'

'Yes, sir.'

A woman now came. 'Yes, 'tis so, sir. She went off quite sudden-like about two hours ago. Well, you see, sir, she was over seventy years of age, and last Sunday she was rather late in starting for church, having to put her bit o' dinner ready before going out; and was very anxious to be in time. So she hurried overmuch, and runned up the hill, which at her time of life she ought not to have done. It upset her heart, and she's been poorly all the week since, and that made her send for 'ee. Two or three times she said she hoped you would come soon, as you'd promised to, and you were so staunch and faithful in wishing to do her good, that she knew 'twas not by your own wish you didn't arrive. But she would not let us send again, as it might trouble 'ee too much, and there might be other poor folks needing you. She worried to think she might not be able to listen to 'ee next Sunday, and feared you'd be hurt at it, and think her remiss. But she was eager to hear you again later on. However, 'twas ordained otherwise for the poor soul, and she was soon gone. "I've found a real friend at last," she said. "He's a man in a thousand. He's not ashamed of a' old woman, and he holds that her soul is worth saving as well as richer people's." She said I was to give you this.'

It was a small folded piece of paper, directed to him and sealed with a thimble. On opening it he found it to be what she called her will, in which she had left him her bureau, case-clock, four-post bedstead, and framed sampler – in fact all the furniture of any account that she possessed.

The curate went out, like Peter at the cock-crow. He was a meek young man, and as he went his eyes were wet. When he reached a lonely place in the lane he stood still thinking, and kneeling down in the dust of the road rested his elbow in one hand and covered his face with the other.

Thus he remained some minutes or so, a black shape on the hot white of the sunned trackway; till he rose, brushed the knees of his trousers, and walked on.

Destiny and a Blue Cloak

'GOOD morning, Miss Lovill!' said the young man, in the free manner usual with him toward pretty and inexperienced country girls.

Agatha Pollin – the maiden addressed – instantly perceived how the mistake had arisen. Miss Lovill was the owner of a blue autumn wrapper, exceptionally gay for a village; and Agatha, in a spirit of emulation rather than originality, had purchased a similarly enviable article for herself, which she wore to-day for the first time. It may be mentioned that the two young women had ridden together from their homes to Maiden-Newton on this foggy September morning, Agatha prolonging her journey thence to Weymouth by train, and leaving her acquaintance at the former place. The remark was made to her on Weymouth esplanade.

Agatha was now about to reply very naturally, 'I am not Miss Lovill,' and she went so far as to turn up her face to him for the purpose, when he added, 'I've been hoping to meet you. I have heard of your – well, I must say it – beauty, long ago, though I only came to Beaminster yesterday.'

Agatha bowed – her contradiction hung back – and they walked slowly along the esplanade together without speaking another word after the above point-blank remark of his. It was evident that her new friend could never have seen either herself or Miss Lovill except from a distance.

And Agatha trembled as well as bowed. This Miss Lovill – Frances Lovill – was of great and long renown as the beauty of Cloton village, near Beaminster. She was five and twenty and fully developed, while Agatha was only the niece of the miller of the same place, just nineteen, and of no repute as yet for comeliness, though she undoubtedly could boast of much. Now, were the speaker, Oswald Winwood, to be told that he had not lighted upon the true Helen, he would instantly apologize for his mistake and leave her side, a contingency of no great matter but for

one curious emotional circumstance – Agatha had already lost her heart
to him. Only in secret had she acquired this interest in Winwood – by
hearing much report of his talent and by watching him several times
from a window; but she loved none the less in that she had discovered
that Miss Lovill's desire to meet and talk with the same intellectual
luminary was in a fair way of approaching the intensity of her own.
We are never unbiased appraisers, even in love, and rivalry usually
operates as a stimulant to esteem even while it is acting as an obstacle
to opportunity. So it had been with Agatha in her talk to Miss Lovill
that morning concerning Oswald Winwood.

The Weymouth season was almost at an end, and but few loungers
were to be seen on the parades, particularly at this early hour. Agatha
looked over the iridescent sea, from which the veil of mist was slowly
rising, at the white cliffs on the left, now just beginning to gleam in a
weak sunlight, at the one solitary yacht in the midst, and still delayed
her explanation. Her companion went on:

'The mist is vanishing, look, and I think it will be fine, after all. Shall
you stay in Weymouth the whole day?'

'No. I am going to Portland by the twelve o'clock steam-boat. But I
return here again at six to go home by the seven o'clock train.'

'I go to Maiden-Newton by the same train, and then to Beaminster
by the carrier.'

'So do I.'

'Not, I suppose, to walk from Beaminster to Cloton at that time in the
evening?'

'I shall be met by somebody – but it is only a mile, you know.'

That is how it all began; the continuation it is not necessary to detail
at length. Both being somewhat young and impulsive, social forms were
not scrupulously attended to. She discovered him to be on board the
steamer as it plowed the emerald waves of Weymouth Bay, although he
had wished her a formal good-bye at the pier. He had altered his mind,
he said, and thought that he would come to Portland too. They returned
by the same boat, walked the velvet sands till the train started, and
entered a carriage together.

All this time, in the midst of her happiness, Agatha's conscience was
sombre with guiltiness at not having yet told him of his mistake. It was
true that he had not more than once or twice called her by Miss Lovill's
name since the first greeting in the morning; but he certainly was still
under the impression that she was Frances Lovill. Yet she perceived that

though he had been led to her by another's name, it was her own proper person that he was so rapidly getting to love, and Agatha's feminine insight suggested blissfully to her that the face belonging to the name would after this encounter have no power to drag him away from the face of the day's romance.

They reached Maiden-Newton at dusk, and went to the inn door, where stood the old-fashioned hooded van which was to take them to Beaminster. It was on the point of starting, and when they had mounted in front the old man at once drove up the long hill leading out of the village.

'This has been a charming experience to me, Miss Lovill,' Oswald said, as they sat side by side. 'Accidental meetings have a way of making themselves pleasant when contrived ones quite fail to do it.'

It was absolutely necessary to confess this time, though all her bliss were at once destroyed.

'I am not really Miss Lovill!' she faltered.

'What! not the young lady – and are you really not Frances Lovill?' he exclaimed, in surprise.

'O forgive me, Mr Winwood! I have wanted so to tell you of your mistake; indeed I have, all day – but I couldn't – and it is so wicked and wrong of me! I am only poor Agatha Pollin, at the mill.'

'But why couldn't you tell me?'

'Because I was afraid that if I did you would go away from me and not care for me any more and I l-l-love you so dearly!'

The carrier being on foot beside the horse, the van being so dark, and Oswald's feelings being rather warm, he could not for his life avoid kissing her there and then.

'Well,' he said, 'it doesn't matter; you are yourself anyhow. It is you I like, and nobody else in the world – not the name. But, you know, I was really looking for Miss Lovill this morning. I saw the back of her head yesterday, and I have often heard how very good-looking she is. Ah! suppose you had been she. I wonder—'

He did not complete the sentence. The driver mounted again, touched the horse with the whip, and they jogged on.

'You forgive me?' she said.

'Entirely – absolutely – the reason justified everything. How strange that you should have been caring deeply for me, and I ignorant of it all the time!'

They descended into Beaminster and alighted, Oswald handing her down. They had not moved from the spot when another female figure also alighted, dropped her fare into the carrier's hand, and glided away.

'Who is that?' said Oswald to the carrier. 'Why, I thought we were the only passengers!'

'What?' said the carrier, who was rather stupid.

'Who is that woman?'

'Miss Lovill, of Cloton. She altered her mind about staying at Beaminster, and is come home again.'

'Oh!' said Agatha, almost sinking to the earth. 'She has heard it all. What shall I do, what shall I do?'

'Never mind it a bit,' said Oswald.

II

The mill stood beside the village high-road, from which it was separated by the stream, the latter forming also the boundary of the mill garden, orchard, and paddock on that side. A visitor crossed a little wood bridge imbedded in oozy, aquatic growths, and found himself in a space where usually stood a wagon laden with sacks, surrounded by a number of bright-feathered fowls.

It was now, however, just dusk, but the mill was not closed, a stripe of light stretching as usual from the open door across the front, across the river, across the road, into the hedge beyond. On the bridge, which was aside from the line of light, a young man and a girl stood talking together. Soon they moved a little way apart, and then it was apparent that their right hands were joined. In receding one from the other they began to swing their arms gently backward and forward between them.

'Come a little way up the lane, Agatha, since it is the last time,' he said. 'I don't like parting here. You know your uncle does not object.'

'He doesn't object because he knows nothing to object to,' she whispered. And they both then contemplated the fine, stalwart figure of the said uncle, who could be seen moving about inside the mill, illuminated by the candle, and circumscribed by a faint halo of flour, and hindered by the whirr of the mill from hearing anything so gentle as lovers' talk.

Oswald had not relinquished her hand, and, submitting herself to a bondage she appeared to love better than freedom, Agatha followed him across the bridge, and they went down the lane engaged in the low, sad talk common to all such cases, interspersed with remarks peculiar to their own.

'It is nothing so fearful to contemplate,' he said. 'Many live there for years in a state of rude health, and return home in the same happy condition. So shall I.'

'I hope you will.'

'But aren't you glad I am going? It is better to do well in India than badly here. Say you are glad, dearest; it will fortify me when I am gone.'

'I am glad,' she murmured faintly. 'I mean I am glad in my mind. I don't think that in my heart I am glad.'

'Thanks to Macaulay, of honoured memory, I have as good a chance as the best of them!' he said, with ardour. 'What a great thing competitive examination is; it will put good men in good places, and make inferior men move lower down; all bureaucratic jobbery will be swept away.'

'What's bureaucratic, Oswald?'

'Oh! that's what they call it, you know. It is – well, I don't exactly know what it is. I know this, that it is the name of what I hate, and that it isn't competitive examination.'

'At any rate it is a very bad thing,' she said, conclusively.

'Very bad, indeed; you may take my word for that.'

Then the parting scene began, in the dark, under the heavy-headed trees which shut out sky and stars. 'And since I shall be in London till the spring,' he remarked, 'the parting doesn't seem so bad – so all at once. Perhaps you may come to London before the spring, Agatha.'

'I may; but I don't think I shall.'

'We must hope on all the same. Then there will be the examination, and then I shall know my fate.'

'I hope you'll fail! – there I've said it; I couldn't help it, Oswald!' she exclaimed, bursting out crying. 'You would come home again then!'

'How could you be so disheartening and wicked, Agatha! I – I didn't expect—'

'No, no; I don't wish it; I wish you to be best, top, very very best!' she said. 'I didn't mean the other; indeed, dear Oswald, I didn't. And will you be sure to come to me when you are rich? Sure to come?'

'If I'm on this earth I'll come home and marry you.'

And then followed the good-bye.

III

In the spring came the examination. One morning a newspaper directed by Oswald was placed in her hands, and she opened it to find it was a copy of the *Times*. In the middle of the sheet, in the most conspicuous place, in the excellent neighbourhood of the leading articles, was a list of names, and the first on the list was Oswald Winwood. Attached to his name, as showing where he was educated, was the simple title of some obscure little academy, while underneath came public school and college men in shoals. Such a case occurs sometimes, and it occurred then.

How Agatha clapped her hands! For her selfish wish to have him in England at any price, even that of failure, had been but a paroxysm of the wretched parting, and was now quite extinct. Circumstances combined to hinder another meeting between them before his departure, and, accordingly, making up her mind to the inevitable in a way which would have done honour to an older head, she fixed her mental vision on that sunlit future – far away, yet always nearing – and contemplated its probabilities with a firm hope.

At length he had arrived in India, and now Agatha had only to work and wait; and the former made the latter more easy. In her spare hours she would wander about the river brinks and into the coppices, and there weave thoughts of him by processes that young women understand so well. She kept a diary, and in this, since there were few events to chronicle in her daily life, she sketched the changes of the landscape, noted the arrival and departure of birds of passage, the times of storms and foul weather – all which information, being mixed up with her life and taking colour from it, she sent as scraps in her letters to him, deriving most of her enjoyment in contemplating his.

Oswald, on his part, corresponded very regularly. Knowing the days of the Indian mail, she would go at such times to meet the post-man in the early morning, and to her unvarying inquiry, 'A letter for me?' it was seldom, indeed, that there came a disappointing answer. Thus the season passed, and Oswald told her he should be a judge some day, with many other details, which, in her mind, were viewed chiefly in their bearing on the grand consummation – that he was to come home and marry her.

Meanwhile, as the girl grew older and more womanly, the woman whose name she had once stolen for a day grew more of an old maid, and showed symptoms of fading. One day Agatha's uncle, who, though still a handsome man in the prime of life, was a widower with four children, to whom she acted the part of eldest sister, told Agatha that Frances Lovill was about to become his second wife.

'Well!' said Agatha, and thought, 'What an end for a beauty!'

And yet it was all reasonable enough, notwithstanding that Miss Lovill might have looked a little higher. Agatha knew that this step would produce great alterations in the small household of Cloton Mill, and the idea of having as aunt and ruler the woman to whom she was in some sense indebted for a lover, affected Agatha with a slight thrill of dread. Yet nothing had ever been spoken between the two women to show that Frances had heard, much less resented, the explanation in the van on that night of the return from Weymouth.

IV

On a certain day old Farmer Lovill called. He was of the same family as Frances, though their relationship was distant. A considerable business in corn had been done from time to time between miller and farmer, but the latter had seldom called at Pollin's house. He was a bachelor, or he would probably never have appeared in this history, and he was mostly full of a boyish merriment rare in one of his years. To-day his business with the miller had been so imperative as to bring him in person, and it was evident from their talk in the mill that the matter was payment. Perhaps ten minutes had been spent in serious converse when the old farmer turned away from the door, and without saying good-morning, went toward the bridge. This was unusual for a man of his temperament.

He was an old man – really and fairly old – sixty-five years of age at least. He was not exactly feeble, but he found a stick useful when walking in a high wind. His eyes were not yet bleared, but in their corners was occasionally a moisture like majolica glaze – entirely absent in youth. His face was not shrivelled, but there were unmistakable puckers in some places. And hence the old gentleman, unmarried, substantial, and cheery as he was, was not doted on by the young girls of Cloton as he had been by their mothers in former time. Each year his breast impended a little further over his toes, and his chin a little further over his breast, and in proportion as he turned down his nose to earth did pretty females turn up theirs at him. They might have liked him as a friend had he not shown the abnormal wish to be regarded as a lover. To Agatha Pollin this aged youth was positively distasteful.

It happened that at the hour of Mr Lovill's visit Agatha was bending over the pool at the mill head, sousing some white fabric in the water. She was quite unconscious of the farmer's presence near her, and continued dipping and rinsing in the idlest phase possible to industry, until she remained quite still, holding the article under the water, and looking at her own reflection within it. The river, though gliding slowly, was yet so smooth that to the old man on the bridge she existed in duplicate – the pouting mouth, the little nose, the frizzed hair, the bit of blue ribbon, as they existed over the surface, being but a degree more distinct than the same features beneath.

'What a pretty maid!' said the old man to himself. He walked up the margin of the stream, and stood beside her.

'Oh!' said Agatha, starting with surprise. In her flurry she relinquished the article she had been rinsing, which slowly turned over and sank deeper, and made toward the hatch of the mill-wheel.

'There – it will get into the wheel, and be torn to pieces!' she exclaimed.

'I'll fish it out with my stick, my dear,' said Farmer Lovill, and kneeling cautiously down he began hooking and crooking with all his might. 'What thing is it – of much value?'

'Yes; it is my best one!' she said involuntarily.

'It – what is the it?'

'Only something – a piece of linen.' Just then the farmer hooked the endangered article, and dragging it out, held it high on his walking-stick – dripping, but safe.

'Why, it is a chemise!' he said.

The girl looked red, and instead of taking it from the end of the stick, turned away.

'Hee-hee!' laughed the ancient man. 'Well, my dear, there's nothing to be ashamed of that I can see in owning to such a necessary and innocent article of clothing. There, I'll put it on the grass for you, and you shall take it when I am gone.'

Then Farmer Lovill retired, lifting his fingers privately, to express amazement on a small scale, and murmuring, 'What a nice young thing! Well, to be sure. Yes, a nice child – young woman rather; indeed, a marriageable woman, come to that; of course she is.'

The doting old person thought of the young one all this day in a way that the young one did not think of him. He thought so much about her, that in the evening, instead of going to bed, he hobbled privately out by the back door into the moonlight, crossed a field or two, and stood in the lane, looking at the mill – not more in the hope of getting a glimpse of the attractive girl inside than for the pleasure of realizing that she was there.

A light moved within, came nearer, and ascended. The staircase window was large, and he saw his goddess going up with a candle in her hand. This was indeed worth coming for. He feared he was seen by her as well, yet hoped otherwise in the interests of his passion, for she came and drew down the window blind, completely shutting out his gaze. The light vanished from this part, and reappeared in a window a little further on.

The lover drew nearer; this, then, was her bedroom. He rested vigorously on his stick, and straightening his back nearly to a perpendicular, turned up his amorous face.

She came to the window, paused, then opened it.

'Bess its deary-eary heart! it is going to speak to me!' said the old man, moistening his lips, resting still more desperately upon his stick, and straightening himself yet an inch taller. 'She saw me then!'

Agatha, however, made no sign; she was bent on a far different purpose. In a box on her window-sill was a row of mignonette, which had been sadly neglected since her lover's departure, and she began to water it, as if inspired by a sudden recollection of its condition. She poured from her water-jug slowly along the plants, and then, to her astonishment, discerned her elderly friend below.

'A rude old thing!' she murmured.

Directing the spout of the jug over the edge of the box, and looking in another direction that it might appear to be an accident, she allowed the stream to spatter down upon her admirer's face, neck, and shoulders, causing him to beat a quick retreat. Then Agatha serenely closed the window, and drew down that blind also.

'Ah! she did not see me; it was evident she did not, and I was mistaken!' said the trembling farmer, hastily wiping his face, and mopping out the rills trickling down within his shirt-collar, as far as he could get at them, which was by no means to their termination. 'A pretty creature, and so innocent, too! Watering her flowers; how I like a girl who is fond of flowers! I wish she had spoken, and I wish I was younger. Yes, I know what I'ld do with the little mouse!' And the old gentleman tapped emotionally upon the ground with his stick.

V

'Agatha, I suppose you have heard the news from somebody else by this time?' said her uncle Humphrey some two or three weeks later. 'I mean what Farmer Lovill has been talking to me about.'

'No, indeed,' said Agatha.

'He wants to marry ye if you be willing.'

'Oh, I never!' said Agatha with dismay. 'That old man!'

'Old? He's hale and hearty; and, what's more, a man very well-to-do. He'll make you a comfortable home, and dress ye up like a doll, and I'm sure you'll like that, or you baint a woman of woman born.'

'But it *can't be*, uncle! – other reasons—'

'What reasons?'

'Why, I've promised Oswald Winwood – years ago!'

'Promised Oswald Winwood years ago, have you?'

'Yes; surely you know it, Uncle Humphrey. And we write to one another regularly.'

'Well, I can just call to mind that ye are always scribbling and getting letters from somewhere. Let me see – where is he now? I quite forget.'

'In India still. Is it possible that you don't know about him, and what a great man he's getting? There are paragraphs about him in our paper very often. The last was about some translation from Hindustani that he'd been making. And he's coming home for me.'

'I very much question it. Lovill will marry you at once, he says.'

'Indeed, he will not.'

'Well, I don't want to force you to do anything against your will, Agatha, but this is how the matter stands. You know I am a little behind-hand in my dealings with Lovill – nothing serious, you know, if he gives me time – but I want to be free of him quite in order to go to Australia.'

'Australia!'

'Yes. There's nothing to be done here. I don't know what business is coming to – can't think. But never mind that; this is the point: if you will marry Farmer Lovill, he offers to clear off the debt, and there will be no longer any delay about my own marriage; in short, away I can go. I mean to, and there's an end on't.'

'What, and leave me at home alone?'

'Yes, but a married woman, of course. You see, the children are getting big now. John is twelve and Nathaniel ten, and the girls are growing fast, and when I am married again I shall hardly want you to keep house for me – in fact, I must reduce our family as much as possible. So that if you could bring your mind to think of Farmer Lovill as a husband, why, 'twould be a great relief to me after having the trouble and expense of bringing you up. If I can in that way edge out of Lovill's debt I shall have a nice bit of money in hand.'

'But Oswald will be richer even than Mr Lovill,' said Agatha, through her tears.

'Yes, yes. But Oswald is not here, nor is he likely to be. How silly you be.'

'But he will come, and soon, with his eleven hundred a year and all.'

'I wish to Heaven he would. I'm sure he might have you.'

'Now, you promise that, uncle, don't you?' she said, brightening. 'If he comes with plenty of money before you want to leave, he shall marry me, and nobody else.'

'Ay, if he comes. But, Agatha, no nonsense. Just think of what I've been telling you. At any rate be civil to Farmer Lovill. If this man Winwood were here and asked for ye, and married ye, that would be a very different thing. I do mind now that I saw something about him and his doings in the papers; but he's a fine gentleman by this time, and won't think of stooping to a girl like you. So you had better take the one who is ready; old men's darlings fare very well as the world goes. We shall be off in nine months, mind; that I've settled. And you must be a married woman afore that time, and wish us good-bye upon your husband's arm.'

'That old arm couldn't support me.'

'And if you don't agree to have him, you'll take a couple of hundred pounds out of my pocket; you'll ruin my chances altogether – that's the long and the short of it.'

Saying which the floury man turned his back upon her, and his footsteps became drowned in the rumble of the mill.

VI

Nothing so definite was said to her again on the matter for some time. The old yeoman hovered round her, but, knowing the result of the interview between Agatha and her uncle, he forbore to endanger his suit by precipitancy. But one afternoon he could not avoid saying, 'Aggy, when may I speak to you upon a serious subject?'

'Next week,' she replied, instantly.

He had not been prepared for such a ready answer, and it startled him almost as much as it pleased him. Had he known the cause of it his emotions might have been different. Agatha, with all the womanly strategy she was capable of, had written post-haste to Oswald after the conversation with her uncle, and told him of the dilemma. At the end of the present week his answer, if he replied with his customary punctuality, would be sure to come. Fortified with his letter, she thought she could meet the old man. Oswald she did not doubt.

Nor had she any reason to. The letter came prompt to the day. It was short, tender, and to the point. Events had shaped themselves so fortunately that he was able to say he would return and marry her before the time named for the family's departure for Queensland.

She danced about for joy. But there was a postscript to the effect that she might as well keep this promise a secret for the present, if she conveniently could, that his intention might not become a public talk in Cloton. Agatha knew that he was a rising and aristocratic young man, and saw at once how proper this was.

So she met Mr Lovill with a simple flat refusal, at which her uncle was extremely angry, and her disclosure to him afterward of the arrival of the letter went but a little way in pacifying him. Farmer Lovill would put in upon him for the debt, he said, unless she could manage to please him for a short time.

'I don't want to please him,' said Agatha. 'It is wrong to encourage him if I don't mean it.'

'Will you behave toward him as the parson advises you?'

The parson! That was a new idea, and from her uncle, unexpected.

'I will agree to what Mr Davids advises about my mere daily behaviour before Oswald comes, but nothing more,' she said. 'That is, I will if you know for certain that he's a good man, who fears God and keeps the commandments.'

'Mr Davids fears God, for sartin, for he never ventures to name Him outside the pulpit; and as for the commandments, 'tis knowed how he swore at the church-restorers for taking them away from the chancel.'

'Uncle, you always jest when I am serious.'

'Well, well! at any rate his advice on a matter of this sort is good.'

'How is it you think of referring me to him?' she asked, in perplexity; 'you so often speak slightingly of him.'

'Oh – well,' said Humphrey, with a faintly perceptible desire to parry the question, 'I have spoken roughly about him once now and then; but perhaps I was wrong. Will ye go?'

'Yes, I don't mind,' she said, languidly.

When she reached the vicar's study Agatha began her story with reserve, and said nothing about the correspondence with Oswald; yet an intense longing to find a friend and confidant led her to indulge in more feeling than she had intended, and as a finale she wept. The genial incumbent, however, remained quite cool, the secret being that his heart was involved a little in another direction – one, perhaps, not quite in harmony with Agatha's interests – of which more anon.

'So the difficulty is,' he said to her, 'how to behave in this trying time of waiting for Mr Winwood, that you may please parties all round and give offence to none.'

'Yes, sir, that's it,' sobbed Agatha, wondering how he could have realized her position so readily. 'And uncle wants to go to Australia.'

'One thing is certain,' said the vicar; 'you must not hurt the feelings of Mr Lovill. Wonderfully sensitive man – a man I respect much as a godly doer.'

'Do you, sir?'

'I do. His earnestness is remarkable.'

'Yes, in courting.'

'The cue is: treat Mr Lovill gently – gently as a babe! Love opposed, especially an old man's, gets all the stronger. It is your policy to give him seeming encouragement, and so let his feelings expend themselves and die away.'

'How am I to? To advise is so easy.'

'Not by acting untruthfully, of course. You say your lover is sure to come back before your uncle leaves England.'

'I know he will.'

'Then pacify old Mr Lovill in this way: Tell him you'll marry him when your uncle wants to go, if Winwood doesn't come for you before that time. That will quite content Mr Lovill, for he doesn't in the least expect Oswald to return, and you will see that his persecution will cease at once.'

'Yes; I'll agree to it,' said Agatha promptly.

Mr Davids had refrained from adding that neither did he expect Oswald to come, and hence his advice. Agatha on her part too refrained from stating the good reasons she had for the contrary expectation, and hence her assent. Without the last letter perhaps even her faith would hardly have been bold enough to allow this palpable driving of her into a corner.

'It would be as well to write Mr Lovill a little note, saying you agree to what I have advised,' said the parson evasively.

'I don't like writing.'

'There is no harm. "If Mr Winwood doesn't come I'll marry you", &c. Poor Mr Lovill will be content, thinking Oswald will not come; you will be content, knowing he will come; your uncle will be content, being indifferent which of two rich men has you and relieves him of his difficulties. Then, if it is the will of Providence, you'll be left in peace. Here's a pen and ink; you can do it at once.'

Thus tempted, Agatha wrote the note with a trembling hand. It really did seem upon the whole a nicely strategic thing to do in her present environed situation. Mr Davids took the note with the air of a man who did not wish to take it in the least, and placed it on the mantelpiece.

'I'll send it down to him by one of the children,' said Aggy, looking wistfully at her note with a little feeling that she would like to have it back again.

'Oh, no, it is not necessary,' said her pleasant adviser. He had rung the bell; the servant now came, and the note was sent off in a trice.

When Agatha got into the open air her confidence returned, and it was with a mischievous sense of enjoyment that she considered how she was duping her persecutors by keeping secret Oswald's intention of a speedy return. If they only knew what a firm foundation she had for her belief in what they all deemed but an improbable contingency, what a life they would lead her; how the old man would worry her uncle for payment, and what general confusion there would be. Mr Davids' advice was very shrewd, she thought, and she was glad she had called upon him.

Old Lovill came that very afternoon. He was delighted, and danced a few bars of a hornpipe in entering the room. So lively was the antique boy that Agatha was rather alarmed at her own temerity when she considered what was the basis of his gaiety; wishing she could get from him some such writing as he had got from her, that the words of her promise might not in any way be tampered with, or the conditions ignored.

'I only accept you conditionally, mind,' she anxiously said. 'That is distinctly understood.'

'Yes, yes,' said the yeoman. 'I am not so young as I was, little dear, and beggars mustn't be choosers. With my ra-ta-ta – say, dear, shall it be the first of November?'

'It will really never be.'

'But if he doesn't come, it shall be the first of November?'

She slightly nodded her head.

'Clk! – I think she likes me!' said the old man aside to Aggy's uncle, which aside was distinctly heard by Aggy.

One of the younger children was in the room, drawing idly on a slate. Agatha at this moment took the slate from the child, and scribbled something on it.

'Now you must please me by just writing your name here,' she said in a voice of playful indifference.

'What is it?' said Lovill, looking over and reading. ' "If Oswald Winwood comes to marry Agatha Pollin before November, I agree to give her up to him without objection." Well, that is cool for a young lady under six feet, upon my word – hee-hee!' He passed the slate to the miller, who read the writing and passed it back again.

'Sign – just in courtesy,' she coaxed.

'I don't see why—'

'I do it to test your faith in me; and now I find you have none. Don't you think I should have rubbed it out instantly? Ah, perhaps I can be obstinate too!'

He wrote his name then. 'Now I have done it, and shown my faith,' he said, and at once raised his fingers as if to rub it out again. But with hands that moved like lightning she snatched up the slate, flew up the stairs, locked it in her box, and came down again.

'Souls of men – that's sharp practice,' said the old gentleman.

'Oh, it is only a whim – a mere memorandum,' said she. 'You had my promise, but I had not yours.'

'Ise wants my slate,' cried the child.

'I'll buy you a new one, dear,' said Agatha, and soothed her.

When she had left the room old Lovill spoke to her uncle somewhat uneasily of the event, which, childish as it had been, discomposed him for the moment.

'Oh, that's nothing,' said Miller Pollin assuringly; 'only play – only play. She's a mere child in nater even now, and she did it only to tease ye. Why, she overheard your whisper that you thought she liked ye, and that was her playful way of punishing ye for your confidence. You'll have to put up with these worries, farmer. Considering the difference in your ages, she is sure to play pranks. You'll get to like 'em in time.'

'Ay, ay, faith, so I shall! I was always a Turk for sprees! – eh, Pollin? Hee-hee!' And the suitor was merry again.

VII

Her life was certainly much pleasanter now. The old man treated her well, and was almost silent on the subject nearest his heart. She was obliged to be very stealthy in receiving letters from Oswald, and on this account was bound to meet the post-man, let the weather be what it would. These transactions were easily kept secret from people out of the house, but it was a most difficult task to hide her movements from her uncle. And one day brought utter failure.

'How's this – out already, Agatha?' he said, meeting her in the lane at dawn on a foggy morning. She was actually reading a letter just received, and there was no disguising the truth.

'I've been for a letter from Oswald.'

'Well, but that won't do. Since he don't come for ye, ye must think no more about him.'

'But he's coming in six weeks. He tells me all about it in this very letter.'

'What – really to marry you?' said her uncle incredulously.

'Yes, certainly.'

'But I hear that he is wonderfully well off.'

'Of course he is; that's why he's coming. He'll agree in a moment to be your surety for the debt to Mr Lovill.'

'Has he said so?'

'Not yet; but he will.'

'I'll believe it when I see him and he tells me so. It is very odd, if he means so much, that he hev never wrote a line to me.'

'We thought – you would force me to have the other at once if he wrote to you,' she murmured.

'Not I, if he comes rich. But it is rather a cock-and-bull story, and since he didn't make up his mind before now, I can't say I be much in his favour. Agatha, you had better not say a word to Mr Lovill about these letters; it will make things deuced unpleasant if he hears of such goings on. You are to reckon yourself bound by your word. Oswald won't hold water, I'm afeared. But I'll be fair. If he do come, proves his income, marries ye willy-nilly, I'll let it be, and the old man and I must do as we can. But barring that – you keep your promise to the letter.'

'That's what it will be, uncle. Oswald will come.'

'Write you must not. Lovill will smell it out, and he'll be sharper than you will like. 'Tis not to be supposed that you are to send love-letters to one man as if nothing was going to happen between ye and another man. The first of November is drawing nearer every day. And be sure and keep this a secret from Lovill for your own sake.'

The more clearly that Agatha began to perceive the entire contrast of expectation as to issue between herself and the other party to the covenant, the more alarmed she became. She had not anticipated such a narrowing of courses as had occurred. A malign influence seemed to be at work without any visible human agency. The critical time drew nearer, and, though no ostensible preparation for the wedding was made, it was evident to all that Lovill was painting and papering his house for somebody's reception. He made a lawn where there had existed a nook of refuse; he bought furniture for a woman's room. The greatest horror was that he insisted upon her taking his arm one day, and there being no help for it she assented, though her distaste was unutterable. She felt the skinny arm through his sleeve, saw over the wry shoulders, looked upon the knobby feet, and shuddered. What if Oswald should not come; the time for her uncle's departure was really getting near. When she reached home she ran up to her bedroom.

On recovering from her dreads a little, Agatha looked from the window. The deaf lad John, who assisted in the mill, was quietly glancing toward her, and a gleam of friendship passed over his kindly face as he caught sight of her form. This reminded her that she had, after all, some sort of friend close at hand. The lad knew pretty well how events stood in Agatha's life, and he was always ready to do on her part whatever lay in his power. Agatha felt stronger, and resolved to bear up.

VIII

Heavens! how anxious she was! It actually wanted only ten days to the first of November, and no new letter had come from Oswald.

Her uncle was married, and Frances was in the house, and the preliminary steps for emigration to Queensland had been taken. Agatha surreptitiously obtained newspapers, scanned the Indian shipping news till her eyes ached, but all to no purpose, for she knew nothing either of route or vessel by which Oswald would return. He had mentioned nothing more than the month of his coming, and she had no way of making that single scrap of information the vehicle for obtaining more.

'In ten days, Agatha,' said the old farmer. 'There is to be no show or fuss of any kind; the wedding will be quite private, in consideration of your feelings and wishes. We'll go to church as if we were taking a morning walk, and nobody will be there to disturb you. Tweedledee!' He held up his arm and crossed it with his walking-stick, as if he were playing the fiddle, at the same time cutting a caper.

'He will come, and then I shan't be able to marry you, even th-th-though I may wish to ever so much,' she faltered, shivering. 'I have promised him, and I *must* have him, you know, and you have agreed to let me.'

'Yes, yes,' said Farmer Lovill, pleasantly. 'But that's a misfortune you need not fear at all, my dear; he won't come at this late day and compel you to marry him in spite of your attachment to me. But, ah – it is only a joke to tease me, you little rogue! Your uncle says so.'

'Agatha, come, cheer up, and think no more of that fellow,' said her uncle when they chanced to be alone together. ' 'Tis ridiculous, you know. We always knew he wouldn't come.'

The day passed. The sixth morning came, the noon, the evening. The fifth day came and vanished. Still no sound of Oswald. His friends now lived in London and there was not a soul in the parish, save herself, that he corresponded with, or one to whom she could apply in such a delicate matter as this.

It was the evening before her wedding-day, and she was standing alone in the gloom of her bedchamber looking out on the plot in front of the mill. She saw a white figure moving below, and knew him to be the deaf miller lad, her friend. A sudden impulse animated Agatha. She had been making desperate attempts during the last two days to like the old man, and since Oswald did not come, to marry him without further resistance, for the sheer good of the family of her uncle, to whom she was indeed indebted for much; but had only got so far in her efforts as not to positively hate him. Now rebelliousness came unsought. The lad knew her case, and upon this fact she acted. Gliding downstairs, she beckoned to him, and as they stood together in the stream of light from the open mill door, she communicated her directions, partly by signs, partly by writing, for it was difficult to speak to him without being heard all over the premises.

He looked in her face with a glance of confederacy, and said that he understood it all. Upon this they parted.

The old man was at her house that evening, and when she withdrew wished her good-bye 'for the present' with a dozen smiles of meaning. Agatha had retired early, leaving him still there, and when she reached her room, instead of looking at the new dress she was supposed to be going to wear on the morrow, busied herself in making up a small bundle of ordinary articles of clothing. Then she extinguished her light, lay down upon the bed without undressing, and waited for a preconcerted time.

In what seemed to her the dead of night, but which she concluded must be the time agreed upon – half-past five – there was a slight noise as of gravel being thrown against her window. Agatha jumped up, put on her bonnet and cloak, took up her bundle, and went downstairs without a light. At the bottom she slipped on her boots, and passed amid the chirping crickets to the door. It was unbarred. Her uncle, then, had risen, as she had half expected, and it necessitated a little more caution. The morning was dark as a cavern, not a star being visible; but knowing the bearings well, she went cautiously and in silence to the mill-door. A faint light shone from inside, and the form of the mill-cart appeared without, the horse ready harnessed to it. Agatha did not see John for the moment, but concluded that he was in the mill with her uncle, who had just at this minute started the wheel for the day. She at once slipped into the vehicle and under the tilt, pulling some empty sacks over, as it had been previously agreed that she should do, to avoid the risk of discovery. After a few minutes of suspense she heard John coming from under the wall, where he had apparently been standing and watching her safely in, and mounting in front, away he drove at a walking pace.

Her scheme had been based upon the following particulars of mill business: Thrice a week it was the regular custom for John and another young man to start early in the morning, each with a horse and covered cart, and go in different directions to customers a few miles off, the carts being laden overnight. All that she had asked John to do this morning was to take her with him to a railway station about ten miles distant, where she might safely wait for an up train.

How will John act on returning – what will he say – how will he excuse himself? she thought as they jogged along. 'John!' she said, meaning to ask him about these things; but he did not hear, and she was too confused and weary after her wakeful night to be able to think consecutively on any subject. But the relief of finding that her uncle did not look into the cart caused a delicious lull in her, and while listlessly watching the dark gray sky through the triangular opening between the curtains at the fore part of the tilt, and John's elbow projecting from the folds of one of them, showing where he was sitting on the outside, she fell asleep.

She awoke after a short interval – everything was just the same – jog, jog, on they went; there was the dim slit between the curtains in front, and, after slightly wondering that John had not troubled himself to see that she was comfortable, she dozed again. Thus Agatha remained until she had a clear consciousness of the stopping of the cart. It aroused her, and looking at once through a small opening at the back, she perceived in the dim dawn that they were turning right about; in another moment the horse was proceeding on the way back again.

'John, what are you doing?' she exclaimed, jumping up and pulling aside the curtain which parted them.

John did not turn.

'How fearfully deaf he is!' she thought, 'and how odd he looks behind, and he hangs forward as if he were asleep. His hair is snow-white with flour; does he never clean it, then?' She crept across the sacks and slapped him on the shoulder. John turned then.

'Hee-hee, my dear!' said the blithe old gentleman; and the moisture of his aged eye glistened in the dawning light, as he turned and looked into her horrified face. 'It is all right; I am John, and I have given ye a nice morning's airing to refresh ye for the uncommon duties of to-day; and now we are going back for the ceremony – hee-hee!'

He wore a miller's smock-frock on this interesting occasion, and had been enabled to play the part of John in the episode by taking the second cart and horse and anticipating by an hour the real John in calling her.

Agatha sank backward. How on earth had he discovered the scheme of escape so readily; he, an old and by no means suspicious man? But what mattered a solution! Hope was crushed, and her rebellion was at an end. Agatha was awakened from thought by another stopping of the horse, and they were again at the mill-door.

She dimly recognized her uncle's voice speaking in anger to her when the old farmer handed her out of the vehicle, and heard the farmer reply, merrily, that girls would be girls and have their freaks, that it didn't matter, and that it was a pleasant jest on this auspicious morn. For himself, there was nothing he had enjoyed all his life so much as a practical joke which did no harm. Then she had a sensation of being told to go into the house, have some food, and dress for her marriage with Mr Lovill, as she had promised to do on that day.

All this she did, and at eleven o'clock became the wife of the old man.

When Agatha was putting on her bonnet in the dusk that evening, for she would not illuminate her ghastly face by a candle, a rustling came against the door. Agatha turned. Her uncle's wife, Frances, was looking into the room, and Agatha could just discern upon her aunt's form the blue cloak which had ruled her destiny.

The sight was almost more than she could bear. If, as seemed likely, this effect was intended, the trick was certainly successful. Frances did not speak a word.

Then Agatha said in quiet irony, and with no evidence whatever of regret, sadness, or surprise at what the fact revealed: 'And so you told Mr Lovill of my flight this morning, and set him on the track? It would be amusing to know how you found out my plan, for he never could have done it by himself, poor old darling.'

'Oh, I was a witness of your arrangement with John last night – that was all, my dear,' said her aunt pleasantly. 'I mentioned it then to Mr Lovill, and helped him to his joke of hindering you. . . . You remember the van, Agatha, and how you made use of my name on that occasion, years ago, now?'

'Yes, and did you hear our talk that night? I always fancied otherwise.'

'I heard it all. It was fun to you; what do you think it was to me – fun, too? – to lose the man I longed for, and to become the wife of a man I care not an atom about?'

'Ah, no. And how you struggled to get him away from me, dear aunt!'

'And have done it, too!'

'Not you, exactly. The parson and fate.'

'Parson Davids kindly persuaded you, because I kindly persuaded him, and persuaded your uncle to send you to him. Mr Davids is an old admirer of mine. Now do you see a wheel within a wheel, Agatha?'

Calmness was almost insupportable by Agatha now, but she managed to say: 'Of course you have kept back letters from Oswald to me?'

'No, I have not done that,' said Frances. 'But I told Oswald, who landed at Southampton last night, and called here in great haste at seven this morning that you had gone out for an early drive with the man you were to marry to-day, and that it might cause confusion if he remained. He looked very pale, and went away again at once to catch the next London train, saying something about having been prevented by a severe illness from sailing at the time he had promised and intended for the last twelvemonths.'

The bride, though nearly slain by the news, would not flinch in the presence of her adversary. Stilling her quivering flesh, she said smiling: 'That information is deeply interesting, but does not concern me at all, for I am my husband's darling now, you know, and I wouldn't make the dear man jealous for the world.' And she glided downstairs to the chaise.

The Doctor's Legend

I

'NOT more than half a dozen miles from the Wessex coast' (said the doctor) 'is a mansion which appeared newer in the last century than it appears at the present day after years of neglect and occupation by inferior tenants. It was owned by a man of five-and-twenty, than whom a more ambitious personage never surveyed his face in a glass. His name I will not mention out of respect to those of his blood and connections who may remain on earth, if any such there be. In the words of a writer of that time who knew him well, he was "one whom anything would petrify but nothing would soften".

'This worthy gentleman was of so elevated and refined a nature that he never gave a penny to women who uttered bad words in their trouble and rage, or who wore dirty aprons in view of his front door. On those misguided ones who did not pull the forelock to him in passing, and call him "your Honour" and "Squire", he turned the shoulder of scorn, especially when he wore his finer ruffles and gold seals.

'Neither his personal nor real estate at this time was large; but the latter he made the most of by jealously guarding it, as of the former by his economies. Yet though his fields and woods were well-watched by his gamekeepers and other dependants, such was his dislike to intrusion that he never ceased to watch the watchers. He stopped footpaths and enclosed lands. He made no exceptions to these sentiments in the case of his own villagers, whose faces were never to be seen in his private grounds except on pressing errands.

'Outside his garden-wall, near the entrance to the park, there lived a poor woman with an only child. This child had been so unfortunate as to trespass upon the Squire's lawn on more than one occasion, in search of flowers; and on this incident, trivial as it was, hung much that was afterwards of concern to the house and lineage of the Squire. It seems that the Squire had sent a message to the little girl's mother concerning the nuisance; nevertheless, only a few days afterwards, he saw the child there again. This unwarrantable impertinence, as the owner and land-lord deemed it to be, irritated him exceedingly; and, with his walking cane elevated, he began to pursue the child to teach her by chastisement what she would not learn by exhortation.

'Naturally enough, as soon as the girl saw the Squire in pursuit of her she gave a loud scream, and started off like a hare; but the only entrance to the grounds being on the side which the Squire's position commanded, she could not escape, and endeavoured to elude him by winding, and doubling in her terrified course. Finding her, by reason of her fleetness, not so easy to chastise as he had imagined, her assailant lost his temper – never a very difficult matter – and the more loudly she screamed the more angrily did he pursue. A more untoward interruption to the peace of a beautiful and secluded spot was never seen.

'The race continued, and the Squire, now panting with rage and exertion, drew closer to his victim. To the horrified eyes of the child, when she gazed over her shoulder, his face appeared like a crimson mask set with eyes of fire. The glance sealed her fate in the race. By a sudden start forward he caught hold of her by the skirt of her short frock flying behind. The clutch so terrified the child that, with a louder shriek than ever, she leapt from his grasp, leaving the skirt in his hand. But she did not go far; in a few more moments she fell on the ground in an epileptic fit.

'This strange, and, but for its painfulness, even ludicrous scene, was witnessed by one of the gardeners who had been working near, and the Squire haughtily directed him to take the prostrate and quivering child home; after which he walked off, by no means pleased with himself at the unmanly and undignified part which a violent temper had led him to play.

'The mother of the girl was in great distress when she saw her only child brought home in such a condition; she was still more distressed, when in the course of a day or two, it became doubtful if fright had not deprived the girl entirely of her reason, as well as of her health. In the singular, nervous malady which supervened the child's hair came off and her teeth fell from her gums; till no one could have recognised in the mere scare-crow that she appeared, the happy and laughing young-ster of a few weeks before.

'The mother was a woman of very different mettle from her poor child. Impassioned and determined in character, she was not one to provoke with impunity. And her moods were as enduring as they were deep. Seeing what a wreck her darling had become she went on foot to the manor-house, and, contrary to the custom of the villagers, rang at the front door, where she asked to see that ruffian the master of the mansion who had ruined her only child. The Squire sent out a reply that he was very sorry for the girl, but that he could not see her mother, accompanying his message by a *solatium* of five shillings.

'In the bitterness of her hate, the woman threw the five-shilling piece through the panes of the dining-room window, and went home to brood again over her idolized child.

'One day a little later, when the girl was well enough to play in the lane, she came in with a bigger girl who took care of her.

' "Death's Head – I be Death's Head – hee, hee!" said the child.

' "What?" said the mother, turning pale.

'The girl in charge explained that the other children had nicknamed her daughter "Death's Head" since she had lost her hair, from her resemblance to a skull.

'When the elder girl was gone the mother carefully regarded the child from the distance. In a moment she saw how cruelly apt the *sobriquet* was. The bald scalp, the hollow cheeks – by reason of the absence of teeth – and the saucer eyes, the cadaverous hue, had, indeed, a startling likeness to that bony relic of mortality.

'At this time the Squire was successfully soliciting in marriage a certain Lady Cicely, the daughter of an ancient and noble house in that county. During the ensuing summer their nuptials were celebrated, and the young wife brought home amid great rejoicing, and ringing of bells, and dancing on the green, followed by a bonfire after dark on the hill. The woman, whose disfigured child was as the apple of her eye to her, saw all this, and the greater the good fortune that fell to the Squire, the more envenomed did she become.

'The newly-wedded lady was much liked by the villagers in general, to whom she was very charitable, intelligently entering into their lives and histories, and endeavouring to relieve their cares. On a particular evening of the ensuing autumn when she had been a wife but a few months, after some parish-visiting, she was returning homeward to dinner on foot, her way to the mansion lying by the churchyard wall. It was barely dusk, but a full harvest moon was shining from the east. At this moment of the Lady Cicely's return it chanced that the widow with her afflicted girl was crossing the churchyard by the footpath from gate to gate. The churchyard was in obscurity, being shaded by the yews. Seeing the lady in the adjoining highway, the woman hastily left the footpath with the child, crossed the graves to the shadow of the wall outside which the lady was passing, and pulled off the child's hood so that the baldness was revealed. Whispering to the child, "Grin at her, my deary!" she held up the little girl as high as she could, which was just sufficient to disclose her face over the coping of the wall to a person on the other side.

'The moonlight fell upon the sepulchral face and head, intensifying the child's daytime aspect till it was only too much like that which had suggested the nickname. The unsuspecting and timid lady – a perfect necrophobist by reason of the care with which everything unpleasant had been kept out of her dainty life – saw the death-like shape, and, shrieking with sudden terror, fell to the ground. The lurking woman with her child disappeared in another direction, and passed through the churchyard gate homeward.

'The Lady Cicely's shriek brought some villagers to the spot. They found her quivering, but not senseless; and she was taken home. There she lay prostrate for some time under the doctor's hands.

II

'It was the following spring, and the time drew near when an infant was to be born to the Squire. Great was the anxiety of all concerned, by reason of the fright and fall from which the Lady Cicely had suffered in the latter part of the preceding year. However, the event which they were all expecting took place, and, to the joy of her friends, no evil consequences seemed to have ensued from the terrifying incident before-mentioned. The child of Lady Cicely was a son and heir.

'Meanwhile the mother of the afflicted child watched these things in silence. Nothing – not even malevolent tricks upon those dear to him – seemed to interrupt the prosperity of the Squire. An uncle of his, a money-lender in some northern city, died childless at this time and left an immense fortune to his nephew the Lady Cicely's husband; who, fortified by this acquisition, now bethought himself of a pedigree as a necessity, so as to be no longer beholden to his wife for all the ancestral credit that his children would possess. By searching in the County history, he happily discovered that one of the Knights who came over

with William the Conqueror bore a name which somewhat resembled
his own, and from this he constructed an ingenious and creditable
genealogical tree; the only rickety point in which occurred at a certain
date in the previous century. It was the date whereat it became necessary to show that his great-grandfather (in reality a respectable village
tanner) was the indubitable son of a scion of the Knightly family before
alluded to, despite the fact that this scion had lived in quite another part
of the county. This little artistic junction, however, was satisfactorily
manipulated, and the grafting was only to be perceived by the curious.

'His upward progress was uninterrupted. His only son grew to be an
interesting lad, though, like his mother, exceedingly timid and impressionable. With his now great wealth, the Squire began to feel that his
present modest country-seat was insufficient, and there being at this
time an Abbey and its estates in the market by reason of some dispute
in the family hitherto its owners, the wealthy gentleman purchased it.
The Abbey was of large proportions and stood in a lovely and fertile
valley surrounded by many attached estates. It had a situation fit for the
home of a prince, still more for that of an Archbishop. This historic
spot, with its monkish associations, its fish-ponds, woods, village, abbey-
church, and abbots' bones beneath their incised slabs, all passed into
the possession of our illustrious self-seeker.

'Meeting his son when the purchase was completed, he smacked the
youth on the shoulder.

' "We've estates, and rivers, and hills, and woods, and a beautiful
Abbey unrivalled in the whole of Wessex – Ha, ha!" he cried.

' "I don't care about abbeys," said the gentle son. "They are gloomy;
this one particularly."

' "Nonsense!" said the father. "And we've a village, and the Abbey
church into the bargain."

' "Yes."

' "And dozens of mitred abbots in their stone coffins underground,
and tons of monks – all for the same money. . . . Yes, the very dust of
those old rascals is mine! Ho, ho!"

'The son turned pale. "Many were holy men," he murmured, "despite
the errors in their creed."

' "D— ye, grow up, and get married, and have a wife who'll disabuse
you of that ghostly nonsense!" cried the Squire.

'Not more than a year after this, several new peers were created for
political reasons with which we have no concern. Among them was the

subject of this legend, much to the chagrin of some of his neighbours, who considered that such rapid advancement was too great for his deserts. On this point I express no opinion.

'He now resided at the Abbey, outwardly honoured by all in his vicinity, though perhaps less honoured in their hearts; and many were the visitors from far and near. In due course his son grew to manhood and married a beautiful woman, whose beauty nevertheless was no greater than her taste and accomplishments. She could read Latin and Greek, as well as one or two modern languages; above all she had great skill as a sculptress in marble and other materials.

'The poor widow in the other village seemed to have been blasted out of existence by the success of her long-time enemy. The two could not thrive side by side. She declined and died; her death having, happily, been preceded by that of her child.

'Though the Abbey, with its little cells and quaint turnings, satisfied the curiosity of visitors, it did not satisfy the noble lord (as the Squire had now become). Except the Abbot's Hall, the rooms were miserably small for a baron of his wealth, who expected soon to be an earl, and the parent of a line of earls.

'Moreover the village was close to his very doors – on his very lawn, and he disliked the proximity of its inhabitants, his old craze for seclusion remaining with him still. On Sundays they sat at service in the very Abbey Church which was part of his own residence. Besides, as his son had said, the conventual buildings formed a gloomy dwelling, with its dark corridors, monkish associations, and charnel-like smell.

'So he set to work, and did not spare his thousands. First, he carted the village bodily away to a distance of a mile or more, where he built new, and, it must be added, convenient cottages, and a little barn-like church. The spot on which the old village had stood was now included in his lawn. But the villagers still intruded there, for they came to ring the Abbey-Church bells – a fine peal, which they professed (it is believed truly) to have an immemorial right to chime.

'As the natives persistently came and got drunk in the ringing-loft, the peer determined to put a stop to it. He sold the ring of bells to a founder in a distant city, and to him one day the whole beautiful set of them was conveyed on waggons away from the spot on which they had hung and resounded for so many centuries, and called so many devout souls to prayer. When the villagers saw their dear bells going off in procession, never to return, they stood in their doors and shed tears.

'It was just after this time that the first shadow fell upon the new lord's life. His wife died. Yet the renovation of the residence went on apace. The Abbey was pulled down wing by wing, and a fair mansion built on its site. An additional lawn was planned to extend over the spot where the cloisters had been, and for that purpose the ground was to be lowered and levelled. The flat tombs covering the Abbots were removed one by one, as a necessity of the embellishment, and the bones dug up.

'Of these bones it seemed as if the excavators would never reach the end. It was necessary to dig ditches and pits for them in the plantations, and from their quantity there was not much respect shown to them in wheeling them away.

III

'One morning, when the family were rising from breakfast, a message was brought to my lord that more bones than ever had been found in clearing away the ground for the ball-room, and for the foundations of the new card-parlour. One of the skeletons was that of a mitred abbot – evidently a very holy person. What were they to do with it?

' "Put him into any hole," says my Lord.

'The foreman came a second time. "There is something strange in those bones, my lord," he said; "we remove them by barrowfuls, and still they seem never to lessen. The more we carry away, the more there are left behind."

'The son looked disturbed, rose from his seat, and went out of the room. Since his mother's death he had been much depressed, and seemed to suffer from nervous debility.

' "Curse the bones," said the peer, angry at the extreme sensitiveness of his son, whose distress and departure he had observed. "More, do ye say? Throw the wormy rubbish into any ditch you can find."

'The servants looked uneasily at each other, for the old Catholicism had not at that time ceased to be the religion of these islands so long as it has now, and much of its superstition and weird fancy still lingered in the minds of the simple folk of this remote nook.

'The son's wife, the bright and accomplished woman aforesaid, to enliven the subject told her father-in-law that she was designing a marble tomb for one of the London churches, and the design was to be a very artistic allegory of Death and the Resurrection; the figure of an

Angel on one side, and that of Death on the other (according to the extravagant symbolism of that date, when such designs as this were much in vogue). Might she, the lady asked, have a skull to copy in marble for the head of Death?

'She might have them all, and welcome, her father-in-law said. He would only be too glad.

'She went out to the spot where the new foundations were being dug, and from the heap of bones chose the one of those sad relics which seemed to offer the most perfect model for her chisel.

' "It is the last Abbot's, my lady," said the clerk of the works.

' "It will do," said she; and directed it to be put into a box and sent to the house in London where she and her husband at present resided.

'When she met her husband that day he proposed that they should return to town almost immediately. "This is a gloomy place," said he. "And if ever it comes into my hands I shan't live here much. I've been telling the old man of my debts, too, and he said he won't pay them – be hanged if he will, until he has a grandson at least – So let's be off."

'They returned to town. This young man, the son and heir, though quiet and nervous, was not a very domestic character; he had many friends of both sexes with whom his refined and accomplished wife was unacquainted. Therefore she was thrown much upon her own resources; and her gifts in carving were a real solace to her. She proceeded with her design for the tomb of her acquaintance, and the Abbot's skull having duly arrived, she made use of it as her model as she had planned.

'Her husband being as usual away from home, she worked at her self-imposed task until bed-time – and then retired. When the house had been wrapped in sleep for some hours, the front door was opened, and the absent one entered, a little the worse for liquor – for drinking in those days was one of a nobleman's accomplishments. He ascended the stairs, candle in hand, and feeling uncertain whether his wife had gone to bed or no, entered her studio to look for her. Holding the candle unsteadily above his head, he perceived a heap of modelling clay; behind it a sheeted figure with a death's head above it – this being in fact the draped dummy arrangement that his wife had built up to be ultimately copied in marble for the allegory she had designed to support the mural tablet.

'The sight seemed to overpower the gazer with horror; the candle fell from his hand, and in the darkness he rushed downstairs and out of the house.

' "I've seen it before!" he cried in mad and maudlin accents. "Where? When?"

'At four o'clock the next morning news was brought to the house that my lord's heir had shot himself dead with a pistol at a tavern not far off.

'His reason for the act was absolutely inexplicable to the outer world. The heir to an enormous property and a high title, the husband of a wife as gifted as she was charming; of all the men in English society he seemed to be the least likely to undertake such a desperate deed.

'Only a few persons – his wife not being one of them, though his father was – knew of the sad circumstances in the life of the suicide's mother, the late Lady Cicely, a few months before his birth – in which she was terrified nearly to death by the woman who held up poor little "Death's Head" over the churchyard wall.

'Then people said that in this there was retribution upon the ambitious lord for his wickedness, particularly that of cursing the bones of the holy men of God. I give the superstition for what it is worth. It is enough to add, in this connection, that the old lord died, some say like Herod, of the characteristics he had imputed to the inoffensive human remains. However that may be, in a few years the title was extinct, and now not a relative or scion remains of the family that bore his name.

'A venerable dissenter, a fearless ascetic of the neighbourhood, who had been deprived of his opportunities through some objections taken by the peer, preached a sermon the Sunday after his funeral, and mentioning no names, significantly took as his text Isaiah, XIV, 10–23:

' "Art thou also become weak as we? Art thou become like unto us? Thy pomp is brought down to the grave, and the noise of thy viols: the worm is spread under thee, and the worms cover thee. How art thou fallen from Heaven, O Lucifer, son of the morning! How art thou cut down to the ground, which didst weaken the nations. . . . I will rise up against him, saith the Lord of hosts, and cut off from Babylon the name, and remnant, and son, and nephew, saith the Lord."

'Whether as a Christian moralist he was justified in doing this I leave others to judge.'

Here the doctor concluded his story, and the thoughtfulness which it had engendered upon his own features spread over those of his hearers, as they sat with their eyes fixed upon the fire.

AN INDISCRETION IN THE LIFE
OF AN HEIRESS

Part One

CHAPTER ONE

When I would pray and think, I think and pray
To several subjects: heaven hath my empty words;
Whilst my invention, hearing not my tongue,
Anchors on Isabel.

THE congregation in Tollamore Church were singing the evening hymn, the people gently swaying backwards and forwards like trees in a soft breeze. The heads of the village children, who sat in the gallery, were inclined to one side as they uttered their shrill notes, their eyes listlessly tracing some crack in the old walls, or following the movement of a distant bough or bird, with features rapt almost to painfulness.

In front of the children stood a thoughtful young man, who was plainly enough the schoolmaster; and his gaze was fixed on a remote part of the aisle beneath him. When the singing was over, and all had sat down for the sermon, his eyes still remained in the same place. There was some excuse for their direction, for it was in a straight line forwards; but their fixity was only to be explained by some object before them. This was a square pew, containing one solitary sitter. But that sitter was a young lady, and a very sweet lady was she.

Afternoon service in Tollamore parish was later than in many others in that neighbourhood; and as the darkness deepened during the progress of the sermon, the rector's pulpit-candles shone to the remotest nooks of the building, till at length they became the sole lights of the congregation. The lady was the single person besides the preacher whose face was turned westwards, the pew that she occupied being the only one in the church in which the seat ran all around. She reclined in her corner, her bonnet and dark dress growing by degrees invisible, and at last only her upturned face could be discerned, a solitary white spot against the black surface of the wainscot. Over her head rose a vast marble monument, erected to the memory of her ancestors, male and female; for she was one of high standing in that parish. The design consisted of a winged skull and two cherubim, supporting a pair of tall Corinthian columns, between which spread a broad slab, containing the roll of ancient names, lineages, and deeds, and surmounted by a pediment, with the crest of the family at its apex.

As the youthful schoolmaster gazed, and all these details became dimmer, her face was modified in his fancy, till it seemed almost to resemble the carved marble skull immediately above her head. The thought was unpleasant enough to arouse him from his half-dreamy state, and he entered on rational considerations of what a vast gulf lay between that lady and himself, what a troublesome world it was to live in where such divisions could exist, and how painful was the evil when a man of his unequal history was possessed of a keen susceptibility.

Now a close observer, who should have happened to be near the large pew, might have noticed before the light got low that the interested gaze of the young man had been returned from time to time by the young lady, although he, towards whom her glances were directed, did not perceive the fact. It would have been guessed that something in the past was common to both, notwithstanding their difference in social standing. What that was may be related in a few words.

One day in the previous week there had been some excitement in the parish on account of the introduction upon the farm of a steam threshing-machine for the first time, the date of these events being some thirty years ago. The machine had been hired by a farmer who was a relative of the schoolmaster's, and when it was set going all the people round about came to see it work. It was fixed in a corner of a field near the main road, and in the afternoon a passing carriage stopped outside the hedge. The steps were let down, and Miss Geraldine Allenville, the young woman whom we have seen sitting in the church pew, came through the gate of the field towards the engine. At that hour most of the villagers had been to the spot, had gratified their curiosity, and afterwards gone home again; so that there were only now left standing beside the engine the engine-man, the farmer, and the young school-master, who had come like the rest. The labourers were at the other part of the machine, under the cornstack some distance off.

The girl looked with interest at the whizzing wheels, asked questions of the old farmer, and remained in conversation with him for some time, the schoolmaster standing a few paces distant, and looking more or less towards her. Suddenly the expression of his face changed to one of horror; he was by her side in a moment, and, seizing hold of her, he swung her round by the arm to a distance of several feet.

In speaking to the farmer she had inadvertently stepped backwards, and had drawn so near to the band which ran from the engine to the drum of the thresher that in another moment her dress must have been caught, and she would have been whirled round the wheel as a mangled carcase. As soon as the meaning of the young man's act was understood by her she turned deadly pale and nearly fainted. When she was well enough to walk, the two men led her to the carriage, which had been standing outside the hedge all the time.

'You have saved me from a ghastly death!' the agitated girl murmured to the schoolmaster. 'Oh! I can never forget it!' and then she sank into the carriage and was driven away.

On account of this the schoolmaster had been invited to Tollamore House to explain the incident to the Squire, the young lady's only living parent. Mr Allenville thanked her preserver, inquired the history of his late father, a painter of good family, but unfortunate and improvident; and finally told his visitor that, if he were fond of study, the library of the house was at his service. Geraldine herself had spoken very impulsively to the young man – almost, indeed, with imprudent warmth – and his tender interest in her during the church service was the result of the sympathy she had shown.

And thus did an emotion, which became this man's sole motive power through many following years, first arise and establish itself. Only once more did she lift her eyes to where he sat, and it was when they all stood up before leaving. This time he noticed the glance. Her look of recognition led his feelings onward yet another stage. Admiration grew to be attachment; he even wished that he might own her, not exactly as a wife, but as a being superior to himself – in the sense in which a servant may be said to own a master. He would have cared to possess her in order to exhibit her glories to the world, and he scarcely even thought of her ever loving him.

There were two other stages in his course of love, but they were not reached until some time after today. The first was a change from this proud desire to a longing to cherish. The last stage, later still, was when her very defects became rallying-points for defence, when every one of his senses became special pleaders for her; and that not through blindness, but from a tender inability to do aught else than defend her against all the world.

CHAPTER TWO

She was active, stirring, all fire –
Could not rest, could not tire –
Never in all the world such an one!
And here was plenty to be done,
And she that could do it, great or small,
She was to do nothing at all.

Five mornings later the same young man was looking out of the window
of Tollamore village school in a fixed and absent manner. The weather
was exceptionally mild, though scarcely to the degree which would have
justified his airy situation at such a month of the year. A hazy light
spread through the air, the landscape on which his eyes were resting
being enlivened and lit up by the spirit of an unseen sun rather than by
its direct rays. Every sound could be heard for miles. There was a great
crowing of cocks, bleating of sheep, and cawing of rooks, which proceeded from all points of the compass, rising and falling as the origin of
each sound was near or far away. There were also audible the voices of
the people in the village, interspersed with hearty laughs, the bell of a
distant flock of sheep, a robin close at hand, vehicles in the neighbouring
roads and lanes. One of these latter noises grew gradually more distinct,
and proved itself to be rapidly nearing the school. The listener blushed
as he heard it.

'Suppose it should be!' he said to himself.

He had said the same thing at every such noise that he had heard
during the foregoing week, and had been mistaken in his hope. But this
time a certain carriage did appear in answer to his expectation. He came
from the window hastily; and in a minute a footman knocked and opened
the school door.

'Miss Allenville wishes to speak to you, Mr Mayne.'

The schoolmaster went to the porch – he was a very young man to be
called a schoolmaster – his heart beating with excitement.

'Good morning,' she said, with a confident yet girlish smile. 'My
father expects me to inquire into the school arrangements, and I wish
to do so on my own account as well. May I come in?'

She entered as she spoke, telling the coachman to drive to the village
on some errand, and call for her in half an hour.

Mayne could have wished that she had not been so thoroughly free
from all apparent consciousness of the event of the previous week, of the
fact that he was considerably more of a man than the small persons by

whom the apartment was mainly filled, and that he was as nearly as possible at her own level in age, as wide in sympathies, and possibly more inflammable in heart. But he soon found that a sort of fear to entrust her voice with the subject of that link between them was what restrained her. When he had explained a few details of routine she moved away from him round the school.

He turned and looked at her as she stood among the children. To his eyes her beauty was indescribable. Before he had met her he had scarcely believed that any woman in the world could be so lovely. The clear, deep eyes, full of all tender expressions; the fresh, subtly-curved cheek, changing its tones of red with the fluctuation of each thought; the ripe tint of her delicate mouth, and the indefinable line where lip met lip; the noble bend of her neck, the wavy lengths of her dark brown hair, the soft motions of her bosom when she breathed, the light fall of her little feet, the elegant contrivances of her attire, all struck him as something he had dreamed of and was not actually seeing. Geraldine Allenville was, in truth, very beautiful; she was a girl such as his eyes had never else-where beheld; and her presence here before his face kept up a sharp struggle of sweet and bitter within him.

He had thought at first that the flush on her face was caused by the fresh air of the morning; but, as it quickly changed to a lesser hue, it occurred to Mayne that it might after all have arisen from shyness at meeting him after her narrow escape. Be that as it might, their conversation, which at first consisted of bald sentences, divided by wide inter-vals of time, became more frequent, and at last continuous. He was painfully soon convinced that her tongue would never have run so easily as it did had it not been that she thought him a person on whom she could vent her ideas without reflection or punctiliousness – a thought, perhaps, expressed to herself by such words as, 'I will say what I like to him, for he is only our schoolmaster.'

'And you have chosen to keep a school,' she went on, with a shade of mischievousness in her tone, looking at him as if she thought that, had she been a man capable of saving people's lives, she would have done something much better than teaching. She was so young as to habitually think thus of other persons' courses.

'No,' he said, simply; 'I don't choose to keep a school in the sense you mean, choosing it from a host of pursuits, all equally possible.'

'How came you here, then?'

'I fear more by chance than by aim.'

'Then you are not very ambitious ?'

'I have my ambitions, such as they are.'

'I thought so. Everybody has nowadays. But it is a better thing not to be too ambitious, *I* think.'

'If we value ease of mind, and take an economist's view of our term of life, it may be a better thing.'

Having been tempted, by his unexpectedly cultivated manner of speaking, to say more than she had meant to say, she found it embarrassing either to break off or say more, and in her doubt she stooped to kiss a little girl.

'Although I spoke lightly of ambition,' she observed, without turning to him, 'and said that easy happiness was worth most, I could defend ambition very well, and in the only pleasant way.'

'And that way ?'

'On the broad ground of the loveliness of any dream about future triumphs. In looking back there is a pleasure in contemplating a time when some attractive thing of the future appeared possible, even though it never came to pass.'

Mayne was puzzled to hear her talk in this tone of maturity. That such questions of success and failure should have occupied his own mind seemed natural, for they had been forced upon him by the difficulties he had encountered in his pursuit of a career. He was not just then aware how very unpractical the knowledge of this sage lady of seventeen really was; that it was merely caught up by intercommunication with people of culture and experience, who talked before her of their theories and beliefs until she insensibly acquired their tongue.

The carriage was heard coming up the road. Mayne gave her the list of the children, their ages, and other particulars which she had called for, and she turned to go out. Not a word had been said about the incident by the threshing-machine, though each one could see that it was constantly in the other's thoughts. The roll of the wheels may or may not have reminded her of her position in relation to him. She said, bowing, and in a somewhat more distant tone: 'We shall all be glad to learn that our schoolmaster is so – nice; such a philosopher.' But, rather surprised at her own cruelty in uttering the latter words, she added one of the sweetest laughs that ever came from lips, and said, in gentlest tones, 'Good morning; I shall *always* remember what you did for me. Oh! it makes me sick to think of that moment. I came on purpose to thank you again, but I could not say it till now!'

Mayne's heart, which had felt the rebuff, came round to her with a rush; he could have almost forgiven her for physically wounding him if she had asked him in such a tone not to notice it. He watched her out of sight, thinking in rather a melancholy mood how time would absorb all her beauty, as the growing distance between them absorbed her form. He then went in, and endeavoured to recall every word that he had said to her, troubling and racking his mind to the utmost of his ability about his imagined faults of manner. He remembered that he had used the indicative mood instead of the proper subjunctive in a certain phrase. He had given her to understand that an old idea he had made use of was his own, and so on through other particulars, each of which was an item of misery.

The place and the manner of her sitting were defined by the position of her chair, and by the books, maps, and prints scattered round it. Her 'I shall always remember,' he repeated to himself, aye, a hundred times; and though he knew the plain import of the words, he could not help toying with them, looking at them from all points, and investing them with extraordinary meanings.

CHAPTER THREE

But what is this ? I turn about
And find a trouble in thine eye.

Egbert Mayne, though at present filling the office of village school-master, had been intended for a less narrow path. His position at this time was entirely owing to the death of his father in embarrassed circum-stances two years before. Mr Mayne had been a landscape and animal painter, and had settled in the village in early manhood, where he set about improving his prospects by marrying a small farmer's daughter. The son had been sent away from home at an early age to a good school, and had returned at seventeen to enter upon some professional life or other. But his father's health was at this time declining, and when the painter died, a year and a half later, nothing had been done for Egbert. He was now living with his maternal grandfather, Richard Broadford, the farmer, who was a tenant of Squire Allenville's. Egbert's ideas did not incline to painting, but he had ambitious notions of adopting a liter-ary profession, or entering the Church, or doing something congenial to his tastes whenever he could set about it. But first it was necessary to read, mark, learn, and look around him; and, a master being temporarily required for the school until such time as it should be placed under Government inspection, he stepped in and made use of the occupation as a stop-gap for a while.

He lived in his grandfather's farmhouse, walking backwards and forwards to the school every day, in order that the old man, who would otherwise be living quite alone, might have the benefit of his society during the long winter evenings. Egbert was much attached to his grandfather, and so, indeed, were all who knew him. The old farmer's amiable disposition and kindliness of heart, while they had hindered him from enriching himself one shilling during the course of a long and laborious life, had also kept him clear of every arrow of antagonism. The house in which he lived was the same that he had been born in, and was almost a part of himself. It had been built by his father's father; but on the dropping of the lives for which it was held, some twenty years earlier, it had lapsed to the Squire.

Richard Broadford was not, however, dispossessed: after his father's death the family had continued as before in the house and farm, but as yearly tenants. It was much to Broadford's delight, for his pain at the thought of parting from those old sticks and stones of his ancestors, before it had been known if the tenure could be continued, was real and great.

On the evening of the day on which Miss Allenville called at the school Egbert returned to the farmhouse as usual. He found his grandfather sitting with his hands on his knees, and showing by his countenance that something had happened to disturb him greatly. Egbert looked at him inquiringly, and with some misgiving.

'I have got to go at last, Egbert,' he said, in a tone intended to be stoical, but far from it. 'He is my enemy after all.'

'Who?' said Mayne.

'The Squire. He's going to take seventy acres of neighbour Greenman's farm to enlarge the park; and Greenman's acreage is to be made up to him, and more, by throwing my farm in with his. Yes, that's what the Squire is going to have done. . . . Well, I thought to have died here; but 'tisn't to be.'

He looked as helpless as a child, for age had weakened him. Egbert endeavoured to cheer him a little, and vexed as the young man was, he thought there might yet be some means of tiding over this difficulty.

'Mr Allenville wants seventy acres more in his park, does he?' he echoed mechanically. 'Why can't it be taken entirely out of Greenman's farm? His is big enough, Heaven knows; and your hundred acres might be left you in peace.'

'Well mayest say so! Oh, it is because he is tired of seeing old-fashioned farming like mine. He likes the young generation's system best, I suppose.'

'If I had only known this this afternoon,' Egbert said.

'You could have done nothing.'

'Perhaps not.' Egbert was, however, thinking that he would have mentioned the matter to his visitor, and told her such circumstances as would have enlisted her sympathies in the case.

'I thought it would come to this,' said old Richard, vehemently. 'The present Squire Allenville has never been any real friend to me. It was only through his wife that I have stayed here so long. If it hadn't been for her we should have gone the very year that my poor father died, and the house fell into hand. I wish we had now. You see, now she's dead, there's nobody to counteract him in his schemes; and I am to be swept away.'

They talked on thus, and by bed-time the old man was in better spirits. But the subject did not cease to occupy Egbert's mind, and that anxiously. Were the house and farm which his grandfather had occupied so long to be taken away, Egbert knew it would affect his life to a degree out of all proportion to the seriousness of the event. The transplanting of old people is like the transplanting of old trees; a twelvemonth usually sees them wither and die away.

The next day proved that his anticipations were likely to be correct, his grandfather being so disturbed that he could scarcely eat or drink. The remainder of the week passed in just the same way. Nothing now occupied Egbert's mind but a longing to see Miss Allenville. To see her would be bliss; to ask her if anything could be done by which his grandfather might retain the farm and premises would be nothing but duty. His hope of good results from the course was based on the knowledge that Allenville, cold and hard as he was, had some considerable affection for or pride in his daughter, and that thus she might influence him.

It was not likely that she would call at the school for a week or two at least, and Mayne therefore tried to meet with her elsewhere. One morning early he was returning from the remote hamlet of Hawksgate, on the further side of the parish, and the nearest way to the school was across the park. He read as he walked, as was customary with him, though at present his thoughts wandered incessantly. The path took him through a shrubbery running close up to a remote wing of the mansion. Nobody seemed to be stirring in that quarter, till, turning an angle, he saw Geraldine's own graceful figure close at hand, robed in fur, and standing at ease outside an open French casement.

She was startled by his sudden appearance, but her face soon betrayed a sympathetic remembrance of him. Egbert scarcely knew whether to stop or to walk on, when, casting her eyes upon his book, she said, 'Don't let me interrupt your reading.'

'I am glad to have—' he stammered, and for the moment could get no further. His nervousness encouraged her to continue. 'What are you reading?' she said.

The book was, as may possibly be supposed by those who know the mood inspired by hopeless attachments, 'Childe Harold's Pilgrimage', a poem which at that date had never been surpassed in congeniality to the minds of young persons in the full fever of virulent love. He was rather reluctant to let her know this; but as the inquiry afforded him an opening for conversation he held out the book, and her eye glanced over the page.

'Oh thank you,' she said hastily, 'I ought not to have asked that – only I am interested always in books. Is your grandfather quite well, Mr Mayne? I saw him yesterday, and thought he seemed to be not in such good health as usual.'

'His mind is disturbed,' said Egbert.

'Indeed, why is that?'

'It is on account of his having to leave the farm. He is old and was born in that house.'

'Ah, yes, I have heard something of that,' she said with a slightly regretful look. 'Mr Allenville has decided to enlarge the park. Born in the house, was he?'

'Yes. His father built it. May I ask your opinion on the point, Miss Allenville? Don't you think it would be possible to enlarge the park without taking my grandfather's farm? Greenman has already five hundred acres.'

She was perplexed how to reply, and evading the question said, 'Your grandfather much wishes to stay?'

'He does, intensely – more than you can believe or think. But he will not ask to be let remain. I dread the effect of leaving upon him. If it were possible to contrive that he should not be turned out I should be grateful indeed.'

'I – I will do all I can that things may remain as they are,' she said with a deepened colour. 'In fact, I am almost certain that he will not have to go, since it is so painful to him,' she added in the sanguine tones of a child. 'My father could not have known that his mind was so bent on staying.'

Here the conversation ended, and Egbert went on with a lightened heart. Whether his pleasure arose entirely from having done his grand-father a good turn, or from the mere sensation of having been near her, he himself could hardly have determined.

CHAPTER FOUR

Oh, for my sake, do you with fortune chide,
The guilty goddess of my harmful deed
That did not better for my life provide.

Now commenced a period during which Egbert Mayne's emotions burnt in a more unreasoning and wilder worship than at any other time in his life. The great condition of idealization in love was present here, that of an association in which, through difference in rank, the petty human elements that enter so largely into life are kept entirely out of sight, and there is hardly awakened in the man's mind a thought that they appertain to her at all.

He deviated frequently from his daily track to the spot where the last meeting had been, till, on the fourth morning after, he saw her there again; but she let him pass that time with a bare recognition. Two days later the carriage drove down the lane to the village as he was walking away. When they met she told the coachman to stop.

'I am glad to tell you that your grandfather may be perfectly easy about the house and farm,' she said; as if she took unfeigned pleasure in saying it. 'The question of altering the park is postponed indefinitely. I have resisted it: I could do no less for one who did so much for me.'

'Thank you very warmly,' said Egbert so earnestly, that she blushed crimson as the carriage rolled away.

The spring drew on, and he saw and spoke with her several times. In truth he walked abroad much more than had been usual with him formerly, searching in all directions for her form. Had she not been unreflecting and impressionable – had not her life dragged on as un-eventfully as that of one in gaol, through her residing in a great house with no companion but an undemonstrative father; and, above all, had not Egbert been a singularly engaging young man of that distracting order of beauty which grows upon the feminine gazer with every glance, this tender waylaying would have made little difference to anybody. But such was not the case. In return for Egbert's presence of mind at the threshing she had done him a kindness, and the pleasure that she took in the act shed an added interest upon the object of it. Thus, on both sides it had happened that a deed of solicitude casually performed gave each doer a sense of proprietorship in its recipient, and a wish still further to establish that position by other deeds of the same sort.

To still further kindle Geraldine's indiscreet interest in him, Egbert's devotion became perceptible ere long even to her inexperienced eyes; and it was like a new world to the young girl. At first she was almost frightened at the novelty of the thing. Then the fascination of the dis-covery caused her ready, receptive heart to palpitate in an ungovernable manner whenever he came near her. She was not quite in love herself, but she was so moved by the circumstance of her deliverer being in love, that she could think of nothing else. His appearing at odd places startled her; and yet she rather liked that kind of startling. Too often her eyes rested on his face; too often her thoughts surrounded his figure and dwelt on his conversation.

One day, when they met on a bridge, they did not part till after a long and interesting conversation on books, in which many opinions of Mayne's (crude and unformed enough, it must be owned) that happened to take her fancy, set her glowing with ardour to unfold her own.

After any such meeting as this, Egbert would go home and think for hours of her little remarks and movements. The day and minute of her accidental rencounter became registered in his mind with the in-delibility of ink. Years afterwards he could recall at a moment's notice that he saw her at eleven o'clock on the third of April, a Sunday; at four on Tuesday, the twelfth; at a quarter to six on Thursday the twenty-eighth; that on the ninth it rained at a quarter past two, when she was walking up the avenue; that on the seventeenth the grass was rather too wet for a lady's feet; and other calendrical and meteorological facts of no value whatever either to science or history.

On a Tuesday evening, when they had had several conversations out of doors, and when a passionate liking for his society was creeping over the reckless though pure girl, slowly, insidiously, and surely, like ripeness over fruit, she further committed herself by coming alone to the school. A heavy rain had threatened to fall all the afternoon, and just as she entered it began. School hours were at that moment over; but he waited a few moments before dismissing the children, to see if the storm would clear up. After looking round at the classes, and making sundry inquiries of the little ones in the usual manner of ladies who patronize a school, she came up to him.

'I listened outside before I came in. It was a great pleasure to hear the voices – three classes reading at three paces.' She continued with a laugh: 'There was a rough treble voice bowling easily along, an ambling sweet voice earnest about fishes in the sea, and a shrill voice spelling out letter by letter. Then there was a shuffling of feet – then you sang. It seemed quite a little poem.'

'Yes,' Egbert said. 'But perhaps, like many poems, it was hard prose to the originators.'

She remained thinking, and Mayne looked out at the weather. Judging from the sky and wind that there was no likelihood of a change that night, he proceeded to let the children go. Miss Allenville assisted in wrapping up as many of them as possible in the old coats and other apparel which Egbert kept by him for the purpose. But she touched both clothes and children rather gingerly, and as if she did not much like the contact.

Egbert's sentiments towards her that evening were vehement and curious. Much as he loved her, his liking for the peasantry about him – his mother's ancestry – caused him sometimes a twinge of self-reproach for thinking of her so exclusively, and nearly forgetting his old acquaintance, neighbours, and his grandfather's familiar friends, with their rough but honest ways. To further complicate his feelings tonight there was the sight, on the one hand, of the young lady with her warm rich dress and glowing future, and on the other of the weak little boys and girls – some only five years old, and none more than twelve, going off in their different directions in the pelting rain, some for a walk of more than two miles, with the certainty of being drenched to the skin, and with no change of clothes when they reached their home. He watched the rain spots thickening upon the faded frocks, worn-out tippets, yellow straw hats and bonnets, and coarse pinafores of his unprotected little flock as they walked down the path, and was thereby reminded of the hopelessness of his attachment, by perceiving how much more nearly akin was his lot to theirs than to hers.

Miss Allenville, too, was looking at the children, and unfortunately she chanced to say, as they toddled off, 'Poor little wretches!'

A sort of despairing irritation at her remoteness from his plane, as implied by her pitying the children so unmercifully impelled him to remark, 'Say poor little *children*, madam.'

She was silent – awkwardly silent.

'I suppose I must walk home,' she said, when about half a minute had passed. 'Nobody knows where I am, and the carriage may not find me for hours.'

'I'll go for the carriage,' said Egbert readily.

But he did not move. While she had been speaking, there had grown up in him a conviction that these opportunities of seeing her would soon necessarily cease. She would get older, and would perceive the incorrectness of being on intimate terms with him merely because he had snatched her from danger. He would have to engage in a more active career, and go away. Such ideas brought on an irresistible climax to an intense and long-felt desire. He had just reached that point in the action of passion upon mind at which it masters judgment.

It was almost dark in the room, by reason of the heavy clouds and nearness of the night. But the fire had just flamed up brightly in the grate, and it threw her face and form into ruddy relief against the gray wall behind.

Suddenly rushing towards her, he seized her hand before she comprehended his intention, kissed it tenderly, and clasped her in his arms. Her soft body yielded like wool under his embrace. As suddenly releasing her he turned, and went back to the other end of the room.

Egbert's feeling as he retired was that he had committed a crime. The madness of the action was apparent to him almost before it was completed. There seemed not a single thing left for him to do, but to go into life-long banishment for such sacrilege. He faced round and regarded her. Her features were not visible enough to judge of their expression. All that he could discern through the dimness and his own agitation was that for some time she remained quite motionless. Her state was probably one of suspension; as with Ulysses before Melanthus, she may have –

Entertained a breast
That in the strife of all extremes did rest.

In one, two, or five minutes – neither of them ever knew exactly how long – apparently without the motion of a limb, she glided noiselessly to the door and vanished.

Egbert leant himself against the wall, almost distracted. He could see absolutely no limit to the harm that he had done by his wild and unreasoning folly. 'Am I a man to thus ill-treat the loveliest girl that ever was born? Sweet injured creature – how she will hate me!' These were some of the expressions that he murmured in the twilight of that lonely room.

Then he said that she certainly had encouraged him, which, unfortunately for her, was only too true. She had seen that he was always in search of her, and she did not put herself out of his way. He was sure that she liked him to admire her. 'Yet, no,' he murmured, 'I will not excuse myself at all.'

The night passed away miserably. One conviction by degrees overruled all the rest in his mind – that if she knew precisely how pure had been his longing towards her, she could not think badly of him. His reflections resulted in a resolve to get an interview with her, and make his defence and explanation in full. The decision come to, his impatience could scarcely preserve him from rushing to Tollamore House that very daybreak, and trying to get into her presence, though it was the likeliest of suppositions that she would never see him.

Every spare minute of the following days he hovered round the house, in hope of getting a glimpse of her; but not once did she make herself visible. He delayed taking the extreme step of calling, till the hour came when he could delay no longer. On a certain day he rang the bell with a mild air, and disguised his feelings by looking as if he wished to speak to her merely on copy-books, slates, and other school matters, the school being professedly her hobby. He was told that Miss Allenville had gone on a visit to some relatives thirty-five miles off, and that she would probably not return for a month.

As there was no help for it, Egbert settled down to wait as he best could, not without many misgivings lest his rash action, which a prompt explanation might have toned down and excused, would now be the cause of a total estrangement between them, so that nothing would restore him to the place he had formerly held in her estimation. That she had ever seriously loved him he did not hope or dream; but it was intense pain to him to be out of her favour.

CHAPTER FIVE

So I soberly laid my last plan
To extinguish the man.
Round his creep-hole, with never a break,
Ran my fires for his sake;
Over-head did my thunder combine
With my underground mine:
Till I looked from my labour content
To enjoy the event.
When sudden – how think ye the end?

A week after the crisis mentioned above, it was secretly whispered to
Egbert's grandfather that the park enlargement scheme was after all to
be proceeded with; that Miss Allenville was extremely anxious to have
it put in hand as soon as possible. Farmer Broadford's farm was to be
added to Greenman's, as originally intended, and the old house that
Broadford lived in was to be pulled down as an encumbrance.

'It is she this time!' murmured Egbert, gloomily. 'Then I did offend
her, and mortify her; and she is resentful.'

The excitement of his grandfather again caused him much alarm, and
even remorse. Such was the responsiveness of the farmer's physical to
his mental state that in the course of a week his usual health failed, and
his gloominess of mind was followed by dimness of sight and giddiness.
By much persuasion Egbert induced him to stay at home for a day or
two; but indoors he was the most restless of creatures, through not being
able to engage in the pursuits to which he had been accustomed from
his boyhood. He walked up and down, looking wistfully out of the
window, shifting the positions of books and chairs, and putting them
back again, opening his desk and shutting it after a vacant look at the
papers, saying he should never get settled in another farm at his time
of life, and evincing all the symptoms of nervousness and excitability.

Meanwhile Egbert anxiously awaited Miss Allenville's return, more
resolved than ever to obtain audience of her, and beg her not to visit
upon an unoffending old man the consequences of a young one's folly.
Any retaliation upon himself he would accept willingly, and own to be
well deserved.

At length, by making off-hand inquiries (for he dared not ask directly
for her again) he learnt that she was to be at home on the Thursday.
The following Friday and Saturday he kept a sharp lookout; and, when

lingering in the park for at least the tenth time in that half-week, a sudden rise in the ground revealed her coming along the path.

Egbert stayed his advance, in order that, if she really objected to see him, she might easily strike off into a side path or turn back.

She did not accept the alternatives, but came straight on to where he lingered, averting her face waywardly as she approached. When she was within a few steps of him he could see that the trimmings of her dress trembled like leaves. He cleared his dry throat to speak.

'Miss Allenville,' he said, humbly taking off his hat, 'I should be glad to say one word to you, if I may.'

She looked at him for just one moment, but said nothing; and he could see that the expression of her face was flushed, and her mood skittish. The place they were standing in was a remote nook, hidden by the trunks and boughs, so that he could afford to give her plenty of time, for there was no fear of their being observed or overheard. Indeed, knowing that she often walked that way, Egbert had previously surveyed the spot and thought it suitable for the occasion, much as Wellington antecedently surveyed the field of Waterloo.

Here the young man began his pleading speech to her. He dilated upon his sensations when first he saw her; and as he became warmed by his oratory he spoke of all his inmost perturbations on her account without the slightest reserve. He related with much natural eloquence how he had tried over and over again not to love her, and how he had loved her in spite of that trying; of his intention never to reveal his passion, till their situation on that rainy evening prompted the impulse which ended in that irreverent action of his; and earnestly asked her to forgive him – not for his feelings, since they were his own to command or blame – but for the way in which he testified of them to one so cultivated, and so beautiful.

Egbert was flushed and excited by the time that he reached this point in his tale.

Her eyes were fixed on the grass; and then a tear stole quietly from its corner, and wandered down her cheek. She tried to say something, but her usually adroit tongue was unequal to the task. Ultimately she glanced at him, and murmured, 'I forgive you'; but so inaudibly, that he only recognized the words by their shape upon her lips.

She looked not much more than a child now, and Egbert thought with sadness that her tear and her words were perhaps but the result, the one of a transitory sympathy, the other of a desire to escape. They stood

silent for some seconds, and the dressing-bell of the house began ringing. Turning slowly away without another word she hastened out of his
sight.

When Egbert reached home some of his grandfather's old friends
were gathered there, sympathizing with him on the removal he would
have to submit to if report spoke truly. Their sympathy was rather more
for him to bear than their indifference; and as Egbert looked at the old
man's bent figure, and at the expression of his face, denoting a wish to
sink under the earth, out of sight and out of trouble, he was greatly
depressed, and he said inwardly, 'What a fool I was to ask forgiveness
of a woman who can torture my only relative like this! Why do I feel
her to be glorious? Oh that I had never seen her!'

The next day was Sunday, and his grandfather being too unwell to
go out, Egbert went to the evening service alone. When it was over, the
rector detained him in the churchyard to say a few words about the next
week's undertakings. This was soon done, and Egbert turned back to
leave the now empty churchyard. Passing the porch he saw Miss Allenville coming out of the door.

Egbert said nothing, for he knew not what to say; but she spoke. 'Ah,
Mr Mayne, how beautiful the west sky looks! It is the finest sunset we
have had this spring.'

'It is very beautiful,' he replied, without looking westward a single
degree. 'Miss Allenville,' he said reproachfully, 'you might just have
thought whether, for the sake of reaching one guilty person, it was worth
while to deeply wound an old man.'

'I do not allow you to say that,' she answered with proud quickness.
'Still, I will listen just this once.'

'Are you glad you asserted your superiority to me by putting in
motion again that scheme for turning him out?'

'I merely left off hindering it,' she said.

'Well, we shall go now,' continued Egbert, 'and make room for newer
people. I hope you forgive what caused it all.'

'You talk in that strain to make me feel regrets; and you think that
because you are read in a few books you may say or do anything.'

'No, no. That's unfair.'

'I will try to alter it – that your grandfather may not leave. Say that
you forgive me for thinking he and yourself had better leave – as I forgive you for what you did. But remember, nothing of that sort ever
again.'

'Forgive you? Oh, Miss Allenville!' said he in a wild whisper, 'I wish you had sinned a hundred times as much, that I might show how readily I can forgive all.'

She had looked as if she would have held out her hand; but, for some reason or other, directly he had spoken with emotion it was not so well for him as when he had spoken to wound her. She passed on silently, and entered the private gate to the house.

A day or two after this, about three o'clock in the afternoon, and whilst Egbert was giving a lesson in geography, a lad burst into the school with the tidings that Farmer Broadford had fallen from a corn-stack they were threshing, and hurt himself severely.

The boy had borrowed a horse to come with, and Mayne at once made him gallop off with it for a doctor. Dismissing the children, the young man ran home full of forebodings. He found his relative in a chair, held up by two of his labouring-men. He was put to bed, and seeing how pale he was, Egbert gave him a little wine, and bathed the parts which had been bruised by the fall.

Egbert had at first been the more troubled at the event through believing that his grandfather's fall was the result of his low spirits and mental uneasiness; and he blamed himself for letting so infirm a man go out upon the farm till quite recovered. But it turned out that the actual cause of the accident was the breaking of the ladder that he had been standing on. When the surgeon had seen him he said that the external bruises were mere trifles; but that the shock had been great, and had produced internal injuries highly dangerous to a man in that stage of life.

His grandson was of opinion in later years that the fall only hastened by a few months a dissolution which would soon have taken place under any circumstances, from the natural decay of the old man's constitution. His pulse grew feeble and his voice weak, but he continued in a comparatively firm state of mind for some days, during which he talked to Egbert a great deal.

Egbert trusted that the illness would soon pass away; his anxiety for his grandfather was great. When he was gone not one of the family would be left but himself. But in spite of hope the younger man perceived that death was really at hand. And now arose a question. It was certainly a time to make confidences, if they were ever to be made; should he, then, tell his grandfather, who knew the Allenvilles so well, of his love for Geraldine? At one moment it seemed duty; at another it seemed a graceful act, to say the least.

Yet Egbert might never have uttered a word but for a remark of his grandfather's which led up to the very point. He was speaking of the farm and of the Squire, and thence he went on to the daughter.

'She, too,' he said, 'seems to have that reckless spirit which was in her mother's family, and ruined her mother's father at the gaming table, though she's too young to show much of it yet.'

'I hope not,' said Egbert fervently.

'Why? What be the Allenvilles to you – not that I wish the girl harm?'

'I think that she is the very best thing in the world. I – love her deeply.'

His grandfather's eyes were set on the wall. 'Well, well, my poor boy,' came softly from his mouth. 'What made ye think of loving her? Ye may as well love a mountain, for any return you'll ever get. Do she know of it?'

'She guesses it. It was my saving her from the threshing-machine that began it.'

'And she checks you?'

'Well – no.'

'Egbert,' he said after a silence, 'I am grieved, for it can but end in pain. Mind, she's an inexperienced girl. She never thinks of what trouble she may get herself into with her father and with her friends. And mind this, my lad, as another reason for dropping it; however honourable your love may be, you'll never get credit for your honour. Nothing you can do will ever root out the notion of people that where the man is poor and the woman is high-born he's a scamp and she's an angel.'

'She's very good.'

'She's thoughtless, or she'd never encourage you. You must try not to see her.'

'I will never put myself in her way again.'

The subject was mentioned no more then. The next day the worn-out old farmer died, and his last request to Egbert was that he would do nothing to tempt Geraldine Allenville to think of him further.

CHAPTER SIX

Hath misery made thee blind
To the fond workings of a woman's mind?
And must I say – albeit my heart rebel
With all that woman feels but should not tell;

> Because despite thy faults, that heart is moved –
> It feared thee, thank'd thee, pitied, madden'd, loved?

It was in the evening of the day after Farmer Broadford's death that Egbert first sat down in the house alone. The bandy-legged little man who had acted as his grandfather's groom of the chambers and stables simultaneously had gone into the village. The candles were not yet lighted, and Mayne abstractedly watched upon the pale wall the latter rays of sunset slowly changing into the white shine of a moon a few days old. The ancient family clock had stopped for want of winding, and the intense silence that prevailed seemed more like the bodily presence of some quality than the mere absence of sound.

He was thinking how many were the indifferent expressions which he had used towards the poor body lying cold upstairs – the only relation that he had latterly had upon earth – which might as well have been left unsaid; of how far he had been from practically attempting to do what in theory he called best – to make the most of every pulse of natural affection; that he had never heeded or particularly inquired the meaning of the different pieces of advice which the kind old man had tendered from time to time; that he had never even thought of asking for any details of his grandfather's history.

His musings turned upon Geraldine. He had promised to seek her no more, and he would keep his promise. Her interest in him might only be that of an exceedingly romantic and freakish soul, awakened but through 'lack of other idleness', and because sound sense suggested to her that it was a thing dangerous to do; for it seemed that she was ever and only moved by the superior of two antagonistic forces. She had as yet seen little or no society, she was only seventeen; and hence it was possible that a week of the town and fashion into which she would soon be initiated might blot out his very existence from her memory.

He was sitting with his back to the window, meditating in this minor key, when a shadow darkened the opposite moonlit wall. Egbert started. There was a gentle tap at the door; and he opened it to behold the well-known form of the lady in his mind.

'Mr Mayne, are you alone?' she whispered, full of agitation.

'Quite alone, excepting my poor grandfather's body upstairs,' he answered, as agitated as she.

Then out it all came. 'I couldn't help coming – I hope – oh, I do pray so – that it was not through me that he died. Was it I, indeed, who killed him? They say it was the effect of the news that he was to leave the farm. I would have done anything to hinder his being turned out had I only reflected! And now he is dead. It was so cruel to an old man like him; and now you have nobody in the world to care for you, have you, Egbert – except me?'

The ice was wholly broken. He took her hand in both his own and began to assure her that her alarm was grounded on nothing whatever. And yet he was almost reluctant to assure her out of so sweet a state. And when he had said over and over again that his grandfather's fall had nothing do with his mental condition, that the utmost result of her hasty proceeding was a sadness of spirit in him, she still persisted, as is the custom of women, in holding to that most painful possibility as the most likely, simply because it wounded her most. It was a long while before she would be convinced of her own innocence, but he maintained it firmly, and she finally believed.

They sat down together, restraint having quite died out between them. The fine-lady portion of her existence, of which there was never much, was in abeyance, and they spoke and acted simply as a young man and woman who were beset by common troubles, and who had like hopes and fears.

'And you will never blame me again for what I did?' said Egbert.

'I never blamed you much,' she murmured with arch simplicity. 'Why should it be wrong for me to be honest with you now, and tell everything you want to know?'

Mayne was silent. That was a difficult question for a conscientious man to answer. Here was he nearly twenty-one years of age, and with some experience of life, while she was a girl nursed up like an exotic, with no real experience, and but little over seventeen – though from the fineness of her figure she looked more womanly than she really was. It plainly had not crossed her young mind that she was on the verge of committing the most horrible social sin – that of loving beneath her, and owning that she so loved. Two years thence she might see the imprudence of her conduct, and blame him for having led her on. Ought he not then, considering his grandfather's words, to say that it was wrong for her to be honest; that she should forget him, and fix her mind on matters appertaining to her order? He could not do it – he let her drift sweetly on.

'I think more of you than anybody in the whole world,' he replied.

'And you will allow me to, will you not? – let me always keep you in my heart, and almost worship you?'

'That would be wrong. But you may think of me, if you like to, very much; it will give me great pleasure. I don't think my father thinks of me at all – or anybody, except you. I said the other day I would never think of you again, but I have done it, a good many times. It is all through being obliged to care for somebody whether you will or no.'

'And you will go on thinking of me?'

'I will do anything to – oblige you.'

Egbert, on the impulse of the moment, bent over her and raised her little hand to his lips. He reverenced her too much to think of kissing her cheek. She knew this, and was thrilled through with the delight of being adored as one from above the sky.

Up to this day of its existence their affection had been a battle, a species of antagonism wherein his heart and the girl's had faced each other, and being anxious to do honour to their respective parts. But now it was a truce and a settlement, in which each one took up the other's utmost weakness, and was careless of concealing his and her own.

Surely, sitting there as they sat then, a more unreasoning condition of mind as to how this unequal conjunction would end never existed. They swam along through the passing moments, not a thought of duty on either side, not a further thought on his but that she was the day-spring of his life, that he would die for her a hundred times; superadded to which was a shapeless uneasiness that she would in some manner slip away from him. The solemnity of the event that had just happened would have shown up to him any ungenerous feeling in strong colours – and he had reason afterwards to examine the epoch narrowly; but it only seemed to demonstrate how instinctive and uncalculating was the love that worked within him.

It was almost time for her to leave. She held up her watch to the moonlight. Five minutes more she would stay; then three minutes, and no longer. 'Now I'm going,' she said. 'Do you forgive me entirely?'

'How shall I say "Yes" without assuming that there was something to forgive?'

'Say "Yes". It is sweeter to fancy I am forgiven than to think I have not sinned.'

With this she went to the door. Egbert accompanied her through the wood, and across a portion of the park, till they were about a hundred yards from the house, when he was forced to bid her farewell.

The old man was buried on the following Sunday. During several weeks afterwards Egbert's sole consolation under his loss was in thinking of Geraldine, for they did not meet in private again till some time had elapsed. The ultimate issue of this absorption in her did not concern him at all: it seemed to be in keeping with the system of his existence now that he should have an utterly inscrutable tomorrow.

CHAPTER SEVEN

*Come forward, some great marshal
and organize equality in society.*

The month of August came around and Miss Allenville was to lay the foundation-stone of a tower or beacon which her father was about to erect on the highest hill of his estate, to the memory of his brother, the General. It was arranged that the school children should sing at the ceremony. Accordingly, at the hour fixed, Egbert was on the spot; a crowd of villagers had also arrived, and carriages were visible in the distance, wending their way towards the scene. When they had drawn up alongside and the visitors alighted, the master-mason appeared nervous.

'Mr Mayne,' he said to Egbert, 'you had better do what's to be done for the lady. I shall speak too loud, or too soft, or handle things wrong. Do you attend upon her, and I'll lower the stone.'

Several ladies and gentlemen now gathered round, and presently Miss Allenville stood in position for her office, supported on one side by her father, a hard featured man of five-and-forty, and some friends who were visiting at the house; and on the other by the school children, who began singing a song in keeping with the occasion. When this was done, Geraldine laid down the sealed bottle with its enclosed memorandum, which had been prepared for the purpose, and taking a trowel from her father's hand, dabbled confusedly in the mortar, accidentally smearing it over the handle of the trowel.

'Lower the stone,' said Egbert, who stood close by, to the mason at the winch; and the stone began to descend.

The dainty-handed young woman was looking as if she would give anything to be relieved of the dirty trowel; but Egbert, the only one who observed this, was guiding the stone with both hands into its place, and could not receive the tool of her. Every moment increased her perplexity.

'Take it, take it, will you?' she impatiently whispered to him, blush-

ing the consciousness that people began to perceive her awkward hand-
ling.

'I must just finish this first,' he said.

She was resigned in an instant. The stone settled down upon its base,
when Egbert at once took the trowel, and her father came up and wiped
her glove. Egbert then handed her the mallet.

'What must I do with this thing?' she whispered entreatingly, holding
the mallet as if it might bite her.

'Tap with it, madam,' said he.

She did as was directed, and murmured the form of words which she
had been told to repeat.

'Thank you,' she said softly when all was done, restored to herself by
the consciousness that she had performed the last part gracefully. Without lifting her eyes she added, 'It was thoughtful of you to remember
that I shouldn't know, and to stand by to tell me.'

Her friends now moved away, but before she had joined them Egbert
said, chiefly for the pleasure of speaking to her: 'The tower, when it is
built, will be seen many miles off.'

'Yes,' she replied in a discreet tone, for many eyes were upon her.
'The view is very extensive.' She glanced round upon the whole landscape stretched out before her, in the extreme distance of which was
visible the town of Westcombe.

'How long does it take to go to Westcombe across this way?' she
asked of him while they were bringing up the carriage.

'About two hours,' he said.

'Two hours – so long as that, does it? How far is it away?'

'Eight miles.'

'Two hours to drive eight miles – who ever heard of such a thing!'

'I thought you meant walking.'

'Ah, yes; but one hardly means walking without expressly stating it.'

'Well, it seems just the other way to me – that walking is meant unless
you say driving.'

That was the whole of their conversation. The remarks had been
simple and trivial, but they brought a similar thought into the minds of
both of them. On her part it spread a sudden gloom over her face, and
it made him feel dead at heart. It was that horrid thought of their
differing habits and of those contrasting positions which could not be
reconciled.

Indeed, this perception of their disparity weighed more and more heavily upon him as the days went on. There was no doubt about their being lovers, though scarcely recognised by themselves as such; and, in spite of Geraldine's warm and unreflecting impulses, a sense of how little Egbert was accustomed to what is called society, and the polite forms which constant usage had almost made nature with her, would rise on occasion, and rob her of many an otherwise pleasant minute. When any little occurrence had brought this into more prominence than usual, Egbert would go away, wander about the lanes, and be kept awake a great part of the night by the distress of mind such a recognition brought upon him. How their intimacy would end, in what uneasiness, yearning, and misery, he could not guess. As for picturing a future of happiness with her by his side there was not ground enough upon which to rest the momentary imagination of it. Thus they mutually oppressed each other even while they loved.

In addition to this anxiety there was another; what would be thought of their romance by her father, if he were to find it out? It was impossible to tell him, for nothing could come of that but Egbert's dismissal and Geraldine's seclusion; and how could these be borne?

He looked round anxiously for some means of deliverance. There were two things to be thought of, the saving of her dignity, and the saving of his and her happiness. That to accomplish the first he ought voluntarily to leave the village before their attachment got known, and never seek her again, was what he sometimes felt; but the idea brought such misery along with it that it died out under contemplation.

He determined at all events to put the case clearly before her, to heroically set forth at their next meeting the true bearings of their position, which she plainly did not realize to the full as yet. It had never entered her mind that the link between them might be observed by the curious, and instantly talked of. Yes, it was his duty to warn her, even though by so doing he would be heaping coals of fire on his own head. For by acting upon his hint she would be lost to him, and the charm that lay in her false notions of the world be for ever destroyed.

That they would ultimately be found out, and Geraldine be lowered in local estimation, was, indeed, almost inevitable. There was one grain of satisfaction only among this mass of distresses. Whatever should become public, only the fashionable side of her character could be depreciated; the natural woman, the specimen of English girlhood that he loved, no one could impugn or harm.

Meetings had latterly taken place between them without any pretence

of accident, and these were facilitated in an amazing manner by the
duty imposed upon her of visiting the school as the representative of her
father. At her very next appearance he told her all he thought. It was
when the children had left the room for the quarter of an hour's airing
that he gave them in the middle of the morning.

She was quite hurt at being treated with justice, and a crowd of tears
came into her sorrowful eyes. She had never thought of half that he
feared, and almost questioned his kindness in enlightening her.

'Perhaps you are right,' she murmured, with the merest motion of
lip. 'Yes, it is sadly true. Should our conduct become known, nobody
will judge us fairly. "She was a wild, weak girl," they will say.'

'To care for such a man – a village youth. They will even suppress the
fact that his father was a painter of no mean power, and a gentleman by
education, little as it would redeem us; and justify their doing so by
reflecting that in adding to the contrast they improve the tale.

> And calumny meanwhile shall feed on us
> As worms devour the dead: what we have done
> None shall dare vouch, though it be truly known.

And they will continue, "He was an artful fellow to win a girl's affec-
tions in that way – one of the mere scum of the earth," they'll say.'

'Don't, don't make it so bad!' she implored, weeping outright. 'They
cannot go so far. Human nature is not so wicked and blind. And they
dare not speak so disrespectfully of me, or of any one I choose to favour.'
A slight haughtiness was apparent in these words. 'But, oh, don't let us
talk of it – it makes the time miserable.'

However, she had been warned. But the difficulty which presented
itself to her mind was, after all, but a small portion of the whole. It was
how should they meet together without causing a convulsion in neighbouring society. His was more radical and complex. The only natural
drift of love was towards marriage. But how could he picture, at any
length of years ahead, her in a cottage as his wife, or himself in a mansion
as her husband? He in the one case, she in the other, were alike painfully
incredible.

But time had flown, and he conducted her to the door. 'Good-bye,
Egbert,' she said tenderly.

'Good-bye, dear, dear madam,' he answered; and she was gone.

Geraldine had never hinted to him to call her by her Christian name,
and finding that she did not particularly wish it he did not care to do so.

'Madam' was as good a name as any other for her, and by adhering to it and using it at the warmest moments it seemed to change its nature from that of a mere title to a soft pet sound. He often wondered in after days at the strange condition of a girl's heart which could allow so much in reality, and at the same time permit the existence of a little barrier such as that; how the keen intelligent mind of woman could be ever so slightly hoodwinked by a sound. Yet, perhaps, it was womanlike, after all, and she may have caught at it as the only straw within reach of that dignity or pride of birth which was drowning in her impetuous affection.

CHAPTER EIGHT

The world and its ways have a certain worth,
And to press a point while these oppose
Were a simple policy: best wait,
And we lose no friends, and gain no foes.

The inborn necessity of ransacking the future for a germ of hope led Egbert Mayne to dwell for longer and longer periods on the at first rejected possibility of winning and having her. And apart from any thought of marriage, he knew that Geraldine was sometimes a trifle vexed that their experiences contained so little in common – that he had never dressed for dinner, or made use of a carriage in his life; even though in literature he was her master, thanks to his tastes.

For the first time he seriously contemplated a visionary scheme which had been several times cursorily glanced at; a scheme almost as visionary as any ever entertained by a man not yet blinded to the limits of the possible. Lighted on by impulse, it was not taken up without long calculation, and it was one in which every link was reasoned out as carefully and as clearly as his powers would permit. But the idea that he would be able to carry it through was an assumption which, had he bestowed upon it one-hundredth part of the thought spent on the details of its working, he would have thrown aside as unfeasible.

To give up the school, to go to London or elsewhere, and there to try to rise to her level by years of sheer exertion, was the substance of this scheme. However his lady's heart might be grieved by his apparent desertion, he would go. A knowledge of life and of men must be acquired, and that could never be done by thinking at home.

Egbert's abstract love for the gigantic task was but small; but there was absolutely no other honest road to her sphere. That the habits of men should be so subversive of the law of nature as to indicate that he was not worthy to marry a woman whose own instincts said that he was worthy, was a great anomaly, he thought, with some rebelliousness; but this did not upset the fact or remove the difficulty.

He told his fair mistress at their next accidental meeting (much sophistry lay in their definition of 'accidental' at this season) that he had determined to leave Tollamore. Mentally she exulted at his spirit, but her heart despaired. He solemnly assured her that it would be much better for them both in the end; and she became submissive, and entirely agreed with him. Then she seemed to acquire a sort of superior insight by virtue of her superior rank, and murmured, 'You will expand your mind, and get to despise me for all this, and for my want of pride in being so easily won; and it will end unhappily.'

Her imagination so affected her that she could not hinder the tears from falling. Nothing was more effective in checking his despair than the sight of her despairing, and he immediately put on a more hopeful tone.

'No,' he said, taking her by the hand, 'I shall rise, and become so learned and so famous that—' He did not like to say plainly that he really hoped to win her as his wife, but it is very probable that she guessed his meaning nearly enough.

'You have some secret resources!' she exclaimed. 'Some help is promised you in this ambitious plan.'

It was most painful to him to have to tell her the truth after this sanguine expectation, and how uncertain and unaided his plans were. However, he cheered her with the words, 'Wait and see.' But he himself had many misgivings when her sweet face was turned away.

Upon this plan he acted at once. Nothing of moment occurred during the autumn, and the time for his departure gradually came near. The sale of his grandfather's effects having taken place, and notice having been given at the school, there was very little else for him to do in way of preparation, for there was no family to be consulted, no household to be removed. On the last day of teaching, when the afternoon lessons were over, he bade farewell to the school children. The younger ones cried, not from any particular reflection on the loss they would sustain, but simply because their hearts were tender to any announcement couched in solemn terms. The elder children sincerely regretted Egbert, as an acquaintance who had not filled the post of schoolmaster so long as to be quite spoilt as a human being.

On the morning of departure he rose at half-past three, for Tollamore was a remote nook of a remote district, and it was necessary to start early, his plan being to go by packet from Melport. The candle-flame had a sad and yellow look when it was brought into his bedroom by Nathan Brown, one of his grandfather's old labourers, at whose house he had taken a temporary lodging, and who had agreed to awake him and assist his departure. Few things will take away a man's confidence in an impulsive scheme more than being called up by candlelight upon a chilly morning to commence working it out. But when Egbert heard Nathan's great feet stamping spiritedly about the floor downstairs, in earnest preparation of breakfast, he overcame his weakness and bustled out of bed.

They breakfasted together, Nathan drinking the hot tea with rattling sips, and Egbert thinking as he looked at him that Nathan had never appeared so desirable a man to have about him as now when he was about to give him up.

'Well, good mornen, Mistur Mayne,' Nathan said, as he opened the door to let Egbert out. 'And mind this, sir; if they use ye bad up there, th'lt always find a hole to put thy head into at Nathan Brown's, I'll warrant as much.'

Egbert stepped from the door, and struck across to the manor-house. The morning was dark, and the raw wind made him shiver till walking warmed him. 'Good heavens, here's an undertaking!' he sometimes thought. Old trees seemed to look at him through the gloom, as they rocked uneasily to and fro; and now and then a dreary drop of rain beat upon his face as he went on. The dead leaves in the ditches, which could be heard but not seen, shifted their position with a troubled rustle, and flew at intervals with a little rap against his walking-stick and hat. He was glad to reach the north stile, and get into the park, where, with an anxious pulse, he passed beneath the creaking limes.

'Will she wake soon enough; will she be forgetful, and sleep over the time?' He had asked himself this many times since he rose that morning, and still beset by the inquiry, he drew near to the mansion.

Her bedroom was in the north wing, facing towards the church, and on turning the brow of the hill a faint light in the window reassured him. Taking a few little stones from the path he threw them upon the sill, as they had agreed, and she instantly opened the window, and said softly, 'The butler sleeps on the ground floor on this side, go to the bow-window in the shrubbery.'

He went round among the bushes to the place mentioned, which was entirely sheltered from the wind. She soon appeared, bearing in her hand a wax taper, so small that it scarcely gave more light than a glow-worm. She wore the same dress that she had worn when they first met on the previous Christmas, and her hair was loose, at that time. Indeed, she looked throughout much as she had looked then, except that her bright eyes were red, as Egbert could see well enough.

'I have something for you,' she said softly as she opened the window. 'How much time is there?'

'Half-an-hour only, dearest.'

She began a sigh, but checked it, at the same time holding out a packet to him.

'Here are fifty pounds,' she whispered. 'It will be useful to you now, and more shall follow.'

Egbert felt how impossible it was to accept this. 'No, my dear one,' he said, 'I cannot.'

'I don't require it, Egbert. I wish you to have it; I have plenty. Come, do take it.' But seeing that he continued firm on this point she reluctantly gave in, saying that she would keep it for him.

'I fear so much that papa suspects me,' she said. 'And if so, it was my own fault, and all owing to a conversation I began with him without thinking beforehand that it would be dangerous.'

'What did you say?'

'I said,' she whispered, ' "Suppose a man should love me very much, would you mind my being acquainted with him if he were a very worthy man?" "That depends upon his rank and circumstances," he said. "Suppose," I said, "that in addition to his goodness he had much learning, and he had made his name famous in the world, but was not altogether rich?" I think I showed too much earnestness, and I wished that I could have recalled my words. "When the time comes, I will tell you," he said, "and don't speak or think of these matters again." '

In consequence of this new imprudence of hers Egbert doubted if it would be right to correspond with her. He said nothing about it then, but it added a new shade to the parting.

'I think your decision a good and noble one,' she murmured, smiling hopefully. 'And you will come back some day a wondrous man of the world talking of vast Schemes, radical Errors, and saying such words as the "Backbone of Society", the "Tendency of Modern Thought", and other things like that. When papa says to you, "My Lord the Chancellor," you will answer him with "A tall man, with a deep-toned voice – I know him well." When he says, "Such and such were Lord Hatton's words, I think," you will answer, "No, they were Lord Tyrrell's; I was present on the occasion"; and so on in that way. You must get to talk authoritatively about vintages and their dates, and to know all about epicureanism, idleness, and fashion; and so you will beat him with his own weapons, for he knows nothing of these things. He will criticise you; then he will be nettled; then he will admire you.'

Egbert kissed her hand devotedly, and held it long.

'If you cannot in the least succeed,' she added, 'I shall never think the less of you. The truly great stand on no middling ledge; they are either famous or unknown.'

Egbert moved slowly away amongst the laurestines. Holding the light above her bright head she smiled upon him, as if it were unknown to her that she wept at the same time.

He left the park precincts, and followed the turnpike road to Melport. In spite of the misery of parting he felt relieved of a certain oppressiveness, now that his presence at Tollamore could no longer bring disgrace upon her. The threatening rain passed off by the time he reached the ridge dividing the inland districts from the coast. It began to get light, but his journey was still very lonely. Ultimately the yellow shore-line of pebbles grew visible, and the distant horizon of water, spreading like a gray upland against the sky, till he could soon hear the measured flounce of the waves.

He entered the town at sunrise, just as the lamps were extinguished, and went to a tavern to breakfast. At half-past eight o'clock the boat steamed out of the harbour and reached London after a passage of five-and-forty hours.

Part Two

CHAPTER ONE

He, like a captain who beleaguers round
Some strong-built castle on a rising ground,
Views all the approaches with observing eyes;
This and that other part in vain he tries,
And more on industry than force relies.

SINCE Egbert Mayne's situation is not altogether a new and unprecedented one, there will be no necessity for detailing in all its minuteness his attempt to scale the steeps of Fame. For notwithstanding the fact that few, comparatively, have reached the top, the lower tracts of that troublesome incline have been trodden by as numerous a company as any allegorical spot in the world.

The reader must then imagine five years to have elapsed, during which rather formidable slice of human life Egbert had been constantly striving. It had been drive, drive from month to month; no rest, nothing but effort. He had progressed from newspaper work to criticism, from criticism to independent composition of a mild order, from the latter to the publication of a book which nobody ever heard of, and from this to the production of a work of really sterling merit, which appeared anonymously. Though he did not set society in a blaze, or even in a smoke, thereby, he certainly caused a good many people to talk about him, and to be curious as to his name.

The luminousness of nature which had been sufficient to attract the attention and heart of Geraldine Allenville had, indeed, meant much. That there had been power enough in the presence, speech, mind, and tone of the poor painter's son to fascinate a girl of Geraldine's station was of itself a ground for the presumption that he might do a work in the world if he chose. The attachment to her was just the stimulus which such a constitution as his required, and it had at first acted admirably upon him. Afterwards the case was scarcely so happy.

He had investigated manners and customs no less than literature; and for a while the experience was exciting enough. But several habits which he had at one time condemned in the ambitious classes now became his own. His original fondness for art, literature, and science was getting quenched by his slowly increasing habit of looking upon each and all of these as machinery wherewith to effect a purpose.

A new feeling began to animate all his studies. He had not the old interest in them for their own sakes, but a breathless interest in them as factors in the game of sink or swim. He entered picture galleries, not, as formerly, because it was humour to dream pleasantly over the images therein expressed, but to be able to talk on demand about painters and their peculiarities. He examined Correggio to criticize his flesh shades; Angelico, to speak technically of the pink faces of his saints; Murillo, to say fastidiously that there was a certain silliness in the look of his old men; Rubens for his sensuous women; Turner for his Turneresqueness. Romney was greater than Reynolds because Lady Hamilton had been his model, and thereby hung a tale. Bonozzi Gozzoli was better worth study than Raffaelle, since the former's name was a learned sound to utter, and all knowledge got up about him would tell.

Whether an intense love for a woman, and that woman Geraldine, was a justifiable reason for this desire to shine it is not easy to say.

However, as has been stated, Egbert worked like a slave in these causes, and at the end of five full years was repaid with certain public applause, though, unfortunately, not with much public money. But this he hoped might soon come.

Regarding his love for Geraldine, the most noteworthy fact to be recorded of the period was that all correspondence with her had ceased. In spite of their fear of her father, letters had passed frequently between them on his first leaving home, and had been continued with ardour for some considerable time. The reason of its close will be perceived in the following note, which he received from her two years before the date of the present chapter: –

'Tollamore House

'My Dear Egbert,
    'How shall I tell you what has happened! and yet how can I keep silence when sooner or later you will know all?
    'My father has discovered what we feel for each other. He took me into his room and made me promise never to write to you, or seek you, or receive a letter from you. I promised in haste, for I was frightened and excited, and now he trusts me – I wish he did not – for

he knows I would not be mean enough to lie. So don't write, poor Egbert, or expect to hear from miserable me. We must try to hope; yet it is a long dreary thing to do. But I *will* hope, and not be beaten. How could I help promising, Egbert, when he compelled me? He is my father. I cannot think what we shall do under it all. It is cruel of life to be like this towards us when we have done no wrong.

'We are going abroad for a long time. I think it is because of you and me, but I don't know. He does not tell me where we shall go. Just as if a place like Europe could make me forget you. He doesn't know what's in me, and how I can think about you and cry at nights – he cannot. If he did, he must see how silly the plan is.

'Remember that you go to church on Sunday mornings, for then I think that perhaps we are reading in the same place at the same moment; and we are sometimes, no doubt. Last Sunday, when we came to this in the Psalms, "And he shall be like a tree planted by the waterside that will bring forth his fruit in due season: his leaf also shall not wither; and look, whatsoever he doeth, it shall prosper," I thought, "That's Egbert in London." I know you were reading that same verse in your church – I felt that you said it with us. Then I looked up to your old nook under the tower arch. It was a misery to see the wood and the stone just as good as ever, and you not there. It is not only that you are gone at these times, but a heavy creature – blankness – seems to stand in your place.

'But how can I tell you of these thoughts now that I am to write no more? Yet we will hope, and hope. Remember this, that should anything serious happen, I will break the bond and write. Obligation would end then. Good-bye for a time. I cannot put into words what I would finish with. Good-bye, good-bye.

G.A.

'P.S. Might we not write just one line at very wide intervals? It is too much never to write at all.'

On receiving this letter Egbert felt that he could not honourably keep up a regular correspondence with her. But a determination to break it off would have been more than he could have adhered to if he had not been strengthened by the hope that he might soon be able to give a plausible reason for renewing it. He sent her a line, bidding her to expect the best results from the prohibition, which, he was sure, would not be for long. Meanwhile, should she think it not wrong to send a line at very wide intervals, he would promptly reply.

But she was apparently too conscientious to do so, for nothing had reached him since. Yet she was as continually in his thought and heart as before. He felt more misgivings than he had chosen to tell her of on the ultimate effect of the prohibition, but could do nothing to remove it.

And then he had learnt that Miss Allenville and her father had gone to Paris, as the commencement of a sojourn abroad.

These circumstances had burdened him with long hours of depression, till he had resolved to throw his whole strength into a production which should either give him a fair start towards fame, or make him clearly understand that there was no hope in that direction for such as he. He had begun the attempt, and ended it, and the consequences were fortunate to an unexpected degree.

CHAPTER TWO

Towards the loadstar of my one desire
I flitted like a dizzy moth, whose flight
Is as a dead leaf's in the owlet light.

Mayne's book having been launched into the world and well received, he found time to emerge from the seclusion he had maintained for several months, and to look into life again.

One warm, fashionable day, between five and six o'clock, he was walking along Piccadilly, absent-minded and unobservant, when an equipage approached whose appearance thrilled him through. It was the Allenville landau, newly-painted up. Egbert felt almost as if he had been going into battle; and whether he should stand forth visibly before her or keep in the background seemed a question of life or death.

He waited in unobserved retirement, which it was not difficult to do, his aspect having much altered since the old times. Coachman, footman, and carriage advanced, in graceful unity of glide, like a swan. Then he beheld her, Geraldine, after two years of silence, five years of waiting, and nearly three years of separation; for although he had seen her two or three times in town after he had taken up his residence there, they had not once met since the year preceding her departure for the Continent.

She came opposite, now passively looking round, then actively glancing at something which interested her. Egbert trembled a little, or perhaps a great deal, at sight of her. But she passed on, and the back of the carriage hid her from his view.

So much of the boy was left in him still that he could scarcely withhold himself from rushing after her, and jumping into the carriage. She had appeared to be well and blooming, and an instinctive vexation that their long separation had produced no perceptible effect upon her, speedily gave way before a more generous sense of gratification at her well-being. Still, had it been possible, he would have been glad to see some sign upon her face that she yet remembered him.

This sudden discovery that they were in town after their years of travel stirred his lassitude into excitement. He went back to his chambers to meditate upon his next step. A trembling on Geraldine's account was disturbing him. She had probably been in London ever since the beginning of the season, but she had not given him a sign to signify that she was so near; and but for this accidental glimpse of her he might have gone on for months without knowing that she had returned from abroad.

Whether she was leading a dull or an exciting life Egbert had no means of knowing. That night after night the arms of interesting young men rested upon her waist and whirled her round the ball-room he could not bear to think. That she frequented gatherings and assemblies of all sorts he calmly owned as very probable, for she was her father's only daughter, and likely to be made much of. That she had not written a line to him since their return was still the grievous point.

'If I had only risen one or two steps further,' he thought, 'how boldly would I seek her out. But only to have published one successful book in all these years – such grounds are slight indeed.'

For several succeeding days he did nothing but look about the Park, and the streets, and the neighbourhood of Chevron Square, where their town-house stood, in the hope of seeing her again; but in vain. There were moments when his distress that she might possibly be indifferent about him and his affairs was unbearable. He fully resolved that he would on some early occasion communicate with her, and know the worst. Years of work remained to be done before he could think of appearing before her father; but he had reached a sort of half-way stage at which some assurance from herself that his track was a hopeful one was positively needed to keep him firm.

Egbert still kept on the look-out for her at every public place; but nearly a month passed, and she did not appear again. One Sunday evening, when he had been wandering near Chevron Square, and looking at her windows from a distance, he returned past her house after dusk. The rooms were lighted, but the windows were still open, and as he strolled along he heard notes from a piano within. They were the accompaniment to an air from the *Messiah*, though no singer's voice was audible. Egbert readily imagined who the player might be, for the *Messiah* was an oratorio which Geraldine often used to wax eloquent upon in days gone by. He had not walked far when he remembered that there was to be an exceptionally fine performance of that stirring composition during the following week, and it instantly occurred to him that Geraldine's mind was running on the same event, and that she intended to be one of the audience.

He resolved upon doing something at a venture. The next morning he went to the ticket-office, and boldly asked for a place as near as possible to those taken in the name of Allenville.

'There is no vacant one in any of those rows,' the office-keeper said, 'but you can have one very near their number on the other side of the division.'

Egbert was astonished that for once in his life he had made a lucky hit. He booked his place, and returned home.

The evening arrived, and he went early. On taking his seat he found himself at the left-hand end of a series of benches, and close to a red cord, which divided the group of seats he had entered from stalls of a somewhat superior kind. He was passing the time in looking at the extent of orchestra space, and other things, when he saw two ladies and a gentleman enter and sit down in the stalls diagonally before his own, and on the other side of the division. It delighted and agitated him to find that one of the three was Geraldine; her two companions he did not know.

'Policy, don't desert me now,' he thought; and immediately sat in such a way that unless she turned round to a very unlikely position she would not see him.

There was a certain half-pleasant misery in sitting behind her thus as a possibly despised lover. Tonight, at any rate, there would be sights and sounds common to both of them, though they should not communicate to the extent of a word. Even now he could hear the rustle of her garments as she settled down in her seat, and the faint murmur of words that passed between her and her friends.

Never, in the many times that he had listened to that rush of harmonies, had they affected him as they did then; and it was no wonder, considering what an influence upon his own life had been and still was exercised by Geraldine, and that she now sat there before him. The varying strains shook and bent him to themselves as a rippling brook shakes and bends a shadow. The music did not show its power by attracting his attention to its subject; it rather dropped its own libretto and took up in place of that the poem of his life and love.

There was Geraldine still. They were singing the chorus 'Lift up your heads', and he found a new impulse of thought in him. It was towards determination. Should every member of her family be against him he would win her in spite of them. He could now see that Geraldine was moved equally with himself by the tones which entered her ears.

'Why do the nations so furiously rage together' filled him with a gnawing thrill, and so changed him to its spirit that he believed he was capable of suffering in silence for his whole lifetime, and of never appearing before her unless she gave a sign.

The audience stood up, and the 'Hallelujah Chorus' began. The deafening harmonies flying from this group and from that seemed to absorb all the love and poetry that his life had produced, to pour it upon that one moment, and upon her who stood so close at hand. 'I will force Geraldine to be mine,' he thought. 'I will make that heart ache of love for me.' The chorus continued, and her form trembled under its influence. Egbert was for seeking her the next morning and knowing what his chances were, without waiting for further results. The chorus and the personality of Geraldine still filled the atmosphere. 'I will seek her tonight – as soon as we get out of this place,' he said. The storm of sound now reached its climax, and Geraldine's power was proportionately increased. He would give anything for a glance this minute – to look into her eyes, she into his. 'If I can but touch her hand, and get one word from her, I will,' he murmured.

He shifted his position somewhat and saw her face. Tears were in her eyes, and her lips were slightly parted. Stretching a little nearer he whispered, 'My love!' Geraldine turned her wet eyes upon him, almost as if she had not been surprised, but had been forewarned by her previous emotion. With the peculiar quickness of grasp that she always showed under sudden circumstances, she had realized the position at a glance.

'O, Egbert!' she said; and her countenance flagged as if she would have fainted.

'Give me your hand,' he whispered.

She placed her hand in his, under the cord, which it was easy to do without observation; and he held it tight.

'Mine, as before?' he asked.

'Yours now as then,' said she.

They were like frail and sorry wrecks upon that sea of symphony, and remained in silent abandonment to the time, till the strains approached their close.

'Can you meet me tonight?' said Egbert.

She was half frightened at the request, and said, 'Where?'

'At your own front door, at twelve o'clock.' He then was at once obliged to gently withdraw himself, for the chorus was ended, and the people were sitting down.

The remainder was soon over, and it was time to leave. Egbert watched her and her party out of the house, and, turning to the other doorway, went out likewise.

CHAPTER THREE

Bright reason will mock thee,
Like the sun from a wintry sky.

When he reached his chambers he sat down and literally did nothing but watch the hand of the mantel-clock minute by minute, till it marked half-past eleven, scarcely removing his eyes. Then going again into the street he called a cab, and was driven down Park Lane and on to the corner of Chevron Square. Here he alighted, and went round to the number occupied by the Allenvilles.

A lamp stood nearly opposite the doorway, and by receding into the gloom to the railing of the square he could see whatever went on in the porch of the house. The lamps over the doorways were nearly all extinguished, and everything about this part was silent and deserted, except at a house on the opposite side of the square, where a ball was going on. But nothing of that concerned Egbert: his eyes had sought out and remained fixed upon Mr Allenville's front door, in momentary expectation of seeing it gently open.

The dark wood of the door showed a keen and distinct edge upon the pale stone of the porch floor. It must have been about two minutes before the hour he had named when he fancied he saw a slight movement at that point, as of something slipped out from under the door.

'It is but fancy,' he said to himself.

He turned his eyes away, and turned them back again. Some object certainly seemed to have been thrust under the door. At this moment the four quarters of midnight began to strike, and then the hour. Egbert could remain still no longer, and he went into the porch. A note had been slipped under the door from inside.

He took it to the lamp, turned it over, and saw it was directed only with initials, – 'To E.M.' Egbert tore it open and glanced upon the page. With a shiver of disappointment he read these words in her handwriting: –

'It was when under the influence of much emotion, kindled in me by the power of the music, that I half assented to a meeting with you tonight; and I believe that you also were excited when you asked for one. After some quiet reflection I have decided that it will be much better for us both if we do not see each other.

'You will, I know, judge me fairly in this. You have by this time learnt what life is; what particular positions, accidental though they may be, ask, nay, imperatively exact from us. If you say "not imperatively", you cannot speak from knowledge of the world.

'To be woven and tied in with the world by blood, acquaintance, tradition, and external habit, is to a woman to be utterly at the beck of that world's customs. In youth we do not see this. You and I did not see it. We were but a girl and a boy at the time of our meetings at Tollamore. What was our knowledge? A list of other people's words. What was our wisdom? None at all.

'It is well for you to remember now that I am not the unsophisticated girl I was when you first knew me. For better or for worse I have become complicated, exclusive, and practised. A woman who can speak, or laugh, or dance, or sing before any number of men with perfect composure may be no sinner, but she is not what I was once. She is what I am now. She is not the girl you loved. That woman is not here.

'I wish to write kindly to you, as to one for whom, in spite of the unavoidable division between our paths, I must always entertain a heartfelt respect. Is it, after this, out of place in me to remind you how contrasting are all our associations, how inharmonious our times and seasons? Could anything ever overpower this incongruity?

'But I must write plainly, and, though it may grieve you now, it will produce ultimately the truest ease. This is my meaning. If I could accept your addresses without an entire loss of position I would do so; but, since this cannot be, we must forget each other.

'Believe me to be, with wishes and prayers for your happiness,
'Your sincere friend,
'G.A.'

Egbert could neither go home nor stay still; he walked off rapidly in any direction for the sole sake of vehement motion. His first impulse was to get into darkness. He went towards Kensington; thence threaded across to the Uxbridge Road, thence to Kensal Green, where he turned into a lane and followed it to Kilburn, and the hill beyond, at which spot he halted and looked over the vast haze of light extending to the length and breadth of London. Turning back and wandering among some fields by a way he could never afterwards recollect, sometimes sitting down, sometimes leaning on a stile, he lingered on until the sun had risen. He then slowly walked again towards London, and, feeling by this time very weary, he entered the first refreshment-house that he came to, and attempted to eat something. Having sat for some time over this meal without doing much more than taste it, he arose and set out for the street in which he lived. Once in his own rooms he lay down upon the couch and fell asleep.

When he awoke it was four o'clock. Egbert then dressed and went out, partook of a light meal at his club at the dismal hour between luncheon and dinner, and cursorily glanced over the papers and reviews. Among the first things that he saw were eulogistic notices of his own book in three different reviews, each the most prominent and weighty of its class. Two of them, at least, would, he knew, find their way to the drawing room of the Allenvilles, for they were among the periodicals which the Squire regularly patronised.

Next, in a weekly review he read the subjoined note: –

'The authorship of the book —— ——, about which conjecture has lately been so much exercised, is now ascribed to Mr Egbert Mayne, whose first attempt in that kind we noticed in these pages some eighteen months ago.'

He took up a daily paper and presently lighted on the following paragraph: –

'It is announced that a marriage is arranged between Lord Bretton, of Tosthill Park, and Geraldine, only daughter of Foy Allenville, Esq., of Tollamore House, Wessex.'

Egbert arose and went towards home. Arrived there he met the postman at the door, and received from him a small note. The young man mechanically glanced at the direction.

'From her,' he mentally exclaimed: 'What does it—'

This is what the letter contained: –

'Twelve o'clock

'I have just learnt that the anonymous author of the book in which the world has been so interested during the past two months, and which I have read, is none other than yourself. Accept my congratulations. It seems almost madness in me to address you now. But I could not do otherwise on receipt of this news, and after writing my last letter. Let your knowledge of my nature prevent your misconstruing my motives in writing thus on the spur of the moment. I need scarcely add, please keep it a secret forever. I am not morally afraid, but other lives, hopes, and objects than mine have to be considered.

'The announcement of the marriage is premature, to say the least. I would tell you more, but dare not.

'G.A.'

The conjunction of all this intelligence produced in Egbert's heart a stillness which was some time in getting aroused to excitement. His emotion was formless. He knew not what point to take hold of and survey his position from; and, though his faculties grew clearer with the passage of time, he failed in resolving on a course with any deliberateness. No sooner had he thought, 'I will never see her again for my pride's sake,' than he said, 'Why not see her? she is a woman; she may love me yet.'

He went downstairs and out of the house, and walked by way of the Park towards Chevron Square.

Probably nobody will rightly appreciate Mayne's wild behaviour at this juncture, unless, which is very unlikely, he has been in a somewhat similar position himself. It may always appear to cool critics, even if they are generous enough to make allowances for his feelings, as visionary and weak in the extreme. Yet it was scarcely to be expected, after the mental and emotional strain that he had undergone during the preceding five years, that he should have acted much otherwise.

He rang the bell and asked to see Mr Allenville. He, perhaps fortunately, was not at home. 'Miss Allenville, then,' said Mayne.

'She is just driving out,' said the footman dubiously.

Egbert then noticed for the first time that the carriage was at the door, and almost as soon as the words were spoken Geraldine came downstairs.

'The madness of hoping to call that finished creature, wife!' he thought.

Geraldine recognised him and looked perplexed.

'One word, Miss Allenville,' he murmured.

She assented, and he followed her into the adjoining room.

'I have come,' said Egbert. 'I know it is hasty of me; but I must hear my doom from your own lips. Five years ago you spurred me on to ambition. I have followed but too closely the plan I then marked out, for I have hoped all along for a reward. What am I to think? Have you indeed left off feeling what you once felt for me?'

'I cannot speak of it now,' she said hurriedly. 'I told you in my letter as much as I dared. Believe me, I cannot speak – in the way you wish. I will always be your friend.'

'And is this the end? Oh, my God!'

'And we shall hope to see you to dinner some day, now you are famous,' she continued, pale as ashes. 'But I – cannot be with you as we once were. I was such a child at that time, you know.'

'Geraldine, is this all I get after this lapse of time and heat of labour?'

'I am not my own mistress – I have my father to please,' she faintly murmured. 'I must please him. There is no help for this. Go from me – do go!'

Egbert turned and went, for he felt that he had no longer a place beside her.

CHAPTER FOUR

Then I said in my heart, 'As it happeneth
to the fool, so it happeneth even to me; and
why was I then more wise?'

Mayne was in rather an ailing state for several days after the above-mentioned event. Yet the lethean stagnation which usually comes with the realisation that all is over allowed him to take some deep sleeps, to which he latterly had been a stranger.

The hours went by, and he did the best he could to dismiss his regrets for Geraldine. He was assisted to the very little success that he attained in this by reflecting how different a woman she must have become from her old sweet self of five or six years ago.

'But how paltry is my success now she has vanished!' he said. 'What is it worth? What object have I in following it up after this?' It rather startled him to see that the root of his desire for celebrity having been Geraldine, he now was a man who had no further motive in moving on. Town life had for some time been depressing to him. He began to doubt whether he could ever be happy in the course of existence that he had followed through these later years. The perpetual strain, the lack of that quiet to which he had been accustomed in early life, the absence of all personal interest in things around him, was telling upon his health of body and of mind.

Then revived the wish which had for some time been smouldering in his secret heart – to leave off, for the present, at least, his efforts for distinction; to retire for a few months to his old country nook, and there to meditate on his next course.

To set about this was curiously awkward to him. He had planned methods of retrogression in case of defeat through want of ability, want of means, or lack of opportunity; but to retreat because his appetite for advance had gone off was what he had never before thought of.

His reflections turned upon the old home of his mother's family. He knew exactly how Tollamore appeared at that time of the year. The trees with their half-ripe apples, the bees and butterflies lazy from the heat; the haymaking over, the harvest not begun, the people lively and always out of doors. He would visit the spot, and call upon some old and half-forgotten friends of his grandfather in an adjoining parish.

Two days later he left town. The fine weather, his escape from that intricate web of effort in which he had been bound these five years, the sensation that nobody in the world had any claims upon him, imparted some buoyancy to his mind; and it was in a serene if sad spirit that he entered Tollamore Vale, and smelt his native air.

He did not at once proceed to the village, but stopped at Fairland, the parish next adjoining. It was now evening, and he called upon some of the old cottagers whom he knew. Time had set a mark upon them all since he had last been there. Middle-aged men were a little more round-shouldered, their wives had taken to spectacles, young people had grown up out of recognition, and old men had passed into second childhood.

Egbert found here, as he had expected, precisely such a lodging as a hermit would desire. It was an ivy-covered detached house which had been partly furnished for a tenant who had never come, and it was kept clean by an old woman living in a cottage near. She offered to wait upon Egbert whilst he remained there, coming in the morning and leaving in the afternoon, thus giving him the house to himself during the latter part of the day.

When it grew dusk he went out, wishing to ramble for a little time. The gibbous moon rose on his right, the stars showed themselves sleepily one by one, and the far distance turned to a mysterious ocean of grey. He instinctively directed his steps toward Tollamore, and when there towards the school. It looked very little changed since the year in which he had had the memorable meetings with her there, excepting that the creepers had grown higher.

He went on towards the Park. Here was the place whereon he had used to await her coming – he could be sure of the spot to a foot. There was the turn of the hill around which she had appeared. The sentimental effect of the scenes upon him was far greater than he had expected, so great that he wished he had never been so reckless as to come here. 'But this is folly,' he thought. 'The betrothed of Lord Bretton is a woman of the world in whose thoughts, hopes, and habits I have no further interest or share.'

In the lane he heard the church-bells ringing out their five notes, and meeting a shepherd Egbert asked him what was going on.

'Practising,' he said, in an uninterested voice. ' 'Tis against young Miss's wedding, that their hands may be thoroughly in by the day for't.'

He presently came to where his grandfather's old house had stood. It was pulled down, the ground it covered having become a shabby, irregular spot, half grown over with trailing plants. The garden had been grassed down, but the old apple-trees still remained, their trunks and stems being now sheeted on one side with moonlight. He entertained himself by guessing where the front door of the house had been, at which Geraldine had entered on the memorable evening when she came to him full of grief and pity, and a tacit avowal of love was made on each side. Where they had sat together was now but a heap of broken rubbish half covered with grass. Near this melancholy spot was the cottage once inhabited by Nathan Brown. But Nathan was dead now, and his wife and family had gone elsewhere.

Finding the effect of memory to be otherwise than cheerful, Mayne hastened from the familiar spot, and went on to the parish of Fairland in which he had taken his lodging.

It soon became whispered in the neighbourhood that Miss Allenville's wedding was to take place on the 17th October. Egbert heard few particulars of the matter beyond the date, though it is possible that he might have known more if he had tried. He preferred to fortify himself by dipping deeply into the few books he had brought with him; but the most obvious plan of escaping his thoughts, that of a rapid change of scene by travel, he was unaccountably loth to adopt. He felt that he could not stay long in this district; yet an indescribable fascination held him on day after day, till the date of the marriage was close at hand.

CHAPTER FIVE

How all the other passions fleet to air,
As doubtful thoughts, and rash-embraced despair
And shudd'ring fear, and green-eyed jealousy!

On the eve of the wedding people told Mayne that arches and festoons of late summer-flowers and evergreens had been put up across the path between the church porch at Tollamore and the private gate to the Squire's lawn, for the procession of bride and bridesmaids. Before it got dark several villagers went on foot to the church to look at and admire these decorations. Egbert had determined to see the ceremony over. It would do him good, he thought, to be witness of the sacrifice.

Hence he, too, went along the path to Tollamore to inspect the preparations. It was dusk by the time that he reached the churchyard, and he entered it boldly, letting the gate fall together with a loud slam, as if he were a man whom nothing troubled. He looked at the half-completed bowers of green, and passed on into the church, never having entered it since he first left Tollamore.

He was standing by the chancel-arch, and observing the quantity of flowers which had been placed around the spot, when he heard the creaking of a gate on its hinges. Two figures entered the church, and Egbert stepped behind a canopied tomb.

The persons were females, and they appeared to be servants from the neighbouring mansion. They brought more flowers and festoons, and were talking of the event of the morrow. Coming into the chancel they threw down their burdens with a remark that it was too dark to arrange more flowers that night.

'This is where she is to kneel,' said one, standing with her arms akimbo before the altar-railing. 'And I wish 'twas I instead, Lord send if I don't.'

The two girls went on gossiping until other footsteps caused them to turn.

'I won't say 'tisn't she. She has been here two or three times today. Let's go round this way.'

And the servants went towards the door by a circuitous path round the aisle, to avoid meeting with the new-comer.

Egbert, too, thought he would leave the place now that he had heard and seen thus much; but from carelessness or design he went straight down the nave. An instant afterwards he was standing face to face with Geraldine. The servants had vanished.

'Good evening,' she said serenely, not knowing him, and supposing him to be a parishioner.

Egbert returned the words hastily, and, in standing aside to let her pass, looked clearly into her eyes and pale face, as if there never had been a time at which he would have done anything on earth for her sake.

She knew him, and started, uttering a weak exclamation. When he reached the door he turned his head, and saw that she was irresolutely holding up her hand, as if to beckon to him to come back.

'One word, since I have met you,' she said in unequal half-whispered tones. 'I have felt that I was one-sided in my haste on the day you called to see me in London. I misunderstood you.'

Egbert could at least out-do her in self-control, and, astonished that she should have spoken, he answered in a yet colder tone,

'I am sorry for that; very sorry, madam.'

'And you excuse it?'

'Of course I do, readily. And I hope you, too, will pardon my intrusion on that day, and understand the – circumstances.'

'Yes, yes. Especially as I am most to blame for those indiscreet proceedings in our early lives which led to it.'

'Certainly you were not most to blame.'

'How can you say that?' she answered with a slight laugh, 'when you know nothing of what my motives and feelings were?'

'I know well enough to judge, for I was the elder. Let me just recall some points in your own history at that time.'

'No.'

'Will you not hear a word?'

'I cannot. . . . Are you writing another book?'

'I am doing nothing. I am idling at Monk's Hut.'

'Indeed!' she said, slightly surprised. 'Well, you will always have my good wishes, whatever you may do. If any of my relatives can ever help you—'

'Thank you, madam, very much. I think, however, that I can help myself.'

She was silent, looking upon the floor; and Egbert spoke again, successfully hiding the feelings of his heart under a light and untrue tone. 'Miss Allenville, you know that I loved you devotedly for many years, and that that love was the starting point of all my ambition. My sense of it makes this meeting rather awkward. But men survive almost anything. I have proved it. Their love is strong while it lasts, but it soon withers at sight of a new face. I congratulate you on your coming marriage. Perhaps I may marry some day, too.'

'I hope you will find someone worth your love. I am sorry I ever – inconvenienced you as I did. But one hardly knows at that age—'

'Don't think of it for a moment – I really entreat you not to think of that.' What prompted the cruelty of his succeeding words he never could afterwards understand. 'It was a hard matter at first for me to forget you, certainly; but perhaps I was helped in my wish by the strong prejudice I originally had against your class and family. I have fixed my mind firmly upon the differences between us, and my youthful fancy is pretty fairly overcome. Those old silly days of devotion were pretty enough, but the devotion was entirely unpractical, as you have seen, of course.'

'Yes, I have seen it,' she faltered.

'It was scarcely of a sort which survives accident and division, and is strengthened by disaster.'

'Well, perhaps not, perhaps not. You can scarcely care much now whether it was nor not; or, indeed, care anything about me or my happiness.'

'I do care.'

'How much? As you do for that of any other wretched human being?'

'Wretched? No!'

'I will tell you – I must tell you!' she said with rapid utterance. 'This is my secret, this. I don't love the man I am going to marry; but I have agreed to be his wife to satisfy my friends. Say you don't hate me for what I have told. I could not bear that you should know!'

'Hate you? Oh, Geraldine!'

A hair's-breadth further, and they would both have broken down.

'Not a word more. Now you know my unhappy state, and I shall die content.'

'But, darling – my Geraldine!'

'It is too late. Good-night – good-bye!' She spoke in a hurried voice, almost like a low cry, and rushed away.

Here was a revelation. Egbert moved along to the door, and up the path, in a condition in which his mind caused his very body to ache. He gazed vacantly through the railings of the lawn, which came close to the churchyard; but she was gone. He still moved mechanically on. A little further and he was overtaken by the parish clerk, who, addressing a few words to him, soon recognised his voice.

The clerk's talk, too, was about the wedding. 'Is the marriage likely to be a happy one?' asked Egbert, aroused by the subject.

'Well, between you and me, Mr Mayne, 'tis a made up affair. Some says she can't bear the man.'

'Lord Bretton?'

'Yes. I could say more if I dared; but what's the good of it now!'

'I suppose none,' said Egbert wearily.

He was glad to be alone again, and went on towards Fairland slowly and heavily. Had Geraldine forgotten him, and loved elsewhere with a light heart, he could have borne it; but this sacrifice at a time when, left to herself, she might have listened to him, was an intolerable misery. Her inconsistent manner, her appearance of being swayed by two feelings, her half-reservations were all explained. 'Against her wishes,' he said; 'at heart she may still be mine. Oh, Geraldine, my poor Geraldine, is it come to this!'

He bitterly regretted his first manner towards her, and turned round to consider whether he could not go back, endeavour to find her, and ask if he could be of any possible use. But all this was plainly absurd. He again proceeded homeward as before.

Reaching Fairland he sat awhile in his empty house without a light, and then went to bed. Owing to the distraction of his mind he lay for three or four hours meditating, and listening to the autumn wind, turning restlessly from side to side, the blood throbbing in his temples and singing in his ears, and the ticking of his watch waxing apparently loud enough to stun him. He conjured up the image of Geraldine in her various stages of preparation on the following day. He saw her coming in at the well-known door, walking down the aisle in a floating cloud of white, and receiving the eyes of the assembled crowd without a flush, or a sign of consciousness; uttering the words, 'I take thee to my wedded husband', as quietly as if she were dreaming them. And the husband? Egbert shuddered. How could she have consented, even if her memories stood their ground only half so obstinately as his own? As for himself, he perceived more clearly than ever how intricately she had mingled with every motive in his past career. Some portion of the thought, 'marriage with Geraldine', had been marked on every day of his manhood.

Ultimately he fell into a fitful sleep, when he dreamed of fighting, wading, diving, boring, through innumerable multitudes, in the midst of which Geraldine's form appeared flitting about, in the usual confused manner of dreams, – sometimes coming towards him, sometimes receding, and getting thinner and thinner till she was a mere film tossed about upon a seething mass.

He jumped up in the bed, damp with a cold perspiration, and in an agony of disquiet. It was a minute or two before he could collect his senses. He went to the window and looked out. It was quite dark, and the wind moaned and whistled round the corners of the house in the heavy intonations which seem to express that ruthlessness has all the world to itself.

'Egbert, do, do come to me!' reached his ears in a faint voice from the darkness.

There was no mistaking it: it was assuredly the tongue of Geraldine.

He half dressed himself, ran downstairs, and opened the front door, holding the candle above his head. Nobody was visible.

He set down the light, hastened round the back of the house, and saw a dusky figure turning the corner to get to the gate. He then ran diagonally across the plot, and intercepted the form in the path. 'Geraldine!' he said, 'can it indeed be you?'

'Yes, it is, it is!' she cried wildly, and fell upon his shoulder.

The hot turmoil of excitement pervading her hindered her from fainting, and Egbert placed his arm round her, and led her into the house, without asking a question, or meeting with any resistance. He assisted her into a chair as soon as they reached the front room.

'I have run away from home, Egbert, and to you!' she sobbed. 'I am not insane: they and you may think so, but I am not. I came to find you. Such shocking things have happened since I met you just now. Can Lord Bretton come and claim me?'

'Nobody on earth can claim you, darling, against your will. Now tell it all to me.'

She spoke on between her tears. 'I have loved you ever since, Egbert; but such influences have been brought to bear upon me that at last I have hardly known what I was doing. At last, I thought that perhaps, after all, it would be better to become a lady of title, with a large park and houses of my own, than the wife of any man of genius who was poor. I loved you all the time, but I was half ashamed that I loved you. I went out continually, that gaiety might obscure the past. And then dark circles came round my eyes – I grew worn and tired. I am not nearly so nice to look at as at that time when we used to meet in the school, nor so healthy either. . . . I think I was handsome then.' At this she smiled faintly, and raised her eyes to his, with a sparkle of their old mischief in them.

'And now and ever,' he whispered.

'How innocent we were then! Fancy, Egbert, our unreserve would have been almost wrong if we had known the canons of behaviour we learnt afterwards. Ah! who at that time would have thought I was to yield to what I did? I wish now that I had met you at the door in Chevron Square, as I promised. But I feared to – I had promised Lord Bretton – and I that evening received a lecturing from my father, who saw you at the concert – he was in a seat further behind. And then, when I heard of your great success, how I wished I had held out a little longer! for I knew your hard labour had been on my account. When we met again last night it seemed awful, horrible – what I had done. Yet how could I tell you plainly? When I got indoors I felt I should die of misery, and I went to my father, and said I could not be married tomorrow. Oh, how angry he was and what a dreadful scene occurred!' She covered her face with her hands.

'My poor Geraldine!' said Egbert, supporting her with his arm.

'When I was in my room this came into my mind, "Better is it that thou shouldst not vow, than that thou shouldst vow and not pay." I could bear it no longer. I was determined not to marry him, and to see you again, whatever came of it. I dressed, and came downstairs noiselessly, and slipped out. I knew where your house was, and hastened here.'

'You will never marry him now?'

'Never. Yet what can I do? Oh! what can I do? If I go back to my father – no, I cannot go back now – it is too late. But if they should find me, and drag me back, and compel me to perform my promise!'

'There is one simple way to prevent that, if, beloved Geraldine, you will agree to adopt it.'

'Yes.'

'By becoming *my* wife at once. We would return to London as soon as the ceremony was over; and there you may defy them all.'

'Oh, Egbert, I have thought of this—'

'You will have no reason to regret it. Perhaps I can introduce you to as intellectual, if odd-mannered and less aristocratic society than that you have been accustomed to.'

'Yes, I know it – I reflected on it before I came. . . . I will be your wife,' she replied tenderly. 'I have come to you, and to you I will cling.'

Egbert kissed her lips then for the first time in his life. He reflected for some time, if that process could be called reflection which was accompanied with so much excitement.

'The parson of your parish would perhaps refuse to marry us, even if we could get to the church secretly,' he said, with a cloud on his brow. 'That's a difficulty.'

'Oh, don't take me there! I cannot go to Tollamore. I shall be seen, or we shall be parted. Don't take me there.'

'No, no; I will not, love; I was only thinking. Are you known in this parish?'

'Well, yes; not, however, to the clergyman. He is a young man – old Mr Keene is dead, you know.'

'Then I can manage it.' Egbert clasped her in his arms in the delight of his heart. 'Now this is our course. I am first going to the surrogate's, and then further; and while I am gone you must stay in this house absolutely alone, and lock yourself in for safety. There is food in the house, and wine in that cupboard; you must stay here in hiding until I come back. It is now five o'clock. I will be here again at latest by eleven. If anybody knocks, remain silent, and the house will be supposed empty, as it lately has been so for a long time. My old servant and waitress must not come here today – I will manage that. I will light a fire, which will have burnt down by daylight, so that the room will be warmed for you. Sit there while I set about it.'

He lit the fire, placed on the table all the food the house afforded, and went away.

CHAPTER SIX

Hence will I to my ghostly father's cell;
His help to crave, and my dear hap to tell.

In half an hour Egbert returned, leading a horse.

'I have borrowed this from an old neighbour,' he said, 'and I have told the woman that waits upon me that I am going on a journey, and shall lock up the house today, so that she will not be wanted. And now, dearest, I want you to lend me something.'

'Whatever it may be, you know it is yours.'

'It is that,' he answered, lightly touching with the tip of his finger a sparkling ring that she wore on hers – the same she had used to wear at their youthful meetings in past years. 'I want it as a pattern for the size.'

She drew it off and handed it to him, at the same time raising her eyelids and glancing under his with a little laugh of confusion. His heart responded, and he kissed her; but he could not help feeling that she was by far too fair a prize for him.

She accompanied him to the door, and Mayne mounted the horse. They parted, and, waiting to hear her lock herself in, he cantered off by a bridle-path towards a town about five miles off.

It was so early that the surrogate on whom he called had not yet breakfasted, but he was very willing to see Mayne, and took him at once to the study. Egbert briefly told him what he wanted; that the lady he wished to marry was at that very moment in his house, and could go nowhere else for shelter – hence the earliness and urgency of his errand.

The surrogate seemed to see rather less interest in the circumstances than Mayne did himself; but he at once prepared the application for a licence. When it was done, he made it up into a letter, directed it, and placed it on the mantelpiece. 'It shall go by this evening's post,' he said.

'But,' said Egbert, 'considering the awkward position this lady is in, cannot a special messenger be sent for the licence? It is only seven or eight miles to ——, and yet otherwise I must wait for two days' posts.'

'Undoubtedly; if anybody likes to pay for it, a special messenger may be sent.'

'There will be no paying; I am willing to go myself. Do you object?'

'No; if the case is really serious, and the lady is dangerously compromised by every delay.'

Mayne left the vicarage of the surrogate and again rode off; this time it was towards a well-known cathedral town. He felt bewildering sensations during this stroke for happiness, and went on his journey in that state of mind which takes cognizance of little things, without at the time being conscious of them, though they return vividly upon the memory long after.

He reached the city after a ride of seven additional miles, and soon obtained the precious document, and all else that he required. Returning to the inn where the horse had been rested, rubbed down, and fed, he again crossed the saddle, and at ten minutes past eleven he was back at Fairland. Before going to Monk's Hut, where Geraldine was immured, he hastened straight to the parsonage.

The young clergyman looked curiously at him and at the bespattered and jaded horse outside. 'Surely you are too rash in the matter,' he said.

'No,' said Egbert; 'there are weighty reasons why I should be in such haste. The lady has at present no home to go to. She has taken shelter with me. I am doing what I consider best in so awkward a case.'

The parson took down his hat, and said, 'Very well; I will go to the church at once. You must be quick if it is to be done today.'

Mayne left the horse for the present in the parson's yard, ran round to the clerk, thence to Monk's Hut, and called Geraldine.

It was, indeed, a hasty preparation for a wedding ceremony that these two made that morning. She was standing at the window, quite ready, and feverish with waiting. Kissing her gaily and breathlessly he directed her by a slightly circuitous path to the church; and, when she had gone about two minutes, proceeded thither himself by the direct road, so that they met in the porch. Within, the clergyman, clerk and clerk's wife had already gathered; and Geraldine and Egbert advanced to the communion railing.

Thus they became man and wife.

'Now he cannot claim me anyhow,' she murmured when the service was ended, as she sank almost fainting upon the arm of Mayne.

'Mr Mayne,' said the clergyman, aside to him in the vestry, 'what is the name of the family at Tollamore House ?'

'Strangely enough, Allenville – the same as hers,' said he, coolly.

The parson looked keenly and dubiously at Mayne, and Egbert returned the look, whereupon the other turned aside and said nothing.

Egbert and Geraldine returned to their hermitage on foot, as they had left it; and, by rigorously excluding all thoughts of the future, they felt happy with the same old unreasoning happiness as of six years before, now resumed for the first time since that date.

But it was quite impossible that the hastily-married pair should remain at Monk's Hut unseen and unknown, as they fain would have done. Almost as soon as they had sat down in the house they came to the conclusion that there was no alternative for them but to start at once for Melport, if not for London. The difficulty was to get a conveyance. The only horse obtainable here, though a strong one, had already been tired down by Egbert in the morning, and the nearest village at which another could be had was about two miles off.

'I can walk as far as that,' said Geraldine.

'Then walk we will,' said Egbert. 'It will remove all our difficulty.' And, first packing up a small valise, he locked the door and went off with her upon his arm, just as the church clock struck one.

That walk through the woods was as romantic an experience as any they had ever known in their lives, though Geraldine was far from being quite happy. On reaching the village, which was larger than Fairland, they were fortunate enough to secure a carriage without any trouble. The village stood on the turnpike road, and a fly, about to return to Melport, where it had come from, was halting before the inn. Egbert hired it at once, and in little less than an hour and a half bridegroom and bride were comfortably housed in a quiet hotel of the seaport town above mentioned.

CHAPTER SEVEN

How small a part of time they share
That are so wondrous sweet and fair!

They remained three days at Melport without having come to any decision on their future movements.

On the third day, at breakfast, Egbert took up the local newspaper which had been published that morning, and his eye presently glanced upon a paragraph headed 'The Tollamore Elopement'.

Before reading it he considered for a moment whether he should lay the journal aside, and for the present hide its contents from the tremulous creature opposite. But deeming this unadvisable, he gently prepared her for the news, and read the paragraph aloud.

It was to the effect that the village of Tollamore and its neighbourhood had been thrown into an unwonted state of excitement by the disappearance of Miss Allenville on the eve of the preparations for her marriage with Lord Bretton, which had been alluded to in their last number. Simultaneously there had disappeared from a neighbouring village, whither he had come for a few months' retirement, a gentleman named Mayne, of considerable literary reputation in the metropolis, and apparently an old acquaintance of Miss Allenville's. Efforts had been made to trace the fugitives by the young lady's father and the distracted bridegroom, Lord Bretton, but hitherto all their exertions had been unavailing.

Subjoined was another paragraph, entitled 'Latest particulars':

'It has just been discovered that Mr Mayne and Miss Allenville are already man and wife. They were boldly married at the parish church of Fairland, before any person in the village had the least suspicion who or what they were. It appears that the lady joined her intended husband early that morning at the cottage he had taken for the season, that they went to the church by different paths, and after the ceremony walked out of the parish by a route as yet unknown. In consequence of this intelligence Lord Bretton has returned to London, and her father is left alone to mourn the young lady's rashness.'

Egbert lifted his eyes and watched Geraldine as he finished reading. On perceiving his look she tried to smile. The smile thinned away, for there was not cheerfulness enough to support it long, and she said faintly, 'Egbert, what must be done?'

'We must, I suppose, leave this place, darling; as charming as our life is here.'

'Yes; I fear we must.'

'London seems to be the spot for us at once, before we attract the attention of people here.'

'How well everything might end,' she said, 'if my father were induced to welcome you, and make the most of your reputation! I wonder, wonder if he would! In that case there would be little amiss.'

Mayne, after some reflection, said, 'I think that I will go to your father before we leave for town. We are certain to be discovered by somebody or other, either here or in London, and that would bring your father, and there would possibly result a public meeting between him and myself at which words might be uttered which could not be forgotten on either side; so that a private meeting and explanation is safest, before anything of that sort can happen.'

'I think,' she said, looking to see if he approved of her words as they fell, 'I think that a still better course would be for me to go to him – alone.'

Mayne did not care much about this plan at first; but further discussion gave it a more feasible aspect, since Allenville, though stern and proud, was fond of his daughter, and had never crossed her, except when her whims interfered, as he considered, with her interests. Nothing could unmarry them; and Geraldine's mind would be much more at ease after begging her father's forgiveness. The journey was therefore decided on. They waited till nearly evening, and then, ordering round a brougham, Egbert told the man to drive to Tollamore.

The journey to Geraldine was tedious and oppressive to a degree. When, after two hours' driving, they drew near the park precincts, she said shivering:

'I don't like to drive up to the house, Egbert.'

'I will do just as you like. What do you propose?'

'To let him wait in the road, under the three oak trees, while you and I walk to the house.'

Egbert humoured her in everything; and when they reached the designated spot the driver was stopped, and they alighted. Carefully wrapping her up he gave her his arm, and they started for Tollamore House at an easy pace through the moonlit park, avoiding the direct road as much as possible.

Geraldine spoke but little during the walk, especially when they neared the house, and passed across the smooth broad glade which surrounded it. At sight of the door she seemed to droop, and leant heavy upon him. Egbert more than ever wished to confront Mr Allenville himself; morally and socially it appeared to him the right thing to do. But Geraldine trembled when he again proposed it; and he yielded to her entreaty thus far, that he would wait a few minutes till she had entered and seen her father privately, and prepared the way for Egbert to follow, which he would then do in due course.

The spot in which she desired him to wait was a summer-house under a tree about fifty yards from the lawn front of the house, and commanding a view of the door on this side. She was to enter unobserved by the servants, and go straight to her father, when, should he listen to her with the least show of mildness, she would send out for Egbert to follow. If the worst were to happen, and he were to be enraged with her, refusing to listen to entreaties or explanations, she would hasten out, rejoin Egbert and depart.

In this little summer-house he embraced her, and bade her adieu, after their honeymoon of three short days. She trembled so much that she could scarcely walk when he let go her hand.

'Don't go alone – you are not well,' said Egbert.

'Yes, yes, dearest, I am – and I will soon return, so soon!' she answered; and he watched her crossing the grass and advancing, a mere dot, towards the mansion. In a short time the appearance of an oblong of light in the shadowy expanse of wall denoted to him that the door was open: her outline appeared on it; then the door shut her in, and all was shadow as before. Even though they were husband and wife the line of demarcation seemed to be drawn again as rigidly as when he lived at the school.

Egbert waited in the solitude of this place minute by minute, restlessly swinging his foot when seated, at other times walking up and down, and anxiously watching for the arrival of some messenger. Nearly half an hour passed, but no messenger came.

The first sign of life in the neighbourhood of the house was in the shape of a man on horseback, galloping from the stable entrance. Egbert saw this by looking over the wall at the back of the summer-house; and the man passed along the open drive, vanishing in the direction of the lodge. Mayne, not without some presentiment of ill, wondered what it could mean, but thought it just possible that the horseman was a special messenger sent to catch the late post at the nearest town, as was sometimes done by Squire Allenville. So he curbed his impatience for Geraldine's sake.

Next he observed lights moving in the upper windows of the building. 'It has been made known to them all that she is come, and they are preparing a room,' he thought hopefully.

But nobody came from the door to welcome him; his existence was apparently forgotten by the whole world. In another ten minutes he saw the Melport brougham that had brought them, creeping slowly up to the house. Egbert went round to the man, and told him to drive to the stables and wait for orders.

From the length of Geraldine's absence, Mayne could not help concluding that the impression produced on her father was of a doubtful kind, not quite favourable enough to warrant her in telling him at once that her husband was in waiting. Still, a sense of his dignity as her husband might have constrained her to introduce him as soon as possible, and he had only agreed to wait a few minutes. Something unexpected must, after all, have occurred. And this supposition was confirmed a moment later by the noise of a horse and carriage coming up the drive. Egbert again looked over into the open park, and saw the vehicle reach the carriage entrance, where somebody alighted and went in.

'Her father away from home perhaps, and now just returned,' he said.

He lingered yet another ten minutes, and then could endure no longer. Before he could reach the lawn door through which Geraldine had disappeared, it opened. A person came out and, without shutting the door, hastened across to where Egbert stood. The man was a servant, without a hat on, and the moment that he saw Mayne he ran up to him.

'Mr Mayne?' he said.

'It is,' said Egbert.

'Mr Allenville desires that you will come with me. There is something serious the matter. Miss Allenville is taken dangerously ill, and she wishes to see you.'

'What has happened to her?' gasped Egbert breathlessly.

'Miss Allenville came unexpectedly home just now, and directly she saw her father it gave her such a turn that she fainted, and ruptured a blood-vessel internally, and fell upon the floor. They have put her to bed, and the doctor has come, but we are afraid she won't live over it. She has suffered from it before.'

Egbert did not speak, but walked hastily beside the man-servant. The only recollection that he ever had in after years of entering that house was a vague idea of stags' antlers in a long row on the wall, and a sense of great breadth in the stone staircase as he ascended it. Everything else was in a mist.

Mr Allenville, on being informed of his arrival, came out and met him in the corridor.

Egbert's mind was so entirely given up to the one thought that the life of his Geraldine was in danger, that he quite forgot the peculiar circumstances under which he met Allenville, and the peculiar behaviour necessary on that account. He seized her father's hand, and said abruptly,

'Where is she? Is the danger great?'

Allenville withdrew his hand, turned, and led the way into his daughter's room, merely saying in a low hard tone, 'Your wife is in great danger, sir.'

Egbert rushed to the bedside and bent over her in agony not to be described. Allenville sent the attendants from the room, and closed the door.

'Father,' she whispered feebly, 'I cannot help loving him. Would you leave us alone? We are very dear to each other, and perhaps I shall soon die.'

'Anything you wish, child,' he said with stern anguish; 'and anything can hardly include more.' Seeing that she looked hurt at this, he spoke more pleasantly. 'I am glad to please you – you know I am, Geraldine – the utmost.' He then went out.

'They would not have let you know if Dr Williams had not insisted,' she said. 'I could not speak to explain at first – that's how it is you have been left there so long.'

'Geraldine, dear, dear Geraldine, why should all this have come upon us?' he said in unbroken accents.

'Perhaps it is best,' she murmured. 'I hardly knew what I was doing when I entered the door, or how I could explain to my father, or what could be done to reconcile him to us. He kept me waiting a little time before he would see me, but at last he came into the room. I felt a fulness on my chest, I could not speak, and then this happened to me. Papa has asked no questions.'

A silence followed, interrupted only by her fitful breathing:

> A silence which doth follow talk, that causes
> The baffled heart to speak with sighs and tears.

'Do you love me very much now, Egbert?' she said. 'After all my vacillation, do you?'

'Yes – how can you doubt?'

'I do not doubt. I know you love me. But will you stay here till I get better? You must stay. Papa is sure to be friendly with you now.'

'Don't agitate yourself, dearest, about me. All is right with me here. Your health is the one thing to be anxious about now.'

'I have only been taken ill like this once before in my life, and I thought it would never be again.'

As she was not allowed to speak much, he remained holding her hand; and after some time she sank into a light sleep. Egbert then went from the chamber for a moment, and asked the physician, who was in the next room, if there was good hope for her life.

'It is a dangerous attack, and she is very weak,' he replied, concealing, though scarcely able to conceal, the curiosity with which he regarded Egbert; for the marriage had now become generally known.

The evening and night wore on. Great events in which he could not participate seemed to be passing over Egbert's head; a stir was in progress, of whose results he grasped but small and fragmentary notions. And, on the other hand, it was mournfully strange to notice her father's behaviour during these hours of doubt. It was only when he despaired that he looked upon Egbert with tolerance. When he hoped, the young man's presence was hateful to him.

Not knowing what to do when out of her chamber, having nobody near him to whom he could speak on intimate terms, Egbert passed a wretched time of three long days. After watching by her for several hours on the third day, he went downstairs, and into the open air. There intelligence was brought him that another effusion, more violent than any which preceded it, had taken place. Egbert rushed back to her room. Powerful remedies were applied, but none availed. A fainting-fit followed, and in two or three hours it became plain to those who understood that there was no Geraldine for the morrow.

Sometimes she was lethargic, and as if her spirit had already flown; then her mind wandered; but towards the end she was sensible of all that was going on, though unable to speak, her strength being barely enough to enable her to receive an idea.

It was a gentle death. She was as acquiescent as if she had been a saint, which was not the least striking and uncommon feature in the life of this fair and unfortunate lady. Her husband held one tiny hand, remaining all the time on the right side of the bed in a nook beside the curtains, while her father and the rest remained on the left side, never raising their eyes to him, and scarcely ever addressing him.

Everything was so still that her weak act of trying to live seemed a silent wrestling with all the powers of the universe. Pale and hopelessly anxious they all waited and watched the heavy shadows close over her. It might have been thought that death felt for her and took her tenderly. She sighed twice or three times; then her heart stood still; and this strange family alliance was at an end for ever.

OUTLINES FOR STORIES

A

(i) Plot – Girl goes to be schoolmistress: leaves her village lover: loves a school-master: he meets old lady in cathedral: she proposes.

(ii) Plot – Violinist in country town: poorish: is going to marry neighbouring village girl (school-mistress) or one of same town: loses his finger: hopeless case: strolls into cathedral or abbey: old lady meets him there, day after day: she proposes to him – he ascertains that her words are true – muses and muses and puts off [quick ?] answer – at last he says he will marry her in a month: they marry privately: go away to her house. Another man, a school-master, who has long secretly loved the school-mistress now hopes to make way with her – but no: she is firm: meanwhile old lady's husband, the quondam violinist absents himself: she jealously watches him – after a deal of trouble traces him to the school of town he left: before the lady has seen school-mistress latter leaves the place:

Schoolmaster, at loss of school-mistress, is disconsolate: goes looking for her: suspects the musician: goes to old lady's place (or better, is introduced as living there – a sad lonely man crossed in love): discovers her in beautifully furnished little place: old lady discovers her here (instead of at first school): this schoolhouse is either in the lady's own parish or the adjoining one according as the following is introduced, or not – When schoolmistress is discovered she vanishes: Old lady's husband affects to make love to the maid: she is dismissed – a new one, prettier yet chosen because husband says he doesn't like her.

The discovery first is that the 1st sweet heart here is *chère amie* of old lady's husband – then that she is really wife: old lady poisons herself: man convicted: dies: girl marries other lover.

Mysterious noises heard at the school (being the rich furniture) nobody, of course, ever goes upstairs in the schoolmistress's, and here is the furniture, plate, etc., jewellery. It is here she dresses to receive him: her evasions etc., to prevent people going upstairs: Could it be managed that she doesn't know he has actually married the other woman.

All the furniture of the lighter kind, because of getting it there. Old lady titled widow.

In opening, the description of schoolmistress's arrival, or house. state the government requirements – and that it argues well for the courage of English maids that (so many) are every year drafted off to lonely residence, etc.

B
Scheme of Short Story

A girl whose parents wish her to marry A begs to be allowed to marry B, her (secret) lover. They are surprised, as they knew nothing of him.

After much entreaty from her they agree to her wishes. Engagement announced, etc.

The wedding day draws near. Unpleasant traits in her betrothed reveal themselves. She suspects that he drinks (?) and at the same time that worthy qualities reveal themselves in A, the rejected one.

She is frightened at having acted on her own judgment as she finds more and more that theirs was the true one. But she feels bound to keep her engagement. Bitter recriminations between her and her parents at breakfast times etc., *she* passionately reproaching them for not having insisted on her marrying the one they chose.

Her father says that he suspected that B drank. She says: 'Then why didn't you tell me ?' Her father says that he was not sure and that she would listen to nothing he urged against B.

They say it cannot be helped now (as they have just heard that he is engaged to somebody else ?) As she has made her bed so she must lie on it, etc. She puts on a dreadful artificial gaiety. The wedding takes place. (What happens afterwards is not told.)

C
How I Won at Monte Carlo
(Christmas story, say)

'I' assist, or relieve a Frenchman who is ill. On his deathbed he begins to tell me of a system he has discovered for winning at Monaco – dies, without finishing.

I think it over – cannot divine the actual clue, or secret, though I lie awake at night, arranging numbers, etc.

Am at an inn when a stranger begins telling of a system of which he knows only the *last* part.

I put the two together – start – arrive – break the bank. When I have enough, come home, purchase estate, etc.

D

(i) The fiddler/player/bandsman at the dancing-rooms
(Based on Barthélémon at Vauxhall. See Facts.)

sitting fiddling – dancers whirling – haze of candles – beaux leering at frail, fair painted faces flushed with wine. 'O that this should be my trade!' The end of the revel – the entrance – going off in carriages, lovers and mistresses. He turns homeward, wearied and sick of the vicious pleasure of this haunt. Right before him, behind the dome of the Cathedral, the rising sun of June. A feeling of aversion to the night he had passed – a sudden upheaval of antagonistic sentiment.

> Awake my Soul and with the sun
> Thy daily stage of duty run

he said aloud. And as he went the music of a new morning hymn grew up in his mind. He stopped – opened his violin – and touched the new tune with his fingers softly on the strings. Did any citizen hear from his bed the notes below his window? If so, he heard an air that within 50 years would be known to the uttermost parts of the earth. It was the morning hymn.

(ii) The Vauxhall Fiddler

Dawn. The orchestra – the first violin obviously Italian or French blood – dancers finish – violinists leave. The exit from Vauxhall – scene – carriages – dawn lights shining out – painted people – smell of candles. A fine July morning – dusty. He goes along towards Westminster Bridge – oil lamps being put out.

At the west end of the Bridge, or as it is usually called the north end – the old houses of Parliament. His shadow in front of him. He stops, wipes his face – looks across Southwark. The rising sun. He watches the sun awhile. Hums notes – draws violin out of green bag and softly touches the strings to some mental melody. Scribbles on scraps of paper. Then turns up Whitehall.

Reaching home. House silent – a cold supper. He eats and prepares to go to bed. But suddenly turns back to the harpsichord. Takes out the scraps of paper. Roughly sketches staves of music on some sheets at hand, and jots down notes from the scrawls. Tries them over on harpsichord. Quite forgets that he should be going to bed. Wife comes down – an English/Scotch woman – surprised. He jumps up. 'Oh yes – I forgot. I'll just write in the words of this – then I'll go. "Awake my soul and with the sun" . . . who wrote that hymn' 'What, the morning hymn? Bishop Ken – he who' etc. . . . 'Just tell me the rest of the verse—'

> Awake my soul . . .
> . . . .
> . . . .
> . . . .

'How do you come to be writing like that after Vauxhall?'

'Well, I came out – tired and sick of it as usual: the painted dancers made me sick, and the chairs and coaches of women no better than those in the street. 'Tis a mighty distasteful life – I wish I could get away. I thought I'd walk home fortunately. On the bridge I happened to stop . . . and then it all came to me. If I don't mistake that will be a tune that fits like a glove – I must publish it. . . .' She, sadly: 'You've said that so many times!'

He went to bed, and when he got up the air seemed less fascinating, and he threw the notes into a drawer. There they lay for years. He moved house, etc. But a day came. . . . It was the old familiar morning hymn by Barthélémon.

(iii) Title ⎧ The Morning Hymn?
         ⎨ An Incident in the Life of Barthélémon?
         ⎩ The Bandmaster at the Dancing-Rooms

(A story based on incidents in the life of Barthélémon)

He is sitting fiddling – the dancers whirling – a blaze of candles, bowers, trees, etc. – beaux leering at frail fair ones with painted faces – flushed with wine.

He gets very weary. Is there night after night through the summer months. The work is hard but music is not a paying trade – At last the end of the nightly revel comes – carriages and hackney coaches are called up to the gates – and drive off with lovers and mistresses.

He turns and takes his way homeward on foot, the night being fine, and his pockets somewhat empty, sick of the vicious pleasures of the haunt he has to frequent. On Westminster Bridge he turns his head. Not a soul near. Right before him appears the rising sun of June. It shines upon his face – that of a man about 30, thoughtful – dark hair – (son of a French officer and an Irish lady). The sight of the sun causes in him a sudden access of emotion. He opens his violin case and touches the strings to a melody he imagines and there and then composes, to the well-known words of Bishop Ken, who had died some years earlier in the century:

> Awake my soul and with the sun
> Thy daily course of duty run

On reaching home, before going to bed, he seized a pen and a sheet of music paper, and pricked down the air as he had thought it out on his walk. Next morning looks at it, throws it into a drawer, and forgets all about it.

This was about the year 1775. Shortly after he gave up his engagement at Vauxhall and left England for a professional tour on the Continent. A few years later he was again in England and the scenes recalled to him his forgotten composition – hymn to the rising sun – when he was in this country – [MS torn] Oratorios, quartets, concertos, duos and preludes, are all forgotten; his name and nationality are nearly forgotten likewise: but his Morning Hymn is known and sung in the uttermost parts of the earth to which Christianity has penetrated. (See Grove's *Dictionary of Music* article Barthélémon.)

E

Form I Sparrow story
'The mistaken symbol' (or) 'For want of a word'
By the sparrow.

I

I had noticed while hopping round a certain St James's church in a certain London Square on Sunday mornings the assiduity with which a shy mannered young man attended the service . . . (Describe him). His face wore a devotional cast, and yet my experience in watching men from the housetops led me to doubt if devotion was altogether the cause of his regularity. . . . Excited my curiosity. The next Sunday as soon as the church doors were opened I flew into the empty building unobserved, and standing hidden among the timbers of the roof watched the congregation assemble . . . a young lady took her seat in the aisle and, the young man who had interested me entered a little later and sat down in the same pew, and next to her. Contrary to my expectation they did not speak to each other . . . yet something in his manner almost proved to me that she was the cause of his regular presence there. . . .

As I always breakfasted early and had little else to do at this hour I amused myself on several ensuing Sunday mornings by observing the pair. . . . The same regularity. . . . As the weather grew warmer some of the church windows were opened for ventilation, and one of these casements was close to the seat of the young couple, so that by standing on the iron stay that held it I could look right into their faces.

. . . could soon discover that when he uttered his words of praise and prayer he addressed them mentally to her. He looked his love, but could not speak it: his shyness would not allow him to make opportunities. . . . Whether she returned his silent affection was a problem. sometimes a passing look at his face when his eyes were on his book led me to think so. . . . The mutual shyness of the two made their situation a painfully attractive one. Their furthest stage of recognition so far was her offering him her hymn book to look over one day when he had come without his own. This grew into a habit. Every week they sang from the same book. her lemon-gloved thumb and finger nipping one bottom corner of the volume, and his brown gloved ones the other – and their elbows nearly touching.

Where she came from he may or may not have known: at any rate something seemed to prevent his following her. . . .

I had an accidental illumination. . . . As he came from the church door to the pavement I heard him whisper before I had left the window: 'I'll tell her what I feel next Sunday between the psalm and the sermon! . . .

I watched nervously the next Sunday. But he did not tell her. His timidity was too strong for his resolve . . . as indeed was proved, for hopping close by him on his exit I heard him murmur: 'Never mind: I will next Sunday, anyhow!' But never a word passed on the next occasion though he looked more strongly than usual at her. This went on for two or three weeks: by watching closely I could discern him almost making up his mouth for the sentence at momentary intervals, particularly during the calling of banns. But never a word. She looked sad on these latter Sundays, and it occurred to me that it was owing to his silence. But I did not know.

I noticed too with concern that he was getting paler, and on the following Sunday to my great disappointment, he did not appear. At the lessons some stranger was shown into his place. I watched her now to read her mind about him, if it were possible. But she gave no sign. She either was hiding her feeling by a great effort of self repression, or, horrid thought, she was indifferent to his absence.

Several weeks elapsed, but though I occupied regularly my perch on the casement by his pew he did not come. I was convinced that he was ill, and my conjectures proved true. . . . When he did reappear, it was early autumn and after the service had begun. The verger was standing at the door, and when the young man came up the verger spoke: 'I haven't seen you, sir, for many Sundays: and you used to be so regular.'

I have been ill said   not dangerously; but still, enough to make me lie by. . . .'

'I am afraid your seat is filled to-day. . . .'

'Never mind. Put me as near as you can to the same pew.'

It was evident that he was still thinking of the young lady. She too had not attended quite so regularly: but she was there that morning, I knew.

I flew round to the window as the verger showed him in to his temporary seat for that morning. I found that it was two pews behind his own, at a point whence he could see her very well though she was not likely to notice him.

As he stood up and mechanically opened his book I saw his face change to a look of utter misery. His eyes were upon her in front of him, and mine followed his glance. She stood looking in her prayer book quite abstractedly – holding it with her left hand, ungloved. On a particular finger she wore a significant ring. She was engaged to be married.

. . . At last he could keep his seat no longer; and went out. She had not seen him at all. From that morning he seemed to break off attending there. She came, irregularly: and always wore the ring. Yet there was never a young man with her, and her look was grave and abstracted. What was the character of her engagement. Then she, too, left off attending.

II

I still haunted the square in which the church stood . . . but I had nearly forgotten the pair of young people in the stress of looking for food. For it was winter now, and we birds often went hungry nearly all day. Yet curiously enough news came of them, though I did not seek it. . . .

It was on a week day, and two women were sweeping and dusting the church. One had brought some sandwiches I suppose to avoid going home to lunch the days being short – As there was a chance of a few crumbs from these I flew in and waited in the roof. . . . They took up and dusted the books in the pews – and made remarks upon their owners – These were quite irrelevant for a long while; but when they came to the seat formerly occupied by the young man and woman I listened.

'Now she was a curious young lady,' said the charwoman, to the other, who appeared to be a relation, and to have nothing to do with the church. 'Her book may as well be sent home, for she will never use it again, if it's true as I hear, that she's dying/dead.'

I cannot give the woman's exact words, but the information I gathered was briefly this: she had died, unmarried.

What, then, about the engagement?

(The story ends in this way. The old women gossip and reveal that she had not told anyone to whom she was engaged: she asked to be buried with the ring on her finger. They pressed her to tell. At last she said: 'I have secretly plighted myself to a man whose name I never knew. He sat next me Sunday after Sunday, etc. Could not speak. . . . Why should he, to a girl he only met in church? *I* could not. . . . He then disappeared. I pleased my sick heart by imagining myself engaged to him: and wore this ring to keep off other men, whose attentions were intolerable to me. Let me wear it in my tomb. –

Or, another ending: –

The old women tell that the young lady was dying – that she confessed as above – that her friends discovered the young man, who was brought to the house – that all was explained. The joy of finding that he loved her caused her to get well, and they were married.)

Form II For want of a word (told by bachelor in the 1st person)

I

We sat next each other in The Baptist Chapel?/St James's Church/in a

certain St James's Church in a certain London Square Sunday
after Sunday. She had a sitting and I had a sitting in the same
pew. . . .

Describe her.

As I led a lonely life at lodgings the result upon me began soon to be
apparent even to myself. . . . But I was constitutionally shy – some
people said abnormally so – an unhappy failing which had often stood
in the way of my advancement – And now, at five and thirty, the quality
had become, as it were, crystallized in my character into a procrastinating
slowness that was not likely to be overcome during my mortal term of
years. . . .

So we sat, Sunday after Sunday, and as we uttered words of prayer
and praise together I addressed mine essentially to her. . . .

I may have looked my love – indeed, after-events led me to believe I
did so. At any rate I felt it: but I did not speak it. Whether she saw as
much I know not. . . .

I began to be anxious lest she should never know my feeling, for tell
it to her, a stranger, I could not. I was at least 10 years older than herself
and the risk of being treated with surprise and mockery was one too
great for me to run. How did I know that she had not delivered her
heart to a young man her own age, who was calm in the assurance that
no trespassers would be allowed.

One Sunday I had brought no hymn book, and she allowed me to look
over hers. This grew to be customary . . . her lemon-gloved finger and
thumb (say it was in the days of lemon gloves ?) nipping one bottom
corner of the little red edged volume, and my brown ones the other – our
elbows nearly touching.

Where she came from I could not discover. She disappeared round a
corner. But I resolved to find out by some means soon.

'I will whisper what I feel next Sunday, between the psalm and the
sermon.'

But when the time came I did not. . . . I would do so next Sunday.
But I could not find opportunity. . . . I thought she looked sad. . . . The
very next Sunday I would do it, come what might. . . .

The Sunday came, but I was in bed with a chill. . . . I wondered if she
missed me. . . . I could not go to church again for several weeks. . . .

I was late. Verger spoke to me (see other MS) my place was occupied,
etc. Shown into a seat behind her. I could see her very well – though
she did not see me. When we stood up I noticed that her book was

held in her ungloved hand instead of the customary lemon-gloved one. What I saw further sent a shock through me. . . .

On a particular finger of her left hand was a significant ring. . . . She was engaged to be married.

I felt as if my sight were failing, and I sat down. . . . Soon I found I could remain there no longer; and I went out of the church. She had not seen me at all. That was just one grain of relief. I went to the church service no more – and did not go near the square for several months.

II

When I did go near the church again [it] was on a week-day, when I chanced to be passing by. (Hears of her death from the woman: see other MS.)

(If the ending is to be the happy one he goes into the church, or in some way ascertains who she was from the old woman – goes to the house – (her aunt's, say or she is a governess) – enquires for her. Sends up message that the fellow-worshipper with whom she used to share her hymn-book at St James's Church had called to inquire. He is asked to leave his address. A letter comes from a relative of hers asking him to call again. . . . He is told by this relative when he calls that the Dr has advised that she should see him. She tells him (as in other MS). . . . She recovers. They marry.)

F
The Sparrow

Glimpse the First, or No. 1. The Lovers that were (or any other title)
'I had been resting and preening my feathers for some time on an upper window-sill in a dingy street running through a northern suburb of London, and was about to fly across to the roof opposite and seek shelter for the night, when one among the foot-passengers in the street below me attracted my attention by knocking at the door of the house I was perched on. – Although the evening was gloomy I could see that he was a man about 40 – worn face, an anxious reflective look, etc. . . . He knocked twice before he was admitted . . . entered the room, one of whose windows I occupied. I then became aware that the house was let to lodgers, and that the lodger who occupied this room was a lady. . . . Elegant figure, too gloomy in the room to see much of her features,' etc.

The story goes on that she asks him to sit down. The sparrow finds that they are old lovers. . . . Conversations. – He finds out that she is unmarried, and at last asks her if, after all, she will marry him . . . (he may have been abroad and is now a well to do Colonial). After some fluttering she agrees. Then she says she will get a light, and the sparrow, who has delayed his roosting to see the end of the episode, is quite sleepy. She lights the gas. Sparrow sees that when the light shines full on her face the man receives a shock – it is much wrinkled – beyond what might have been expected. She sees his start at her aged appearance, but says nothing. After a pause he stammers, 'Well, it would be a great pleasure if we could hit it off after all. We must think over the feasibility of it – there would of course be difficulties,' etc. (plainly showing that he has changed his mind, now that he has seen her, and is backing out of his offer). She converses pleasantly, as if she has noticed nothing, and he goes – When he is outside the room she calls him in – tells him that, though she did not mean to let him know, she will do so – and charges him with having backed from his word. At last he owns that he has. . . . When he is gone, etc. . . .

Glimpse the Second, No. 2. The. . . .

The sparrow may be perching on the beam of a church, having flown in through an open window. . . . Sees two people enter by different doors . . . a parson arrive . . . a secret wedding. They part at the church door. Sparrow follows her home. . . . She is living with her family, etc. . . .

No. 3.

(A street accident, say, and what arises from it.)

No. 4.

(An assignation on the steps of the National Gallery, etc.)

No. 5 etc.

(Anything suggested by what you read in the papers –)

No. – (the last but one in the series)

(A murder witnessed by the Sparrow – .)

No. – (the last)

(A death, or funeral.)

The stories may be broken off at any convenient point by darkness closing in, and the sparrow being so sleepy that it tucks its head under its wing and sees no more: or by a boy or a cat frightening it away.

For variety of presentation the sparrow may be perched on the edge of a chimney pot, and hear conversation come up the chimney, etc., etc.

A rather grim one in the series would be the watching by the sparrow

of a lonely man much occupied in chemical work. He goes to a friend –
or a friend calls – the lonely man is excited – says he will soon astonish
the world. Then, one morning the sparrow follows him to the Serpen-
tine, and he drowns himself. Going back the sparrow finds he has written
a letter to his friend, and left it on the table – friend enters – sparrow
looks over letter. It says that he (the lonely man) has discovered the
secret of biogenesis (the origin of living species) and has practised their
manufacture – he has thus produced all sorts of strange monsters: but
in a fit of remorse has destroyed them all, and killed himself. But perhaps
it would suit the character of the series better to adhere to natural
stories.

Instead of No. 1, No. 2, etc. they might be called Glimpse the First,
Glimpse the Second, etc. . . . Thus plunging suddenly into scenes,
breaking off in the midst, and resuming (after asterisks) further on,
would be in keeping.

You might introduce pretty touches of what 'I' do – i.e. the sparrow,
by watching some.

STORIES FOR CHILDREN

The Thieves Who Couldn't Help Sneezing

MANY years ago, when oak-trees now past their prime were about as large as elderly gentlemen's walking-sticks, there lived in Wessex a yeoman's son, whose name was Hubert. He was about fourteen years of age, and was as remarkable for his candour and lightness of heart as for his physical courage, of which, indeed, he was a little vain.

One cold Christmas Eve his father, having no other help at hand, sent him on an important errand to a small town several miles from home. He travelled on horseback, and was detained by the business till a late hour of the evening. At last, however, it was completed; he returned to the inn, the horse was saddled, and he started on his way. His journey homeward lay through the Vale of Blackmore, a fertile but somewhat lonely district, with heavy clay roads and crooked lanes. In those days, too, a great part of it was thickly wooded.

It must have been about nine o'clock when, riding along amid the overhanging trees upon his stout-legged cob Jerry, and singing a Christmas carol, to be in harmony with the season, Hubert fancied that he heard a noise among the boughs. This recalled to his mind that the spot he was traversing bore an evil name. Men had been waylaid there. He looked at Jerry, and wished he had been of any other colour than light grey; for on this account the docile animal's form was visible even here in the dense shade. 'What do I care?' he said aloud, after a few minutes of reflection. 'Jerry's legs are too nimble to allow any highwayman to come near me.'

'Ha! ha! indeed,' was said in a deep voice; and the next moment a man darted from the thicket on his right hand, another man from the thicket on his left hand, and another from a tree-trunk a few yards ahead. Hubert's bridle was seized, he was pulled from his horse, and although he struck out with all his might, as a brave boy would naturally do, he was overpowered. His arms were tied behind him, his legs bound tightly together, and he was thrown into the ditch. The robbers, whose faces he could now dimly perceive to be artificially blackened, at once departed, leading off the horse.

As soon as Hubert had a little recovered himself, he found that by great exertion he was able to extricate his legs from the cord; but, in spite of every endeavour, his arms remained bound as fast as before. All, therefore, that he could do was to rise to his feet and proceed on his way with his arms behind him, and trust to chance for getting them unfastened. He knew that it would be impossible to reach home on foot that night, and in such a condition; but he walked on. Owing to the confusion which this attack caused in his brain, he lost his way, and would have been inclined to lie down and rest till morning among the dead leaves had he not known the danger of sleeping without wrappers in a frost so severe. So he wandered further onwards, his arms wrung and numbed by the cord which pinioned him, and his heart aching for the loss of poor Jerry, who never had been known to kick, or bite, or show a single vicious habit. He was not a little glad when he discerned through the trees a distant light. Towards this he made his way, and presently found himself in front of a large mansion with flanking wings, gables, and towers, the battlements and chimneys showing their shapes against the stars.

All was silent; but the door stood wide open, it being from this door that the light shone which had attracted him. On entering he found himself in a vast apartment arranged as a dining-hall, and brilliantly illuminated. The walls were covered with a great deal of dark wainscoting, formed into moulded panels, carvings, closet-doors, and the usual fittings of a house of that kind. But what drew his attention most was the large table in the midst of the hall, upon which was spread a sumptuous supper, as yet untouched. Chairs were placed around, and it appeared as if something had occurred to interrupt the meal just at the time when all were ready to begin.

Even had Hubert been so inclined, he could not have eaten in his helpless state, unless by dipping his mouth into the dishes, like a pig or cow. He wished first to obtain assistance; and was about to penetrate further into the house for that purpose when he heard hasty footsteps in the porch and the words, 'Be quick!' uttered in the deep voice which had reached him when he was dragged from the horse. There was only just time for him to dart under the table before three men entered the dining-hall. Peeping from beneath the hanging edges of the tablecloth, he perceived that their faces, too, were blackened, which at once removed any remaining doubts he may have felt that these were the same thieves.

'Now, then,' said the first – the man with the deep voice – 'let us hide ourselves. They will all be back again in a minute. That was a good trick to get them out of the house – eh?'

'Yes. You well imitated the cries of a man in distress,' said the second. 'Excellently,' said the third.

'But they will soon find out that it was a false alarm. Come, where shall we hide? It must be some place we can stay in for two or three hours, till all are in bed and asleep. Ah! I have it. Come this way! I have learnt that the further closet is not opened once in a twelvemonth; it will serve our purpose exactly.'

The speaker advanced into a corridor which led from the hall. Creeping a little further forward, Hubert could discern that the closet stood at the end, facing the dining-hall. The thieves entered it, and closed the door. Hardly breathing, Hubert glided forward, to learn a little more of their intention, if possible; and, coming close, he could hear the robbers whispering about the different rooms where the jewels, plate, and other valuables of the house were kept, which they plainly meant to steal.

They had not been long in hiding when a gay chattering of ladies and gentlemen was audible on the terrace without. Hubert felt that it would not do to be caught prowling about the house, unless he wished to be taken for a robber himself; and he slipped softly back to the hall, out at the door, and stood in a dark corner of the porch, where he could see everything without being himself seen. In a moment or two a whole troop of personages came gliding past him into the house. There were an elderly gentleman and lady, eight or nine young ladies, as many young men, besides half-a-dozen men-servants and maids. The mansion had apparently been quite emptied of its occupants.

'Now, children and young people, we will resume our meal,' said the old gentleman. 'What the noise could have been I cannot understand. I never felt so certain in my life that there was a person being murdered outside my door.'

Then the ladies began saying how frightened they had been, and how they had expected an adventure, and how it had ended in nothing after all.

'Wait a while,' said Hubert to himself. 'You'll have adventure enough by-and-by, ladies.'

It appeared that the young men and women were married sons and daughters of the old couple, who had come that day to spend Christmas with their parents.

The door was then closed, Hubert being left outside in the porch. He thought this a proper moment for asking their assistance; and, since he was unable to knock with his hands, began boldly to kick the door.

'Hullo! What disturbance are you making here?' said a footman who opened it; and, seizing Hubert by the shoulder, he pulled him into the dining-hall. 'Here's a strange boy I have found making a noise in the porch, Sir Simon.'

Everybody turned.

'Bring him forward,' said Sir Simon, the old gentleman before mentioned. 'What were you doing there, my boy?'

'Why, his arms are tied!' said one of the ladies.

'Poor fellow!' said another.

Hubert at once began to explain that he had been waylaid on his journey home, robbed of his horse, and mercilessly left in this condition by the thieves.

'Only to think of it!' exclaimed Sir Simon.

'That's a likely story,' said one of the gentlemen-guests, incredulously.

'Doubtful, hey?' asked Sir Simon.

'Perhaps he's a robber himself,' suggested a lady.

'There is a curiously wild wicked look about him, certainly, now that I examine him closely,' said the old mother.

Hubert blushed with shame; and, instead of continuing his story, and relating that robbers were concealed in the house, he doggedly held his tongue, and half resolved to let them find out their danger for themselves.

'Well, untie him,' said Sir Simon. 'Come, since it is Christmas Eve, we'll treat him well. Here, my lad; sit down in that empty seat at the bottom of the table, and make as good a meal as you can. When you have had your fill we will listen to more particulars of your story.'

The feast then proceeded; and Hubert, now at liberty, was not at all sorry to join in. The more they eat and drank the merrier did the company become; the wine flowed freely, the logs flared up the chimney, the ladies laughed at the gentlemen's stories; in short, all went as noisily and as happily as a Christmas gathering in old times possibly could do.

Hubert, in spite of his hurt feelings at their doubts of his honesty, could not help being warmed both in mind and in body by the good cheer, the scene, and the example of hilarity set by his neighbours. At last he laughed as heartily at their stories and repartees as the old Baronet, Sir Simon, himself. When the meal was almost over one of the sons, who had drunk a little too much wine, after the manner of men in that century, said to Hubert, 'Well, my boy, how are you? Can you take a pinch of snuff?' He held out one of the snuff-boxes which were then becoming common among young and old throughout the country.

'Thank you,' said Hubert, accepting a pinch.

'Tell the ladies who you are, what you are made of, and what you can do,' the young man continued, slapping Hubert upon the shoulder.

'Certainly,' said our hero, drawing himself up, and thinking it best to put a bold face on the matter. 'I am a travelling magician.'

'Indeed!'

'What shall we hear next?'

'Can you call up spirits from the vasty deep, young wizard?'

'I can conjure up a tempest in a cupboard,' Hubert replied.

'Ha-ha!' said the old Baronet, pleasantly rubbing his hands. 'We must see this performance. Girls, don't go away: here's something to be seen.'

'Not dangerous, I hope?' said the old lady.

Hubert rose from the table. 'Hand me your snuff-box, please,' he said to the young man who had made free with him. 'And now,' he continued, 'without the least noise, follow me. If any of you speak it will break the spell.'

They promised obedience. He entered the corridor, and, taking off his shoes, went on tiptoe to the closet door, the guests advancing in a silent group at a little distance behind him. Hubert next placed a stool in front of the door, and, by standing upon it, was tall enough to reach to the top. He then, just as noiselessly, poured all the snuff from the box along the upper edge of the door, and, with a few short puffs of breath, blew the snuff through the chink into the interior of the closet. He held up his finger to the assembly, that they might be silent.

'Dear me, what's that?' said the old lady, after a minute or two had elapsed.

A suppressed sneeze had come from inside the closet.

Hubert held up his finger again.

'How very singular,' whispered Sir Simon. 'This is most interesting.'

Hubert took advantage of the moment to gently slide the bolt of the closet door into its place. 'More snuff,' he said, calmly.

'More snuff,' said Sir Simon. Two or three gentlemen passed their boxes, and the contents were blown in at the top of the closet. Another sneeze, not quite so well suppressed as the first, was heard: then another, which seemed to say that it would not be suppressed under any circumstances whatever. At length there arose a perfect storm of sneezes.

'Excellent, excellent for one so young!' said Sir Simon. 'I am much interested in this trick of throwing the voice – called, I believe, ventriloquism.'

'More snuff,' said Hubert.

'More snuff,' said Sir Simon. Sir Simon's man brought a large jar of the best scented Scotch.

Hubert once more charged the upper chink of the closet, and blew the snuff into the interior, as before. Again he charged, and again, emptying the whole contents of the jar. The tumult of sneezes became really extraordinary to listen to – there was no cessation. It was like wind, rain, and sea battling in a hurricane.

'I believe there are men inside, and that it is no trick at all!' exclaimed Sir Simon, the truth flashing on him.

'There are,' said Hubert. 'They are come to rob the house; and they are the same who stole my horse.'

The sneezes changed to spasmodic groans. One of the thieves, hearing Hubert's voice, cried, 'Oh! mercy! mercy! let us out of this!'

'Where's my horse?' said Hubert.

'Tied to the tree in the hollow behind Short's Gibbet. Mercy! mercy! let us out, or we shall die of suffocation!'

All the Christmas guests now perceived that this was no longer sport, but serious earnest. Guns and cudgels were procured; all the menservants were called in, and arranged in position outside the closet. At a signal Hubert withdrew the bolt, and stood on the defensive. But the three robbers, far from attacking them, were found crouching in the corner, gasping for breath. They made no resistance; and, being pinioned, were placed in an out-house till the morning.

Hubert now gave the remainder of his story to the assembled company, and was profusely thanked for the services he had rendered. Sir Simon pressed him to stay over the night, and accept the use of the best bed-room the house afforded, which had been occupied by Queen Elizabeth and King Charles successively when on their visits to this part of the country. But Hubert declined, being anxious to find his horse Jerry, and to test the truth of the robbers' statements concerning him.

Several of the guests accompanied Hubert to the spot behind the gibbet, alluded to by the thieves as where Jerry was hidden. When they reached the knoll and looked over, behold! there the horse stood, un-injured, and quite unconcerned. At sight of Hubert he neighed joyfully; and nothing could exceed Hubert's gladness at finding him. He mounted, wished his friends 'Good-night!' and cantered off in the direction they pointed out as his nearest way, reaching home safely about four o'clock in the morning.

Our Exploits at West Poley

I. HOW WE WENT EXPLORING UNDERGROUND

ON a certain fine evening of early autumn – I will not say how many
years ago – I alighted from a green gig, before the door of a farm-house
at West Poley, a village in Somersetshire. I had reached the age of thirteen, and though rather small for my age, I was robust and active. My
father was a schoolmaster, living about twenty miles off. I had arrived
on a visit to my Aunt Draycot, a farmer's widow, who, with her son
Stephen, or Steve, as he was invariably called by his friends, still managed the farm, which had been left on her hands by her deceased husband.

Steve promptly came out to welcome me. He was two or three years
my senior, tall, lithe, ruddy, and somewhat masterful withal. There was
that force about him which was less suggestive of intellectual power than
(as Carlyle said of Cromwell) 'Doughtiness – the courage and faculty
to do.'

When the first greetings were over, he informed me that his mother
was not indoors just then, but that she would soon be home. 'And, do
you know, Leonard,' he continued, rather mournfully, 'she wants me to
be a farmer all my life, like my father.'

'And why not be a farmer all your life, like your father ?' said a voice
behind us.

We turned our heads, and a thoughtful man in a threadbare, yet well-
fitting suit of clothes, stood near, as he paused for a moment on his way
down to the village.

'The straight course is generally the best for boys,' the speaker continued, with a smile. 'Be sure that professions you know little of have
as many drudgeries attaching to them as those you know well – it is only
their remoteness that lends them their charm.' Saying this he nodded
and went on.

'Who is he ?' I asked.

'Oh – he's nobody,' said Steve. 'He's a man who has been all over the world, and tried all sorts of lives, but he has never got rich, and now he has retired to this place for quietness. He calls himself the Man who has Failed.'

After this explanation I thought no more of the Man who had Failed than Steve himself did; neither of us was at that time old enough to know that the losers in the world's battle are often the very men who, too late for themselves, have the clearest perception of what constitutes success; while the successful men are frequently blinded to the same by the tumult of their own progress.

To change the subject, I said something about the village and Steve's farm-house – that I was glad to see the latter was close under the hills, which I hoped we might climb before I returned home. I had expected to find these hills much higher, and I told Steve so without disguise.

'They may not be very high, but there's a good deal inside 'em,' said my cousin, as we entered the house, as if he thought me hypercritical, 'a good deal more than you think.'

'Inside 'em?' said I. 'Stone and earth, I suppose.'

'More than that,' said he. 'You have heard of the Mendip Caves, haven't you?'

'But they are nearer Cheddar,' I said.

'There are one or two in this place, likewise,' Steve answered me. 'I can show them to you to-morrow. People say there are many more, only there is no way of getting into them.'

Being disappointed in the height of the hills, I was rather incredulous about the number of the caves; but on my saying so, Steve rejoined, 'Whatever you may think, I went the other day into one of 'em – Nick's Pocket – that's the cavern nearest here, and found that what was called the end was not really the end at all. Ever since then I've wanted to be an explorer, and not a farmer; and in spite of that old man, I think I am right.'

At this moment my aunt came in, and soon after we were summoned to supper; and during the remainder of the evening nothing more was said about the Mendip Caves. It would have been just as well for us two boys if nothing more had been said about them at all; but it was fated to be otherwise, as I have reason to remember.

Steve did not forget my remarks, which, to him, no doubt, seemed to show a want of appreciation for the features of his native district. The next morning he returned to the subject, saying, as he came indoors to me suddenly, 'I mean to show ye a little of what the Mendips contain,

Leonard, if you'll come with me. But we must go quietly, for my mother does not like me to prowl about such places, because I get muddy. Come here, and see the preparations I have made.'

He took me into the stable, and showed me a goodly supply of loose candle ends; also a bit of board perforated with holes, into which the candles would fit, and shaped to a handle at one extremity. He had provided, too, some slices of bread and cheese, and several apples. I was at once convinced that caverns which demanded such preparations must be something larger than the mere gravel-pits I had imagined; but I said nothing beyond assenting to the excursion.

It being the time after harvest, while there was not much to be attended to on the farm, Steve's mother could easily spare him, 'to show me the neighbourhood', as he expressed it, and off we went, with our provisions and candles.

A quarter of a mile, or possibly a little more – for my recollections on matters of distance are not precise – brought us to the mouth of the cave called Nick's Pocket, the way thither being past the village houses, and the mill, and across the mill-stream, which came from a copious spring in the hillside some distance further up. I seem to hear the pattering of that mill-wheel when we walked by it, as well as if it were going now; and yet how many years have passed since the sound beat last upon my ears.

The mouth of the cave was screened by bushes, the face of the hill behind being, to the best of my remembrance, almost vertical. The spot was obviously well known to the inhabitants, and was the haunt of many boys, as I could see by footprints; though the cave, at this time, with others thereabouts, had been but little examined by tourists and men of science.

We entered unobserved, and no sooner were we inside, than Steve lit a couple of candles and stuck them into the board. With these he showed the way. We walked on over a somewhat uneven floor, the novelty of the proceeding impressing me, at first, very agreeably; the light of the candles was sufficient, at first, to reveal only the nearer stalactites, remote nooks of the cavern being left in well-nigh their original, mystic shadows. Steve would occasionally turn, and accuse me, in arch tones, of being afraid, which accusation I (as a boy would naturally do) steadfastly denied; though even now I can recollect that I experienced more than once some sort of misgiving.

'As for me – I have been there hundreds of times,' Steve said proudly.

'We West Poley boys come here continually to play "I spy", and think nothing of running in with no light of any sort. Come along, it is home to me. I said I would show you the inside of the Mendips, and so I will.'

Thus we went onward. We were now in the bowels of the Mendip hills – a range of limestone rocks stretching from the shores of the Bristol Channel into the middle of Somersetshire. Skeletons of great extinct beasts, and the remains of prehistoric men have been found thereabouts since that time; but at the date of which I write science was not so ardent as she is now, in the pursuit of the unknown; and we boys could only conjecture on subjects in which the boys of the present generation are well informed.

The dim sparkle of stalactites, which had continually appeared above us, now ranged lower and lower over our heads, till at last the walls of the cave seemed to bar further progress.

'There, this spot is what everybody calls the end of Nick's Pocket,' observed Steve, halting upon a mount of stalagmite, and throwing the beams of the candles around. 'But let me tell you,' he added, 'that here is a little arch, which I and some more boys found the other day. We did not go under it, but if you are agreed we will go in now and see how far we can get, for the fun of the thing. I brought these pieces of candle on purpose.' Steve looked what he felt – that there was a certain grandeur in a person like himself, to whom such mysteries as caves were mere playthings, because he had been born close alongside them. To do him justice, he was not altogether wrong, for he was a truly courageous fellow, and could look dangers in the face without flinching.

'I think we may as well leave fun out of the question,' I said, laughing; 'but we will go in.'

Accordingly he went forward, stooped, and entered the low archway, which, at first sight, appeared to be no more than a slight recess. I kept close at his heels. The arch gave access to a narrow tunnel or gallery, sloping downwards, and presently terminating in another cave, the floor of which spread out into a beautiful level of sand and shingle, interspersed with pieces of rock. Across the middle of this subterranean shore, as it might have been called, flowed a pellucid stream. Had my thoughts been in my books, I might have supposed we had descended to the nether regions, and had reached the Stygian shore; but it was out of sight, out of mind, with my classical studies then.

Beyond the stream, at some elevation, we could see a delightful recess in the crystallized stone-work, like the apse of a Gothic church.

'How tantalizing!' exclaimed Steve, as he held the candles above his head, and peered across. 'If it were not for this trickling riband of water, we could get over and climb up into that arched nook, and sit there like kings on a crystal throne!'

'Perhaps it would not look so wonderful if we got close to it,' I suggested. 'But, for that matter, if you had a spade, you could soon turn the water out of the way, and into that hole.' That fact was, that just at that moment I had discovered a low opening on the left hand, like a human mouth, into which the stream would naturally flow, if a slight barrier of sand and pebbles were removed.

On looking there, also, Steve complimented me on the sharpness of my eyes. 'Yes,' he said, 'we could scrape away that bank, and the water would go straight into the hole surely enough. And we will. Let us go for a spade!'

I had not expected him to put the idea into practice; but it was no sooner said than done. We retraced our steps, and in a few minutes found ourselves again in the open air, where the sudden light overpowered our eyes for awhile.

'Stay here, while I run home,' he said. 'I'll not be long.'

I agreed, and he disappeared. In a very short space he came back with the spade in his hand, and we again plunged in. This time the candles had been committed to my charge. When we had passed down the gallery into the second cave, Steve directed me to light a couple more of the candles, and stick them against a piece of rock, that he might have plenty of light to work by. This I did, and my stalwart cousin began to use the spade with a will, upon the breakwater of sand and stones.

The obstacle, which had been sufficient to turn the stream at a right angle, possibly for centuries, was of the most fragile description. Such instances of a slight obstruction diverting a sustained onset often occur in nature on a much larger scale. The Chesil Bank, for example, connecting the peninsula of Portland, in Dorsetshire, with the mainland, is a mere string of loose pebbles; yet it resists, by its shelving surface and easy curve, the mighty roll of the channel seas, when urged upon the bank by the most furious south-west gales.

In a minute or two a portion of the purling stream discovered the opening Steve's spade was making in the sand, and began to flow through. The water assisted him in his remaining labours, supplementing every spadeful that he threw back, by washing aside ten. I remember that I was child enough, at that time, to clap my hands at the sight of

larger and larger quantities of the brook tumbling in the form of a cas-
cade down the dark chasm, where it had possibly never flowed before,
or at any rate, never within the human period of the earth's history. In
less than twenty minutes the whole stream trended off in this new direction, as calmly as if it had coursed there always. What had before been its
bed now gradually drained dry, and we saw that we could walk across
dryshod, with ease.

We speedily put the possibility into practice, and so reached the
beautiful, glistening niche, that had tempted us to our engineering. We
brought up into it the candles we had stuck against the rock-work
further down, placed them with the others around the niche, and prepared to rest awhile, the spot being quite dry.

'That's the way to overcome obstructions!' said Steve triumphantly.
'I warrant nobody ever got so far as this before – at least, without wading
up to his knees, in crossing that water-course.'

My attention was so much attracted by the beautiful natural orna-
ments of the niche, that I hardly heeded his remark. These covered the
greater part of the sides and roof; they were flesh-coloured, and assumed
the form of pills, lace, coats of mail; in many places they quaintly
resembled the skin of geese after plucking, and in others the wattles of
turkeys. All were decorated with water crystals.

'Well,' exclaimed I, 'I could stay here always!'

'So could I,' said Steve, 'if I had victuals enough. And some we'll
have at once.'

Our bread and cheese and apples were unfolded, and we speedily
devoured the whole. We then tried to chip pieces from the rock, and
but indifferently succeeded, though while doing this we discovered
some curious stones, like axe and arrow heads, at the bottom of the
niche; but they had become partially attached to the floor by the limestone deposit, and could not be extracted.

'This is a long enough visit for to-day,' said my cousin, jumping up
as one of the candles went out. 'We shall be left in the dark if we
don't mind, and it would be no easy matter to find our way out without a
light.'

Accordingly we gathered up the candles that remained, descended
from the niche, re-crossed the deserted bed of the stream, and found
our way to the open air, well pleased enough with the adventure, and
promising each other to repeat it at an early day. On which account,
instead of bringing away the unburnt candles, and the wood candlestick,

and the spade, we laid these articles on a hidden shelf near the entrance, to be ready at hand at any time.

Having cleaned the tell-tale mud from our boots, we were on the point of entering the village, when our ears were attracted by a great commotion in the road below.

'What is it?' said I, standing still.

'Voices, I think,' replied Steve. 'Listen!'

It seemed to be a man in a violent frenzy.

'I think it is somebody out of his mind,' continued my cousin. 'I never heard a man rave so in my life.'

'Let us draw nearer,' said I.

We moved on, and soon came in sight of an individual, who, standing in the midst of the street, was gesticulating distractedly, and uttering invectives against something or other, to several villagers that had gathered around.

'Why, 'tis the miller!' said Steve. 'What can be the matter with him?'

We were not kept long in suspense, for we could soon hear his words distinctly. 'The money I've sunk here!' he was saying; 'the time – the honest labour – all for nothing! Only beggary afore me now! One month it was a new pair of mill-stones; then the back wall was cracked with the shaking, and had to be repaired; then I made a bad speculation in corn and dropped money that way! But 'tis nothing to this! My own freehold – the only staff and dependence o' my family – all useless now – all of us ruined!'

'Don't you take on so, Miller Griffin,' soothingly said one who proved to be the Man who had Failed. 'Take the ups with the downs, and maybe 'twill come right again.'

'Right again!' raved the miller; 'how can what's gone forever come back again as 'twere afore – that's what I ask my wretched self – how can it?'

'We'll get up a subscription for ye,' said a local dairyman.

'I don't drink hard; I don't stay away from church, and I only grind into Sabbath hours when there's no getting through the work otherwise, and I pay my way like a man!'

'Yes – you do that,' corroborated the others.

'And yet, I be brought to ruinous despair, on this sixth day of September, Hannah Dominy; as if I were a villain! Oh, my mill, my mill-wheel – you'll never go round any more – never more!' The miller flung his arms upon the rail of the bridge, and buried his face in his hands.

'This raving is but making a bad job worse,' said the Man who had Failed. 'But who will listen to counsel on such matters?'

By this time we had drawn near, and Steve said, 'What's the cause of all this?'

'The river has dried up – all on a sudden,' said the dairyman, 'and so his mill won't go any more.'

I gazed instantly towards the stream, or rather what had been the stream. It was gone; and the mill-wheel, which had pattered so persistently when we entered the cavern, was silent. Steve and I instinctively stepped aside.

'The river gone dry!' Steve whispered.

'Yes,' said I. 'Why, Steve, don't you know why?'

My thoughts had instantly flown to our performance of turning the stream out of its channel in the cave, and I knew in a moment that this was the cause. Steve's silence showed me that he divined the same thing, and we stood gazing at each other in consternation.

II. HOW WE SHONE IN THE EYES OF THE PUBLIC

As soon as we had recovered ourselves we walked away, unconsciously approaching the river-bed, in whose hollows lay the dead and dying bodies of loach, sticklebacks, dace, and other small fry, which before our entrance into Nick's Pocket had raced merrily up and down the waterway. Further on we perceived numbers of people ascending to the upper part of the village, with pitchers on their heads, and buckets yoked to their shoulders.

'Where are you going?' said Steve to one of these.

'To your mother's well for water,' was the answer. 'The river we have always been used to dip from is dried up. Oh, mercy me, what with the washing and cooking and brewing I don't know what we shall do to live, for 'tis killing work to bring water on your back so far!'

As may be supposed, all this gave me still greater concern than before, and I hurriedly said to Steve that I was strongly of opinion that we ought to go back to the cave immediately, and turn the water into the old channel, seeing what harm we had unintentionally done by our manœuvre.

'Of course we'll go back – that's just what I was going to say,' returned Steve. 'We can set it all right again in half an hour, and the river will run the same as ever. Hullo – now you are frightened at what has happened! I can see you are.'

I told him that I was not exactly frightened, but that it seemed to me we had caused a very serious catastrophe in the village, in driving the miller almost crazy, and killing the fish, and worrying the poor people into supposing they would never have enough water again for their daily use without fetching it from afar. 'Let us tell them how it came to pass,' I suggested, 'and then go and set it right.'

'Tell 'em – not I!' said Steve. 'We'll go back and put it right, and say nothing about it to any one, and they will simply think it was caused by a temporary earthquake, or something of that sort.' He then broke into a vigorous whistle, and we retraced our steps together.

It occupied us but a few minutes to rekindle a light inside the cave, take out the spade from its nook, and penetrate to the scene of our morning exploit. Steve then fell to, and first rolling down a few large pieces of stone into the current, dexterously banked them up with clay from the other side of the cave, which caused the brook to swerve back into its original bed almost immediately. 'There,' said he, 'it is all just as it was when we first saw it – now let's be off.'

We did not dally long in the cavern; but when we gained the exterior we decided to wait there a little time till the villagers should have discovered the restoration of their stream, to watch the effect. Our waiting was but temporary; for in quick succession there burst upon our ears a shout, and then the starting of the mill-wheel patter.

At once we walked into the village street with an air of unconcern. The miller's face was creased with wrinkles of satisfaction; the countenances of the blacksmith, shoemaker, grocer and dairyman were perceptibly brighter. These, and many others of West Poley, were gathered on the bridge over the mill-tail, and they were all holding a conversation with the parson of the parish, as to the strange occurrence.

Matters remained in a quiet state during the next two days. Then there was a remarkably fine and warm morning, and we proposed to cross the hills and descend into East Poley, the next village, which I had never seen. My aunt made no objection to the excursion, and we departed, ascending the hill in a straight line without much regard to paths. When we had reached the summit, and were about half-way between the two villages, we sat down to recover breath. While we sat a man overtook us, and Steve recognized him as a neighbour.

'A bad job again for West Poley folks!' cried the man, without halting.

'What's the matter now?' said Steve, and I started with curiosity.

'Oh, the river is dry again. It happened at a quarter past ten this morning, and it is thought it will never flow any more. The miller he's gone crazy, or all but so. And the washerwoman, she will have to be kept by the parish, because she can't get water to wash with; aye, 'tis a terrible time that's come. I'm off to try to hire a water-cart, but I fear I shan't hear of one.'

The speaker passed by, and on turning to Steve I found he was looking on the ground. 'I know how that's happened,' he presently said. 'We didn't make our embankment so strong as it was before, and so the water has washed it away.'

'Let's go back and mend it,' said I; and I proposed that we should reveal where the mischief lay, and get some of the labourers to build the bank up strong, that this might not happen again.

'No,' said Steve, 'since we are half-way we will have our day's pleasure. It won't hurt the West Poley people to be out of water for one day. We'll return home a little earlier than we intended, and put it all in order again, either ourselves, or by the help of some men.'

Having gone about a mile and a half further we reached the brow of the descent into East Poley, the place we had come to visit. Here we beheld advancing towards us a stranger whose actions we could not at first interpret. But as the distance between us and him lessened we discerned, to our surprise, that he was in convulsions of laughter. He would laugh until he was tired, then he would stand still gazing on the ground, as if quite preoccupied, then he would burst out laughing again and walk on. No sooner did he see us two boys than he placed his hat upon his walking-stick, twirled it and cried 'Hurrah!'

I was so amused that I could not help laughing with him; and when he came abreast of us Steve said, 'Good morning; may I ask what it is that makes you laugh so?'

But the man was either too self-absorbed or too supercilious to vouchsafe to us any lucid explanation. 'What makes me laugh?' he said. 'Why, good luck, my boys! Perhaps when you are as lucky, you will laugh too.' Saying which he walked on and left us; and we could hear him exclaiming to himself, 'Well done – hurrah!' as he sank behind the ridge.

Without pausing longer we descended towards the village, and soon reached its outlying homesteads. Our path intersected a green field dotted with trees, on the other side of which was an inn. As we drew near we heard the strains of a fiddle, and presently perceived a fiddler

standing in a chair outside the inn door; whilst on the green in front
were several people seated at a table eating and drinking, and some
younger members of the assembly dancing a reel in the background.

We naturally felt much curiosity as to the cause of the merriment,
which we mentally connected with that of the man we had met just
before. Turning to one of the old men feasting at the table, I said to him
as civilly as I could, 'Why are you all so lively in this parish, sir?'

'Because we are in luck's way just now, for we don't get a new river
every day. Hurrah!'

'A new river?' said Steve and I in one breath.

'Yes,' said one of our interlocutors, waving over the table a ham-bone
he had been polishing. 'Yesterday afternoon a river of beautiful water
burst out of the quarry at the higher end of this bottom; in an hour or
so it stopped again. This morning, about a quarter past ten, it burst out
again, and it is running now as if it would run always.'

'It will make all land and houses in this parish worth double as much
as afore,' said another; 'for want of water is the one thing that has
always troubled us, forcing us to sink deep wells, and even then being
hard put to, to get enough for our cattle. Now, we have got a river,
and the place will grow to a town.'

'It is as good as two hundred pounds to me!' said one who looked like
a grazier.

'And two hundred and fifty to me!' cried another, who seemed to be
a brewer.

'And sixty pound a year to me, and to every man here in the building
trade!' said a third.

As soon as we could withdraw from the company, our thoughts found
vent in words.

'I ought to have seen it!' said Steve. 'Of course if you stop a stream
from flowing in one direction, it must force its way out in another.'

'I wonder where their new stream is,' said I.

We looked round. After some examination we saw a depression in the
centre of a pasture, and, approaching it, beheld the stream meandering
along over the grass, the current not having had as yet sufficient time to
scour a bed. Walking down to the brink, we were lost in wonder at what
we had unwittingly done, and quite bewildered at the strange events we
had caused. Feeling, now, that we had walked far enough from home for
one day, we turned, and, in a brief time, entered a road pointed out by
Steve, as one that would take us to West Poley by a shorter cut than our
outward route.

As we ascended the hill, Steve looked round at me. I suppose my face revealed my thoughts, for he said, 'You are amazed, Leonard, at the wonders we have accomplished without knowing it. To tell the truth, so am I.'

I said that what staggered me was this – that we could not turn back the water into its old bed now, without doing as much harm to the people of East Poley by taking it away, as we should do good to the people of West Poley by restoring it.

'True,' said Steve, 'that's what bothers me. Though I think we have done more good to these people than we have done harm to the others; and I think these are rather nicer people than those in our village, don't you?'

I objected that even if this were so, we could have no right to take water away from one set of villagers and give it to another set without consulting them.

Steve seemed to feel the force of the argument; but as his mother had a well of her own he was less inclined to side with his native place than he might have been if his own household had been deprived of water, for the benefit of the East Poleyites. The matter was still in suspense, when, weary with our day's pilgrimage, we reached the mill.

The mill-pond was drained to its bed; the wheel stood motionless; yet a noise came from the interior. It was not the noise of machinery, but of the nature of blows, followed by bitter expostulations. On looking in, we were grieved to see that the miller, in a great rage, was holding his apprentice by the collar, and beating him with a strap.

The miller was a heavy, powerful man, and more than a match for his apprentice and us two boys besides; but Steve reddened with indignation, and asked the miller, with some spirit, why he served the poor fellow so badly.

'He says he'll leave,' stormed the frantic miller. 'What right hev he to say he'll leave, I should like to know!'

'There is no work for me to do, now the mill won't go,' said the apprentice, meekly; 'and the agreement was that I should be at liberty to leave if work failed in the mill. He keeps me here and don't pay me; and I be at my wits' end how to live.'

'Just shut up!' said the miller. 'Go and work in the garden! Mill-work or no mill-work, you'll stay on.'

Job, as the miller's boy was called, had won the good-will of Steve, and Steve was now ardent to do him a good turn. Looking over the bridge, we saw, passing by, the Man who had Failed. He was considered an authority on such matters as these, and we begged him to come in. In a few minutes the miller was set down, and it was proved to him that, by the terms of Job's indentures, he was no longer bound to remain.

'I have to thank you for this,' said the miller, savagely, to Steve. 'Ruined in every way! I may as well die!'

But my cousin cared little for the miller's opinion, and we came away, thanking the Man who had Failed for his interference, and receiving the warmest expressions of gratitude from poor Job; who, it appeared, had suffered much ill-treatment from his irascible master, and was over-joyed to escape to some other employment.

We went to bed early that night, on account of our long walk; but we were far too excited to sleep at once. It was scarcely dark as yet, and the nights being still warm the window was left open as it had been left during the summer. Thus we could hear everything that passed without. People were continually coming to dip water from my aunt's well; they gathered round it in groups, and discussed the remarkable event which had latterly occurred for the first time in parish history.

'My belief is that witchcraft have done it,' said the shoemaker, 'and the only remedy that I can think o', is for one of us to cut across to Bartholomew Gann, the white wizard, and get him to tell us how to counteract it. 'Tis a long pull to his house for a little man, such as I be, but I'll walk it if nobody else will.'

'Well, there's no harm in your going,' said another. 'We can manage by drawing from Mrs Draycot's well for a few days; but something must be done, or the miller'll be ruined, and the washerwoman can't hold out long.'

When these personages had drawn water and retired, Steve spoke across from his bed to me in mine. 'We've done more good than harm, that I'll maintain. The miller is the only man seriously upset, and he's not a man to deserve consideration. It has been the means of freeing poor Job, which is another good thing. Then, the people in East Poley that we've made happy are two hundred and fifty, and there are only a hundred in this parish, even if all of 'em are made miserable.'

I returned some reply, though the state of affairs was, in truth, one rather suited to the genius of Jeremy Bentham than to me. But the problem in utilitarian philosophy was shelved by Steve exclaiming, 'I have it! I see how to get some real glory out of this!'

I demanded how, with much curiosity.

'You'll swear not to tell anybody, or let it be known anyhow that we are at the bottom of it all?'

I am sorry to say that my weak compunctions gave way under stress of this temptation; and I solemnly declared that I would reveal nothing, unless he agreed with me that it would be best to do so. Steve made me swear, in the tone of Hamlet to the Ghost, and when I had done this, he sat up in his bed to announce his scheme.

'First, we'll go to Job,' said Steve. 'Take him into the secret; show him the cave; give him a spade and pickaxe; and tell him to turn off the water from East Poley at, say, twelve o'clock, for a little while. Then we'll go to the East Poley boys and declare ourselves to be magicians.'

'Magicians?' I said.

'Magicians, able to dry up rivers, or to make 'em run at will,' he repeated.

'I see it!' I almost screamed, in my delight.

'To show our power, we'll name an hour for drying up theirs, and making it run again after a short time. Of course, we'll say the hour we've told Job to turn the water in the cave. Won't they think something of us then?'

I was enchanted. The question of mischief or not mischief was as indifferent to me now as it was to Steve – for which indifference we got rich deserts, as will be seen in the sequel.

'And to look grand and magical,' continued he, 'we'll get some gold lace that I know of in the garret, on an old coat my grandfather wore in the Yeomanry Cavalry, and put it round our caps, and make ourselves great beards with horse-hair. They will look just like real ones at a little distance off.'

'And we must each have a wand!' said I, explaining that I knew how to make excellent wands, white as snow, by peeling a couple of straight willows; and that I could do all that in the morning while he was preparing the beards.

Thus we discussed and settled the matter, and at length fell asleep – to dream of to-morrow's triumphs among the boys of East Poley, till the sun of that morrow shone in upon our faces and woke us. We arose promptly and made our preparations, having carte blanche from my Aunt Draycot to spend the days of my visit as we chose.

Our first object on leaving the farmhouse was to find Job Tray, apprise him of what it was necessary that he should know, and induce him to act as confederate. We found him outside the garden of his lodging; he told us he had nothing to do till the following Monday, when a farmer had agreed to hire him. On learning the secret of the river-head, and what we proposed to do, he expressed his glee by a low laugh of amazed delight, and readily promised to assist as bidden. It took us some little time to show him the inner cave, the tools, and to arrange candles for him, so that he might enter without difficulty just after eleven and do the trick. When this was all settled we put Steve's watch on a ledge in the cave, that Job might know the exact time, and came out to ascend the hills that divided the eastern from the western village.

For obvious reasons we did not appear in magician's guise till we had left the western vale some way behind us. Seated on the limestone ridge, removed from all observation, we set to work at preparing ourselves. I peeled the two willows we had brought with us to be used as magic wands, and Steve pinned the pieces of old lace round our caps, congratulating himself on the fact of the lace not being new, which would thus convey the impression that we had exercised the wizard's calling for some years. Our last adornments were the beards; and, finally equipped, we descended on the other side.

Our plan was now to avoid the upper part of East Poley, which we had traversed on the preceding day, and to strike into the parish at a point farther down, where the humble cottages stood, and where we were both absolutely unknown. An hour's additional walking brought us to this spot, which, as the crow flies, was not more than half so far from West Poley as the road made it.

The first boys we saw were some playing in an orchard near the new stream, which novelty had evidently been the attraction that had brought them there. It was an opportunity for opening the campaign, especially as the hour was long after eleven, and the cessation of water consequent on Job's performance at a quarter past might be expected to take place as near as possible to twelve allowing the five and forty minutes from eleven-fifteen, as the probable time that would be occupied by the stream in travelling to the point we had reached.

I forget at this long distance of years the exact words used by Steve in addressing the strangers; but to the best of my recollection they were, 'How d'ye do, gentlemen, and how does the world use ye?' I distinctly remember the sublimity he threw into his gait, and how slavishly I imitated him in the same.

The boys made some indifferent answer, and Steve continued, 'You will kindly present us with some of those apples, I presume, considering what we are?'

They regarded us dubiously, and at last one of them said, 'What are you, that you should expect apples from us?'

'We are travelling magicians,' replied Steve. 'You may have heard of us, for by our power this new river has begun to flow. Rhombustas is my name, and this is my familiar, Balcazar.'

'I don't believe it,' said an incredulous one from behind.

'Very well, gentlemen; we can't help that. But if you give us some apples we'll prove our right to the title.'

'Be hanged if we will give you any apples,' said the boy who held the basket; 'since it is already proved that magicians are impossible.'

'In that case,' said Steve, 'we – we—'

'Will perform just the same,' interrupted I, for I feared Steve had forgotten that the time was at hand when the stream would be interrupted by Job, whether he willed it or not.

'We will stop the water of your new river at twelve o'clock this day, when the sun crosses the meridian,' said Rhombustas, 'as a punishment for your want of generosity.'

'Do it!' said the boys incredulously.

'Come here, Balcazar,' said Steve. We walked together to the edge of the stream; then we muttered, *Hi, hæ, hæc, horum, harum, horum*, and stood waving our wands.

'The river do run just the same,' said the strangers derisively.

'The spell takes time to work,' said Rhombustas, adding in an aside to me, 'I hope that fellow Job has not forgotten, or we shall be hooted out of the place.'

There we stood, waving and waving our white sticks, hoping and hoping we should succeed; while still the river flowed. Seven or ten minutes passed thus; and then, when we were nearly broken down by ridicule, the stream diminished its volume. All eyes were instantly bent on the water, which sank so low as to be in a short time but a narrow rivulet. The faithful Job had performed his task. By the time that the clock of the church tower struck twelve the river was almost dry.

The boys looked at each other in amazement, and at us with awe. They were too greatly concerned to speak except in murmurs to each other.

'You see the result of your conduct, unbelieving strangers,' said Steve, drawing boldly up to them. 'And I seriously ask that you hand over those apples before we bring further troubles upon you and your village. We give you five minutes to consider.'

'We decide at once!' cried the boys. 'The apples be yours and welcome.'

'Thank you, gentlemen,' said Steve, while I added, 'For your readiness the river shall run again in two or three minutes' time.'

'Oh – ah, yes,' said Steve, adding heartily in undertones, 'I had forgotten that!'

Almost as soon as the words were spoken we perceived a little increase in the mere dribble of water which now flowed, whereupon he waved his wand and murmured more words. The liquid thread swelled and rose; and in a few minutes was the same as before. Our triumph was complete; and the suspension had been so temporary that probably nobody in the village had noticed it but ourselves and the boys.

III. HOW WE WERE CAUGHT IN OUR OWN TRAP

At this acme of our glory who should come past but a hedger whom Steve recognized as an inhabitant of West Poley; unluckily for our greatness the hedger also recognized Steve.

'Well, Maister Stevey, what be you doing over in these parts then? And yer little cousin, too, upon my word! And beards – why ye've made yerselves ornamental! haw, haw!'

In great trepidation Steve moved on with the man, endeavouring, thus, to get him out of hearing of the boys.

'Look here,' said Steve to me on leaving that outspoken rustic; 'I think this is enough for one day. We'd better go further before they guess all.'

'With all my heart,' said I. And we walked on.

'But what's going on here?' said Steve, when, turning a corner of the hedge, we perceived an altercation in progress hard by. The parties proved to be a poor widow and a corn-factor, who had been planning a water-wheel lower down the stream. The latter had dammed the water for his purpose to such an extent as to submerge the poor woman's garden, turning it into a lake.

'Indeed, sir, you need not ruin my premises so!' she said with tears in her eyes. 'The mill-pond can be kept from overflowing my garden by a little banking and digging; it will be just as well for your purpose to keep it lower down, as to let it spread out into a great pool here. The house and garden are yours by law, sir; that's true. But my father built the house, and, oh, sir, I was born here, and I should like to end my days under its roof!'

'Can't help it, mis'ess,' said the corn-factor. 'Your garden is a mill-pond already made, and to get a hollow further down I should have to dig at great expense. There is a very nice cottage up the hill, where you can live as well as here. When your father died the house came into my hands; and I can do what I like with my own.'

The woman went sadly away indoors. As for Steve and myself, we were deeply moved, as we looked at the pitiable sight of the poor woman's garden, the tops of the gooseberry bushes forming small islands in the water, and her few apple trees standing immersed half-way up their stems.

'The man is a rascal,' said Steve. 'I perceive that it is next to impossible, in this world, to do good to one set of folks without doing harm to another.'

'Since we have not done all good to these people of East Poley,' said I, 'there is a reason for restoring the river to its old course through West Poley.'

'But then,' said Steve, 'if we turn back the stream, we shall be starting Miller Griffin's mill; and then, by the terms of his 'prenticeship, poor Job will have to go back to him and be beaten again! It takes good brains no less than a good heart to do what's right towards all.'

Quite unable to solve the problem into which we had drifted, we retraced our steps, till, at a stile, within half a mile of West Poley, we beheld Job awaiting us.

'Well, how did it act?' he asked with great eagerness. 'Just as the hands of your watch got to a quarter past eleven, I began to shovel away, and turned the water in no time. But I didn't turn it where you expected – not I – 'twould have started the mill for a few minutes, and I wasn't going to do that.'

'Then where did you turn it?' cried Steve.

'I found another hole,' said Job.

'A third one?'

'Ay, hee, hee! a third one! So I pulled the stones aside from this new hole, and shovelled the clay, and down the water went with a gush. When it had run down there a few minutes, I turned it back to the East Poley hole, as you ordered me to do. But as to getting it back to the old West Poley hole, that I'd never do.'

Steve then explained that we no more wished the East village to have the river than the West village, on account of our discovery that equal persecution was going on in the one place as in the other. Job's news of a third channel solved our difficulty. 'So we'll go at once and send it down this third channel,' concluded he.

We walked back to the village, and, as it was getting late, and we were tired, we decided to do nothing that night, but told Job to meet us in the cave on the following evening, to complete our work there.

All next day my cousin was away from home, at market for his mother, and he had arranged with me that if he did not return soon enough to join me before going to Nick's Pocket, I should proceed thither, where he would meet me on his way back from the market-town. The day passed anxiously enough with me, for I had some doubts of a very grave kind as to our right to deprive two parishes of water on our own judgment, even though that should be, as it was, honestly based on our aversion to tyranny. However, dusk came on at last, and Steve not appearing from market, I concluded that I was to meet him at the cave's mouth.

To this end I strolled out in that direction, and there being as yet no hurry, I allowed myself to be tempted out of my path by a young rabbit, which, however, I failed to capture. This divergence had brought me inside a field, behind a hedge, and before I could resume my walk along the main road, I heard some persons passing along the other side. The words of their conversation arrested me in a moment.

' 'Tis a strange story if it's true,' came through the hedge in the tones of Miller Griffin. 'We know that East Poley folk will say queer things; but the boys wouldn't say that it was the work of magicians if they hadn't some ground for it.'

'And how do they explain it?' asked the shoemaker.

'They say that these two young fellows passed down their lane about twelve o'clock, dressed like magicians, and offered to show their power by stopping the river. The East Poley boys challenged 'em; when, by George, they did stop the river! They said a few words, and it dried up like magic. Now mark my words, my suspicion is this: these two game-sters have somehow got at the river-head, and been tampering with it in some way. The water that runs down East Poley bottom is the water that ought, by rights, to be running through my mill.'

'A very pretty piece of mischief, if that's the case!' said the shoemaker. 'I've never liked them lads, particularly that Steve – for not a boot or

shoe hev he had o' me since he's been old enough to choose for himself –
not a pair, or even a mending. But I don't see how they could do all this,
even if they had got at the river-head. 'Tis a spring out of the hill, isn't
it? And how could they stop the spring?'

It seemed that the miller could offer no explanation, for no answer
was returned. My course was clear: to join Job and Steve at Nick's
Pocket immediately; tell them that we were suspected, and to get them
to give over further proceeding, till we had stated our difficulties to some
person of experience – say the Man who had Failed.

I accordingly ran like a hare over the clover inside the hedge, and soon
was far away from the interlocutors. Drawing near the cave, I was
relieved to see Steve's head against the sky. I joined him at once, and
recounted to him, in haste, what had passed.

He meditated. 'They don't even now suspect that the secret lies in
the cavern,' said he.

'But they will soon,' said I.

'Well, perhaps they may,' he answered. 'But there will be time for us
to finish our undertaking, and turn the stream down the third hole.
When we've done that we can consider which of the villages is most
worthy to have the river, and act accordingly.'

'Do let us take a good wise man into our confidence,' I said.

After a little demurring, he agreed that as soon as we had completed
the scheme we would state the case to a competent adviser, and let it be
settled fairly. 'And now,' he said, 'where's Job? Inside the cave, no
doubt, as it is past the time I promised to be here.'

Stepping inside the cave's mouth, we found that the candles and other
things which had been deposited there were removed. The probability
being that Job had arrived and taken them in with him, we groped our
way along in the dark, helped by an occasional match which Steve struck
from a box he carried. Descending the gallery at the further end of the
outer cavern, we discerned a glimmer at the remote extremity, and soon
beheld Job working with all his might by the light of one of the candles.

'I've almost got it into the hole that leads to neither of the Poleys, but
I wouldn't actually turn it till you came,' he said, wiping his face.

We told him that the neighbours were on our track, and might soon
guess that we performed our tricks in Nick's Pocket, and come there,
and find that the stream flowed through the cave before rising in the
spring at the top of the village; and asked him to turn the water at once,
and be off with us.

'Ah!' said Job, mournfully, 'then 'tis over with me! They will be here to-morrow, and will turn back the stream, and the mill will go again, and I shall have to finish my time as 'prentice to the man who did this!' He pulled up his shirt sleeve, and showed us on his arm several stripes and bruises – black and blue and green – the tell-tale relics of old blows from the miller.

Steve reddened with indignation. 'I would give anything to stop up the channels to the two Poleys so close that they couldn't be found again!' he said. 'Couldn't we do it with stones and clay? Then, if they come here 'twould make no difference, and the water would flow down the third hole forever, and we should save Job and the widow after all.'

'We can but try it,' said Job, willing to fall in with anything that would hinder his recall to the mill. 'Let's set to work.'

Steve took the spade, and Job the pickaxe. First they finished what Job had begun – the turning of the stream into the third tunnel or crevice, which led to neither of the Poleys. This done, they set to work jamming stones into the other two openings, treading earth and clay around them, and smoothing over the whole in such a manner that nobody should notice they had ever existed. So intent were we on completing it that – to our utter disaster – we did not notice what was going on behind us.

I was the first to look round, and I well remember why. My ears had been attracted by a slight change of tone in the purl of the water down the new crevice discovered by Job, and I was curious to learn the reason of it. The sight that met my gaze might well have appalled a stouter and older heart than mine. Instead of pouring down out of sight, as it had been doing when we last looked, the stream was choked by a rising pool into which it boiled, showing at a glance that what we had innocently believed to be another outlet for the stream was only a blind passage or cul-de-sac, which the water, when first turned that way by Job, had not been left long enough to fill before it was turned back again.

'Oh, Steve – Job!' I cried, and could say no more.

They gazed round at once, and saw the situation. Nick's Pocket had become a cauldron. The surface of the rising pool stood, already, far above the mouth of the gallery by which we had entered, and which was our only way out – stood far above the old exit of the stream to West Poley, now sealed up; far above the second outlet to East Poley, discovered by Steve, and also sealed up by our fatal ingenuity. We had been spending the evening in making a close bottle of the cave, in which the water was now rising to drown us.

'There is one chance for us – only one,' said Steve in a dry voice.

'What one?' we asked in a breath.

'To open the old channel leading to the mill,' said Steve.

'I would almost as soon be drowned as do that,' murmured Job gloomily. 'But there's more lives than my own, so I'll work with a will. Yet how be we to open any channel at all?'

The question was, indeed, of awful aptness. It was extremely improbable that we should have power to reopen either conduit now. Both those exits had been funnel-shaped cavities, narrowing down to mere fissures at the bottom; and the stones and earth we had hurled into these cavities had wedged themselves together by their own weight. Moreover – and here was the rub – it had been possible to pull the stones out while they remained unsubmerged, but the whole mass was now under water, which enlarged the task of reopening the channel to Herculean dimensions.

But we did not know my cousin Steve as yet. 'You will help me here,' he said authoritatively to Job, pointing to the West Poley conduit. 'Lenny, my poor cousin,' he went on, turning to me, 'we are in a bad way. All you can do is to stand in the niche, and make the most of the candles by keeping them from the draught with your hat, and burning only one at a time. How many have we, Job?'

'Ten ends, some long, some short,' said Job.

'They will burn many hours,' said Steve. 'And now we must dive, and begin to get out the stones.'

They had soon stripped off all but their drawers, and, laying their clothes on the dry floor of the niche behind me, stepped down into the middle of the cave. The water here was already above their waists, and at the original gulley-hole leading to West Poley spring was proportionately deeper. Into this part, nevertheless, Steve dived. I have recalled his appearance a hundred – aye, a thousand times since that day, as he came up – his crown bobbing into the dim candle-light like a floating apple. He stood upright, bearing in his arms a stone as big as his head.

'That's one of 'em!' he said as soon as he could speak. 'But there are many, many more!'

He threw the stone behind; while Job, wasting no time, had already dived in at the same point. Job was not such a good diver as Steve, in the sense of getting easily to the bottom; but he could hold his breath longer, and it was an extraordinary length of time before his head emerged above the surface, though his feet were kicking in the air more than once. Clutched to his chest, when he rose, was a second large stone, and a couple of small ones with it. He threw the whole to a distance; and Steve, having now recovered breath, plunged again into the hole.

But I can hardly bear to recall this terrible hour even now, at a distance of many years. My suspense was, perhaps, more trying than that of the others, for, unlike them, I could not escape reflection by superhuman physical efforts. My task of economizing the candles, by shading them with my hat, was not to be compared, in difficulty, to theirs; but I would gladly have changed places, if it had been possible to such a small boy, with Steve and Job, so intolerable was it to remain motionless in the desperate circumstances.

Thus I watched the rising of the waters, inch by inch, and on that account was in a better position than they to draw an inference as to the probable end of the adventure.

There were a dozen, or perhaps twenty, stones to extract before we could hope for an escape of the pent mass of water; and the difficulty of extracting them increased with each successive attempt, in two ways, by the greater actual remoteness of stone after stone, and by its greater relative remoteness through the rising of the pool. However, the sustained, gallant struggles of my two comrades succeeded, at last, in raising the number of stones extracted to seven. Then we fancied that some slight passage had been obtained for the stream; for, though the terrible pool still rose higher, it seemed to rise less rapidly.

After several attempts, in which Steve and Job brought up nothing, there came a declaration from them that they could do no more. The lower stones were so tightly jammed between the sides of the fissure that no human strength seemed able to pull them out.

Job and Steve both came up from the water. They were exhausted and shivering, and well they might be. 'We must try some other way,' said Steve.

'What way?' asked I.

Steve looked at me. 'You are a very good little fellow to stand this so well!' he said, with something like tears in his eyes.

They soon got on their clothes; and, having given up all hope of escape downward, we turned our eyes to the roof of the cave, on the chance of discovering some outlet there.

There was not enough light from our solitary candle to show us all the features of the vault in detail; but we could see enough to gather that it formed anything but a perfect dome. The roof was rather a series of rifts and projections, and high on one side, almost lost in the shades, there was a larger and deeper rift than elsewhere, forming a sort of loft, the back parts of which were invisible, extending we knew not how far. It was through this overhanging rift that the draught seemed to come which had caused our candle to gutter and flare.

To think of reaching an opening so far above our heads, so advanced into the ceiling of the cave as to require a fly's power of walking upside down to approach it, was mere waste of time. We bent our gaze elsewhere. On the same side with the niche in which we stood there was a small narrow ledge quite near at hand, and to gain it my two stalwart companions now exerted all their strength.

By cutting a sort of step with the pickaxe, Job was enabled to obtain a footing about three feet above the level of our present floor, and then he called to me.

'Now, Leonard, you be the lightest. Do you hop up here, and climb upon my shoulder, and then I think you will be tall enough to scramble to the ledge, so as to help us up after you.'

I leapt up beside him, clambered upon his stout back as he bade me, and, springing from his shoulder, reached the ledge. He then handed up the pickaxe, directed me how to make its point firm into one of the crevices on the top of the ledge; next, to lie down, hold on to the handle of the pickaxe and give him my other hand. I obediently acted, when he sprang up, and turning, assisted Steve to do likewise.

We had now reached the highest possible coign of vantage left to us, and there remained nothing more to do but wait and hope that the encroaching water would find some unseen outlet before reaching our level.

Job and Steve were so weary from their exertions that they seemed almost indifferent as to what happened, provided they might only be allowed to rest. However, they tried to devise new schemes, and looked wistfully over the surface of the pool.

'I wonder if it rises still?' I said. 'Perhaps not, after all.'

'Then we shall only exchange drowning for starving,' said Steve.

Job, instead of speaking, had endeavoured to answer my query by stooping down and stretching over the ledge with his arm. His face was very calm as he rose again. 'It will be drowning,' he said almost inaudibly, and held up his hand, which was wet.

IV. HOW OLDER HEADS THAN OURS
BECAME CONCERNED

The water had risen so high that Job could touch its surface from our retreat.

We now, in spite of Job's remark, indulged in the dream that, provided the water would stop rising, we might, in the course of time, find a way out somehow, and Job by-and-by said, 'Perhaps round there in the dark may be places where we could crawl out, if we could only see them well enough to swim across to them. Couldn't we send a candle round that way?'

'How?' said I and Steve.

'By a plan I have thought of,' said he. Taking off his hat, which was of straw, he cut with his pocket-knife a little hole in the middle of the crown. Into this he stuck a piece of candle, lighted it, and lying down to reach the surface of the water as before, lowered the hat till it rested afloat.

There was, as Job had suspected, a slight circular current in the apparently still water, and the hat moved on slowly. Our six eyes became riveted on the voyaging candle as if it were a thing of fascination. It travelled away from us, lighting up in its progress unsuspected protuberances and hollows, but revealing to our eager stare no spot of safety or of egress. It went further and yet further into darkness, till it became like a star alone in a sky. Then it crossed from left to right. Then it gradually turned and enlarged, was lost behind jutting crags, reappeared, and journeyed back towards us, till it again floated under the ledge on which we stood, and we gathered it in. It had made a complete circuit of the cavern, the circular motion of the water being caused by the inpour of the spring, and it had showed us no means of escape at all.

Steve spoke, saying solemnly, 'This is all my fault!'

'No,' said Job. 'For you would not have tried to stop the mill-stream if it had not been to save me.'

'But I began it all,' said Steve, bitterly. 'I see now the foolishness of presumption. What right had I to take upon myself the ordering of a stream of water that scores of men three times my age get their living by?'

'I thought overmuch of myself, too,' said Job. 'It was hardly right to stop the grinding of flour that made bread for a whole parish, for my poor sake. We ought to ha' got the advice of someone wi' more experience than ourselves.'

We then stood silent. The impossibility of doing more pressed in upon our senses like a chill, and I suggested that we should say our prayers.

'I think we ought,' said Steve, and Job assenting, we all three knelt down. After this a sad sense of resignation fell on us all, and there being now no hopeful attempt which they could make for deliverance, the sleep that excitement had hitherto withstood overcame both Steve and Job. They leant back and were soon unconscious.

Not having exerted myself to the extent they had done I felt no sleepiness whatever. So I sat beside them with my eyes wide open, holding and protecting the candle mechanically, and wondering if it could really be possible that we were doomed to die.

I do not know how or why, but there came into my mind during this suspense the words I had read somewhere at school, as being those of Flaminius, the consul, when he was penned up at Thrasymene: 'Friends, we must not hope to get out of this by vows and prayers alone. 'Tis by fortitude and strength we must escape.' The futility of any such resolve in my case was apparent enough, and yet the words were sufficient to lead me to scan the roof of the cave once more.

When the opening up there met my eye I said to myself, 'I wonder where that hole leads to?' Picking up a stone about the size of my fist I threw it with indifference, though with a good aim, towards the spot. The stone passed through the gaping orifice, and I heard it alight within like a tennis ball.

But its noise did not cease with its impact. The fall was succeeded by a helter-skelter kind of rattle which, though it receded in the distance, I could hear for a long time with distinctness, owing, I suppose, to the reflection or echo from the top and sides of the cave. It denoted that on the other side of that dark mouth yawning above me there was a slope downward – possibly into another cave, and that the stone had ricocheted down the incline. 'I wonder where it leads?' I murmured again aloud.

Something greeted my ears at that moment of my pronouncing the words 'where it leads' that caused me well-nigh to leap out of my shoes. Even now I cannot think of it without experiencing a thrill. It came from the gaping hole.

If my readers can imagine for themselves the sensations of a timid bird, who, while watching the approach of his captors to strangle him, feels his wings loosening from the tenacious snare, and flight again possible, they may conceive my emotions when I realized that what greeted my ears from above were the words of a human tongue, direct from the cavity.

'Where, in the name of fortune, did that stone come from?'

The voice was the voice of the miller.

'Be dazed if I know – but 'a nearly broke my head!' The reply was that of the shoemaker.

'Steve – Job!' said I. They awoke with a start and exclamation. I tried to shout, but could not. 'They have found us – up there – the miller – shoemaker!' I whispered, pointing to the hole aloft.

Steve and Job understood. Perhaps the sole ingredient, in this sudden revival of our hopes, which could save us from fainting with joy, was the one actually present – that our discoverer was the adversary whom we had been working to circumvent. But such antagonism as his weighed little in the scale with our present despairing circumstances.

We all three combined our voices in one shout – a shout which roused echoes in the cavern that probably had never been awakened since the upheaval of the Mendips, in whose heart we stood. When the shout died away we listened with parted lips.

Then we heard the miller speak again. 'Faith, and believe me – 'tis the rascals themselves! A-throwing stones – a-trying to terrify us off the premises! Did man ever know the like impudence? We have found the clue to the water mystery at last – may be at their pranks at this very moment! Clamber up here; and if I don't put about their backs the greenest stick that ever growed, I'm no grinder o' corn!'

Then we heard a creeping movement from the orifice over our heads, as of persons on their hands and knees; a puffing, as of fat men out of breath; sudden interjections, such as can be found in a list in any boys' grammar-book, and, therefore, need not be repeated here. All this was followed by a faint glimmer, about equal to that from our own candle, bursting from the gap on high, and the cautious appearance of a head over the ledge.

It was the visage of the shoemaker. Beside it rose another in haste, exclaiming, 'Urrr-r! The rascals!' and waving a stick. Almost before we had recognized this as the miller, he, climbing forward with too great impetuosity, and not perceiving that the edge of the orifice was so near, was unable to check himself. He fell over headlong, and was precipitated a distance of some thirty feet into the whirling pool beneath.

Job's face, which, until this catastrophe, had been quite white and rigid at sight of his old enemy, instantly put on a more humane expression. 'We mustn't let him drown,' he said. 'No,' said Steve, 'but how can we save him in such an awkward place?'

There was, for the moment, however, no great cause for anxiety. The miller was a stout man, and could swim, though but badly – his power to keep afloat being due rather to the adipose tissues which composed his person, than to skill. But his immersion had been deep, and when he rose to the surface he was bubbling and sputtering wildly.

'Hu, hu, hu, hu! O, ho – I am drownded!' he gasped. 'I am a dead man and miller – all on account of those villainous – I mean good boys! – If Job would only help me out I would give him such a dressing – blessing I would say – as he never felt the force of before. Oh, bub, bub, hu, hu, hu!'

Job had listened to this with attention. 'Now, will you let me rule in this matter?' he said to Steve.

'With all my heart,' said Steve.

'Look here, Miller Griffin,' then said Job, speaking over the pool, 'you can't expect me or my comrades to help ye until you treat us civilly. No mixed words o' that sort will we stand. Fair and square, or not at all. You must give us straightforward assurance that you will do us no harm; and that if the water runs in your stream again, and the mill goes, and I finish out my 'prenticeship, you treat me well. If you won't promise this, you are a dead man in that water to-night.'

'A master has a right over his 'prentice, body and soul!' cried the miller, desperately, as he swam round, 'and I have a right over you – and I won't be drownded!'

'I fancy you will,' said Job, quietly. 'Your friends be too high above to get at ye.'

'What must I promise ye, then, Job – hu – hu – hu – bub, bub, bub!'

'Say, if I ever strike Job Tray again, he shall be at liberty to leave my service forthwith, and go to some other employ, and this is the solemn oath of me, Miller Griffin. Say that in the presence of these witnesses.'

'Very well – I say it – bub, bub – I say it.' And the miller repeated the words.

'Now I'll help ye out,' said Job. Lying down on his stomach he held out the handle of the shovel to the floating miller, and hauled him towards the ledge on which we stood. Then Steve took one of the miller's hands, and Job the other, and he mounted up beside us.

'Saved – saved!' cried Miller Griffin.

'You must stand close in,' said Steve, 'for there isn't much room on this narrow shelf.'

'Ay, yes I will,' replied the saved man gladly. 'And now, let's get out of this dark place as soon as we can – Ho! – Cobbler Jones! – here we be coming up to ye – but I don't see him!'

'Nor I,' said Steve. 'Where is he?'

The whole four of us stared with all our vision at the opening the miller had fallen from. But his companion had vanished.

'Well – never mind,' said Miller Griffin, genially; 'we'll follow. Which is the way?'

'There's no way – we can't follow,' answered Steve.

'*Can't follow!*' echoed the miller, staring round, and perceiving for the first time that the ledge was a prison. 'What – *not saved*!' he shrieked. 'Not able to get out from here?'

'We be not saved unless your friend comes back to save us,' said Job. 'We've been calculating upon his help – otherwise things be as bad as they were before. We three have clung here waiting for death these two hours, and now there's one more to wait for death – unless the shoemaker comes back.'

Job spoke stoically in the face of the cobbler's disappearance, and Steve tried to look cool also; but I think they felt as much discouraged as I, and almost as much as the miller, at the unaccountable vanishing of Cobbler Jones.

On reflection, however, there was no reason to suppose that he had basely deserted us. Probably he had only gone to bring further assistance. But the bare possibility of disappointment at such times is enough to take the nerve from any man or boy.

'He *must* mean to come back!' the miller murmured lugubriously, as we all stood in a row on the ledge, like sparrows on the moulding of a chimney.

'I should think so,' said Steve, 'if he's a man.'

'Yes – he must!' the miller anxiously repeated. 'I once said he was a two-penny sort of workman to his face – I wish I hadn't said it, oh – how I wish I hadn't; but 'twas years and years ago, and pray heaven he's forgot it! I once called him a stingy varmint – that I did! But we've made that up, and been friends ever since. And yet there's men who'll carry a snub in their buzzoms; and perhaps he's going to punish me now!'

' 'Twould be very wrong of him,' said I, 'to leave us three to die, because you've been a wicked man in your time, miller.'

'Quite true,' said Job.

'Zounds take your saucy tongues!' said Griffin. 'If I had elbow room on this miserable perch I'd – I'd—'

'Just do nothing,' said Job at his elbow. 'Have you no more sense of decency, Mr Griffin, than to go on like that, and the waters rising to drown us minute by minute?'

'Rising to drown us – hey?' said the miller.

'Yes, indeed,' broke in Steve. 'It has reached my feet.'

V. HOW WE BECAME CLOSE ALLIES WITH THE VILLAGERS

Sure enough, the water – to which we had given less attention since the miller's arrival – had kept on rising with silent and pitiless regularity. To feel it actually lapping over the ledge was enough to paralyze us all. We listened and looked, but no shoemaker appeared. In no very long time it ran into our boots, and coldly encircled our ankles.

Miller Griffin trembled so much that he could scarcely keep his standing. 'If I do get out of this,' he said, 'I'll do good – lots of good – to everybody! Oh, oh – the water!'

'Surely you can hold your tongue if this little boy can bear it without crying out!' said Job, alluding to me.

Thus rebuked, the miller was silent; and nothing more happened till we heard a slight sound from the opening which was our only hope, and saw a slight light. We watched, and the light grew stronger, flickering about the orifice like a smile on parted lips. Then hats and heads broke above the edge of the same – one, two, three, four – then candles, arms and shoulders; and it could be seen then that our deliverers were provided with ropes.

'Ahoy – all right!' they shouted, and you may be sure we shouted back a reply.

'Quick, in the name o' goodness!' cried the miller.

A consultation took place among those above, and one of them shouted, 'We'll throw you a rope's end and you must catch it. If you can make it fast, and so climb up one at a time, do it.

'If not, tie it round the first one, let him jump into the water; we'll tow him across by the rope till he's underneath us, and then haul him up.'

'Yes, yes, that's the way!' said the miller. 'But do be quick – I'm dead drowned up to my thighs. Let me have the rope.'

'Now, miller, that's not fair!' said one of the group above – the Man who had Failed, for he was with them. 'Of course you'll send up the boys first – the little boy first of all.'

'I will – I will – 'twas a mistake,' Griffin replied with contrition.

The rope was then thrown; Job caught it, and tied it round me. It was with some misgiving that I flung myself on the water; but I did it, and, upheld by the rope, I floated across to the spot in the pool that was perpendicularly under the opening, when the men all heaved, and I felt myself swinging in the air, till I was received into the arms of half the parish. For the alarm having been given, the attempt at rescue was known all over the lower part of West Poley.

My cousin Steve was now hauled up. When he had gone the miller burst into a sudden terror at the thought of being left till the last, fearing he might not be able to catch the rope. He implored Job to let him go up first.

'Well,' said Job; 'so you shall – on one condition.'

'Tell it, and I agree.'

Job searched his pockets, and drew out a little floury pocket-book, in which he had been accustomed to enter sales of meal and bran. Without replying to the miller, he stooped to the candle and wrote. This done he said, 'Sign this, and I'll let ye go.'

The miller read: I hereby certify that I release from this time forth Job Tray, my apprentice, by his wish, and demand no further service from him whatever. 'Very well – have your way,' he said; and taking the pencil subscribed his name. By this time they had untied Steve and were flinging the rope a third time; Job caught it as before, attached it to the miller's portly person, shoved him off, and saw him hoisted. The dragging up on this occasion was a test to the muscles of those above; but it was accomplished. Then the rope was flung back for the last time, and fortunate it was that the delay was no longer. Job could only manage to secure himself with great difficulty, owing to the numbness which was creeping over him from his heavy labours and immersions. More dead than alive he was pulled to the top with the rest.

The people assembled above began questioning us, as well they might, upon how we had managed to get into our perilous position. Before we had explained, a gurgling sound was heard from the pool. Several looked over. The water whose rising had nearly caused our death was sinking suddenly; and the light of the candle, which had been left to burn itself out on the ledge, revealed a whirlpool on the surface. Steve, the only one of our trio who was in a condition to observe anything, knew in a moment what the phenomenon meant.

The weight of accumulated water had completed the task of reopening the closed tunnel or fissure which Job's and Steve's diving had begun; and the stream was rushing rapidly down the old West Poley outlet, through which it had run from geological times. In a few minutes – as I was told, for I was not an eyewitness of further events this night – the water had drained itself out, and the stream could be heard trickling across the floor of the lower cave as before the check.

In the explanations which followed our adventure, the following facts were disclosed as to our discovery by the neighbours.

The miller and the shoemaker, after a little further discussion in the road where I overheard them, decided to investigate the caves one by one. With this object in view they got a lantern, and proceeded, not to Nick's Pocket, but to a well-known cave nearer at hand called Grim Billy, which to them seemed a likely source for the river.

This cave was very well known up to a certain point. The floor sloped upwards, and eventually led to the margin of the hole in the dome of Nick's Pocket; but nobody was aware that it was the inner part of Nick's Pocket which the treacherous opening revealed. Rather was the un-plumbed depth beneath supposed to be the mouth of an abyss into which no human being could venture. Thus when a stone ascended from this abyss (the stone I threw) the searchers were amazed, till the miller's intuition suggested to him that we were there. And, what was most curious, when we were all delivered, and had gone home, and had been put into warm beds, neither the miller nor the shoemaker knew for certain that they had lighted upon the source of the mill-stream. Much less did they suspect the contrivance we had discovered for turning the water to East or West Poley, at pleasure.

By a piece of good fortune, Steve's mother heard nothing of what had happened to us till we appeared dripping at the door, and could testify to our deliverance before explaining our perils.

The result which might have been expected to all of us, followed in the case of Steve. He caught cold from his prolonged duckings, and the cold was followed by a serious illness.

The illness of Steve was attended with slight fever, which left him very weak, though neither Job nor I suffered any evil effects from our immersion.

The mill-stream having flowed back to its course, the mill was again started, and the miller troubled himself no further about the river-head; but Job, thanks to his ingenuity, was no longer the miller's apprentice. He had been lucky enough to get a place in another mill many miles off, the very next day after our escape.

I frequently visited Steve in his bed-room, and, on one of these occasions, he said to me, 'Suppose I were to die, and you were to go away home, and Job were always to stay away in another part of England, the secret of that mill-stream head would be lost to our village; so that if by chance the vent this way were to choke, and the water run into the East Poley channel, our people would not know how to recover it. They saved our lives, and we ought to make them the handsome return of telling them the whole manœuvre.'

This was quite my way of thinking, and it was decided that Steve should tell all as soon as he was well enough. But I soon found that his anxiety on the matter seriously affected his recovery. He had a scheme, he said, for preventing such a loss of the stream again.

Discovering that Steve was uneasy in his mind, the doctor – to whom I explained that Steve desired to make personal reparation – insisted that his wish be gratified at once – namely, that some of the leading inhabitants of West Poley should be brought up to his bed-room, and learn what he had to say. His mother assented, and messages were sent to them at once.

The villagers were ready enough to come, for they guessed the object of the summons, and they were anxious, too, to know more particulars of our adventures than we had as yet had opportunity to tell them. Accordingly, at a little past six that evening, when the sun was going down, we heard their footsteps ascending the stairs, and they entered. Among them there were the blacksmith, the shoemaker, the dairyman, the Man who had Failed, a couple of farmers; and some men who worked on the farms were also admitted.

Some chairs were brought up from below, and, when our visitors had settled down, Steve's mother, who was very anxious about him, said, 'Now, my boy, we are all here. What have you to tell?'

Steve began at once, explaining first how we had originally discovered the inner cave, and how we walked on till we came to a
stream.

'What we want to know is this,' said the shoemaker, 'is that great pool
we fetched you out of, the head of the mill-stream?'

Steve explained that it was not a natural pool, and other things which
the reader already knows. He then came to the description of the grand
manœuvre by which the stream could be turned into either the east or
the west valley.

'But how did you get down there?' asked one. 'Did you walk in
through Giant's Ear, or Goblin's Cellar, or Grim Billy?'

'We did not enter by either of these,' said Steve. 'We entered by
Nick's Pocket.'

'Ha!' said the company, 'that explains all the mystery.'

' 'Tis amazing,' said the miller, who had entered, 'that folks should
have lived and died here for generations, and never ha' found out that
Nick's Pocket led to the river spring!'

'Well, that isn't all I want to say,' resumed Steve. 'Suppose any
people belonging to East Poley should find out the secret, they
would go there and turn the water into their own vale; and, perhaps,
close up the other channel in such a way that we could scarcely open it
again. But didn't somebody leave the room a minute ago? – who is it
that's going away?'

'I fancy a man went out,' said the dairyman looking round. One or two
others said the same, but dusk having closed in it was not apparent
which of the company had gone away.

Steve continued: 'Therefore before the secret is known, let somebody
of our village go and close up the little gallery we entered by, and the
upper mouth you looked in from. Then there'll be no danger of our
losing the water again.'

The proposal was received with unanimous commendation, and after
a little more consultation, and the best wishes of the neighbours for
Steve's complete recovery, they took their leave, arranging to go and
stop the cave entrances the next evening.

As the doctor had thought, so it happened. No sooner was his sense of
responsibility gone, than Steve began to mend with miraculous rapidity.
Four and twenty hours made such a difference in him that he said to me,
with animation, the next evening: 'Do, Leonard, go and bring me word
what they are doing at Nick's Pocket. They ought to be going up there

about this time to close up the gallery. But 'tis quite dark – you'll be afraid.'

'No – not I,' I replied, and off I went, having told my aunt my mission.

It was, indeed, quite dark, and it was not till I got quite close to the mill that I found several West Poley men had gathered in the road opposite thereto. The miller was not among them, being too much shaken by his fright for any active enterprise. They had spades, pick-axes, and other tools, and were just preparing for the start to the caves.

I followed behind, and as soon as we reached the outskirts of West Poley, I found they all made straight for Nick's Pocket as planned. Arrived there they lit their candles and we went into the interior. Though they had been most precisely informed by Steve how to find the connecting gallery with the inner cavern, so cunningly was it hidden by Nature's hand that they probably would have occupied no small time in lighting on it, if I had not gone forward and pointed out the nook.

They thanked me, and the dairyman, as one of the most active of the group, taking a spade in one hand, and a light in the other, prepared to creep in first and foremost. He had not advanced many steps before he reappeared in the outer cave, looking as pale as death.

VI. HOW ALL OUR DIFFICULTIES
CAME TO AN END

'What's the matter!' said the shoemaker.

'Somebody's there!' he gasped.

'It can't be,' said a farmer. 'Till those boys found the hole, not a being in the world knew of such a way in.'

'Well, come and harken for yourselves,' said the dairyman.

We crept close to the gallery mouth and listened. Peck, peck, peck; scrape, scrape, scrape, could be heard distinctly inside.

'Whoever they call themselves, they are at work like the busy bee!' said the farmer.

It was ultimately agreed that some of the party should go softly round into Grim Billy, creep up the ascent within the cave, and peer through the opening that looked down through the roof of the cave before us. By this means they might learn, unobserved, what was going on.

It was no sooner proposed than carried out. The baker and shoemaker were the ones that went round, and, as there was nothing to be seen where the others waited, I thought I would bear them company. To get to Grim Billy, a circuit of considerable extent was necessary; moreover, we had to cross the mill-stream. The mill had been stopped for the night, some time before, and, hence, it was by a pure chance we noticed that the river was gradually draining itself out. The misfortune initiated by Steve was again upon the village.

'I wonder if the miller knows it?' murmured the shoemaker. 'If not, we won't tell him, or he may lose his senses outright.'

'Then the folks in the cave are enemies!' said the farmer.

'True,' said the baker, 'for nobody else can have done this – let's push on.'

Grim Billy being entered, we crawled on our hands and knees up the slope, which eventually terminated at the hole above Nick's Pocket – a hole that probably no human being had passed through before we were hoisted up through it on the evening of our marvellous escape. We were careful to make no noise in ascending, and, at the edge, we gazed cautiously over.

A striking sight met our view. A number of East Poley men were assembled below on the floor, which had been for awhile submerged by our exploit; and they were working with all their might to build and close up the old outlet of the stream towards West Poley, having already, as it appeared, opened the new opening towards their own village, discovered by Steve. We understood it in a moment, and, descending with the same softness as before, we returned to where our comrades were waiting for us in the other cave, where we told them the strange sight we had seen.

'How did they find out the secret?' the shoemaker inquired under his breath. 'We have guarded it as we would ha' guarded our lives.'

'I can guess!' replied the baker. 'Have you forgot how somebody went away from Master Steve Draycot's bedroom in the dusk last night, and we didn't know who it was? Half-an-hour after, such a man was seen crossing the hill to East Poley; I was told so to-day. We've been surprised, and must hold our own by main force, since we can no longer do it by stealth.'

'How, main force?' asked the blacksmith and a farmer simultaneously.

'By closing the gallery they went in by,' said the baker. 'Then we shall have them in prison, and bring them to book rarely.'

The rest being all irritated at having been circumvented so slily and selfishly by the East Poley men, the baker's plan met with ready acceptance. Five of our body at once chose hard boulders from the outer cave, of such a bulk that they would roll about half-way into the passage or gallery – where there was a slight enlargement – but which would pass no further. These being put in position, they were easily wedged there, and it was impossible to remove them from within, owing to the diminishing size of the passage, except by more powerful tools than they had, which were only spades. We now felt sure of our antagonists, and in a far better position to argue with them than if they had been free. No longer taking the trouble to preserve silence, we, of West Poley, walked in a body round to the other cave – Grim Billy – ascended the inclined floor like a flock of goats, and arranged ourselves in a group at the opening that impended over Nick's Pocket.

The East Poley men were still working on, absorbed in their labour, and were unconscious that twenty eyes regarded them from above like stars.

'Let's halloo!' said the baker.

Halloo we did with such vigour that the East Poley men, taken absolutely unawares, well-nigh sprang into the air at the shock it produced on their nerves. Their spades flew from their hands, and they stared around in dire alarm, for the echoes confused them as to the direction whence the hallooing came. They finally turned their eyes upwards, and saw us individuals of the rival village far above them, illuminated with candles, and with countenances grave and stern as a bench of unmerciful judges.

'Men of East Poley,' said the baker, 'we have caught ye in the execution of a most unfair piece of work. Because of a temporary turning of our water into your vale by a couple of meddlesome boys – a piece of mischief that was speedily repaired – you have thought fit to covet our stream. You have sent a spy to find out its secret, and have meanfully come here to steal the stream for yourselves forever. This cavern is in our parish, and you have no right here at all.'

'The waters of the earth be as much ours as yours,' said one from beneath. But the remainder were thunderstruck, for they knew that their chance had lain entirely in strategy and not in argument.

The shoemaker then spoke: 'Ye have entered upon our property, and diverted the water, and made our parish mill useless, and caused us other losses. Do ye agree to restore it to its old course, close up the new course

ye have been at such labour to widen – in short, to leave things as they
have been from time immemorial ?'

'No-o-o-o!' was shouted from below in a yell of defiance.

'Very well, then,' said the baker, 'we must make you. Gentlemen, ye
are prisoners. Until you restore that water to us, you will bide where you
be.'

The East Poley men rushed to escape by the way they had entered.
But half-way up the tunnel a barricade of adamantine blocks barred their
footsteps. 'Bring spades!' shouted the foremost. But the stones were so
well wedged, and the passage so small, that, as we had anticipated, no
engineering force at their disposal could make the least impression upon
the blocks. They returned to the inner cave disconsolately.

'D'ye give in ?' we asked them.

'Never!' said they doggedly.

'Let 'em sweat – let 'em sweat,' said the shoemaker, placidly. 'They'll
tell a different tale by to-morrow morning. Let 'em bide for the night,
and say no more.'

In pursuance of this idea we withdrew from our position, and, passing
out of Grim Billy, went straight home. Steve was excited by the length
of my stay, and still more when I told him the cause of it. 'What – got
them prisoners in the cave ?' he said. 'I must go myself to-morrow and
see the end of this!'

Whether it was partly due to the excitement of the occasion, or solely
to the recuperative powers of a strong constitution, cannot be said; but
certain it is that next morning, on hearing the villagers shouting and
gathering together, Steve sprang out of bed, declaring that he must go
with me to see what was happening to the prisoners. The doctor was
hastily called in, and gave it as his opinion that the outing would do
Steve no harm, if he were warmly wrapped up; and soon away we went,
just in time to overtake the men who had started on their way.

With breathless curiosity we entered Grim Billy, lit our candles and
clambered up the incline. Almost before we reached the top, exclama-
tions ascended through the chasm to Nick's Pocket, there being such
words as, 'We give in!' 'Let us out!' 'We give up the water forever!'

Looking in upon them, we found their aspect to be very different
from what it had been the night before. Some had extemporized a couch
with smock-frocks and gaiters, and jumped up from a sound sleep
thereon; while others had their spades in their hands, as if undoing
what they had been at such pains to build up, as was proved in a moment

by their saying eagerly, 'We have begun to put it right, and shall finish soon – we are restoring the river to his old bed – give us your word, good gentlemen, that when it is done we shall be free!'

'Certainly,' replied our side with great dignity. 'We have said so already.'

Our arrival stimulated them in the work of repair, which had hither-to been somewhat desultory. Then shovels entered the clay and rubble like giants' tongues; they lit up more candles, and in half an hour had completely demolished the structure raised the night before with such labour and amazing solidity that it might have been expected to last forever. The final stone rolled away, the much tantalized river withdrew its last drop from the new channel, and resumed its original course once more.

While the East Poley men had been completing this task, some of our party had gone back to Nick's Pocket, and there, after much exertion, succeeded in unpacking the boulders from the horizontal passage admit-ting to the inner cave. By the time this was done, the prisoners within had finished their work of penance, and we West Poley men, who had remained to watch them, rejoined our companions. Then we all stood back, while those of East Poley came out, walking between their van-quishers, like the Romans under the Caudine Forks, when they sur-rendered to the Samnites. They glared at us with suppressed rage, and passed without saying a word.

'I see from their manner that we have not heard the last of this,' said the Man who had Failed, thoughtfully. He had just joined us, and learnt the state of the case.

'I was thinking as much,' said the shoemaker. 'As long as that cave is known in Poley, so long will they bother us about the stream.'

'I wish it had never been found out,' said the baker bitterly. 'If not now upon us, they will be playing that trick upon our children when we are dead and gone.'

Steve glanced at me, and there was sadness in his look.

We walked home considerably in the rear of the rest, by no means at ease. It was impossible to disguise from ourselves that Steve had lost the good feeling of his fellow parishioners by his explorations and their results.

As the West Poley men had predicted, so it turned out. Some months afterwards, when I had gone back to my home and school, and Steve was learning to superintend his mother's farm, I heard that another

midnight entry had been made into the cave by the rougher characters
of East Poley. They diverted the stream as before, and when the miller
and other inhabitants of the west village rose in the morning, behold,
their stream was dry! The West Poley folk were furious, and rushed to
Nick's Pocket. The mischief-makers were gone, and there was no legal
proof as to their identity, though it was indirectly clear enough where
they had come from. With some difficulty the water was again restored,
but not till Steve had again been spoken of as the original cause of the
misfortunes.

About this time I paid another visit to my cousin and aunt. Steve
seemed to have grown a good deal older than when I had last seen him,
and, almost as soon as we were alone, he began to speak on the subject
of the mill-stream.

'I am glad you have come, Leonard,' he said, 'for I want to talk to you.
I have never been happy, you know, since the adventure; I don't like the
idea that by a freak of mine our village should be placed at the mercy of
the East Poleyites; I shall never be liked again unless I make that river
as secure from interruption as it was before.'

'But that can't be,' said I.

'Well, I have a scheme,' said Steve musingly. 'I am not so sure that
the river may not be made as secure as it was before.'

'But how? What is the scheme based on?' I asked, incredulously.

'I cannot reveal to you at present,' said he. 'All I can say is, that I have
injured my native village, that I owe it amends, and that I'll pay the debt
if it's a possibility.'

I soon perceived from my cousin's manner at meals and elsewhere
that the scheme, whatever it might be, occupied him to the exclusion
of all other thoughts. But he would not speak to me about it. I frequently
missed him for spaces of an hour or two, and soon conjectured that these
hours of absence were spent in furtherance of his plan.

The last day of my visit came round, and to tell the truth I was not
sorry, for Steve was so preoccupied as to be anything but a pleasant
companion. I walked up to the village alone, and soon became aware
that something had happened.

During the night another raid had been made upon the river-head –
with but partial success, it is true; but the stream was so much reduced
that the mill-wheel would not turn, and the dipping pools were nearly
empty. It was resolved to repair the mischief in the evening, but the
disturbance in the village was very great, for the attempt proved that the

more unscrupulous characters of East Poley were not inclined to
desist.

Before I had gone much further, I was surprised to discern in the
distance a figure which seemed to be Steve's, though I thought I had
left him at the rear of his mother's premises.

He was making for Nick's Pocket, and following thither I reached the
mouth of the cave just in time to see him enter.

'Steve!' I called out. He heard me and came back. He was pale, and
there seemed to be something in his face which I had never seen there
before.

'Ah – Leonard,' he said, 'you have traced me. Well, you are just in
time. The folks think of coming to mend this mischief as soon as their
day's work is over, but perhaps it won't be necessary. My scheme may
do instead.'

'How – do instead?' asked I.

'Well, save them the trouble,' he said with assumed carelessness. 'I
had almost decided not to carry it out, though I had got the materials in
readiness, but the doings of the night have stung me; I carry out my
plan.'

'When?'

'Now – this hour – this moment. The stream must flow into its right
channel, and stay there, and no man's hands must be able to turn it
elsewhere. Now good-bye, in case of accidents.'

To my surprise, Steve shook hands with me solemnly, and wringing
from me a promise not to follow, disappeared into the blackness of the
cave.

For some moments I stood motionless where Steve had left me, not
quite knowing what to do. Hearing footsteps behind my back, I looked
round. To my great pleasure I saw Job approaching, dressed up in his
best clothes, and with him the Man who had Failed.

Job was glad to see me. He had come to West Poley for a holiday,
from the situation with the farmer which, as I now learned for the first
time, the Man who had Failed had been the means of his obtaining.
Observing, I suppose, the perplexity upon my face, they asked me
what was the matter, and I, after some hesitation, told them of Steve.
The Man who had Failed looked grave.

'Is it serious?' I asked him.

'It may be,' said he, in that poetico-philosophic strain which, under
more favouring circumstances, might have led him on to the intellectual

eminence of a Coleridge or an Emerson. 'Your cousin, like all such natures, is rushing into another extreme, that may be worse than the first. The opposite of error is error still; from careless adventuring at other people's expense he may have flown to rash self-sacrifice. He contemplates some violent remedy, I make no doubt. How long has he been in the cave? We had better follow him.'

Before I could reply, we were startled by a jet of smoke, like that from the muzzle of a gun, bursting from the mouth of Nick's Pocket; and this was immediately followed by a deadened rumble like thunder underground. In another moment a duplicate of the noise reached our ears from over the hill, in the precise direction of Grim Billy.

'Oh – what can it be?' said I.

'Gunpowder,' said the Man who had Failed, slowly.

'Ah – yes – I know what he's done – he has blasted the rocks inside!' cried Job. 'Depend upon it, that's his plan for closing up the way to the river-head.'

'And for losing his life into the bargain,' said our companion. 'But no – he may be alive. We must go in at once – or as soon as we can breathe there.'

Job ran for lights, and before he had returned we heard a familiar sound from the direction of the village. It was the patter of the mill-wheel. Job came up almost at the moment, and with him a crowd of the village people.

'The river is right again,' they shouted. 'Water runs better than ever – a full, steady stream, all on a sudden – just when we heard the rumble underground.'

'Steve has done it!' I said.

'A brave fellow,' said the Man who had Failed. 'Pray that he is not hurt.'

Job had lighted the candles, and, when we were entering, some more villagers, who at the noise of the explosion had run to Grim Billy, joined us. 'Grim Billy is partly closed up inside!' they told us. 'Where you used to climb up the slope to look over into Nick's Pocket, 'tis all altered. There's no longer any opening there; the whole rock has crumbled down as if the mountain had sunk bodily.'

Without waiting to answer, we, who were about to enter Nick's Pocket, proceeded on our way. We soon had penetrated to the outer approaches, though nearly suffocated by the sulphurous atmosphere; but we could get no further than the first cavern. At a point somewhat in advance of the little gallery to the inner cave, Nick's Pocket ceased to exist. Its roof had sunk. The whole superimposed mountain, as it seemed, had quietly settled down upon the hollow places beneath it, closing like a pair of bellows, and barring all human entrance.

But alas, where was Steve? 'I would never have had no water in West Poley forevermore than have lost Steve!' said Job.

'And so would I!' said many of us.

To add to our terror, news was brought into the cave at that moment that Steve's mother was approaching; and how to meet my poor aunt was more than we could think.

But suddenly a shout was heard. A few of the party, who had not penetrated so far into the cave as we had done, were exclaiming, 'Here he is!' We hastened back, and found they were in a small, side hollow, close to the entrance, which we had passed by unheeded. The Man who had Failed was there, and he and the baker were carrying something into the light. It was Steve – apparently dead, or unconscious.

'Don't be frightened,' said the baker to me. 'He's not dead; perhaps not much hurt.'

As he had declared, so it turned out. No sooner was Steve in the open air, than he unclosed his eyes, looked round with a stupefied expression, and sat up.

'Steve – Steve!' said Job and I, simultaneously.

'All right,' said Steve, recovering his senses by degrees. 'I'll tell – how it happened – in a minute or two.'

Then his mother came up, and was at first terrified enough, but on seeing Steve gradually get upon his legs, she recovered her equanimity. He soon was able to explain all. He said that the damage to the village by his tampering with the stream had weighed upon his mind, and led him to revolve many schemes for its cure. With this in view he had privately made examination of the cave; when he discovered that the whole superincumbent mass, forming the roof of the inner cave, was divided from the walls of the same by a vein of sand, and that it was only kept in its place by a slim support at one corner. It seemed to him that if this support could be removed, the upper mass would descend by its own weight, like the brick of a brick-trap when the peg is withdrawn.

He laid his plans accordingly; procuring gunpowder, and scooping out holes for the same, at central points in the rock. When all this was done, he waited awhile, in doubt, as to the effect; and might possibly never have completed his labours, but for the renewed attempt upon the river. He then made up his mind, and attached the fuse. After lighting it, he would have reached the outside safely enough but for the accident of stumbling as he ran, which threw him so heavily on the ground, that, before he could recover himself and go forward, the explosion had occurred.

All of us congratulated him, and the whole village was joyful, for no less than three thousand, four hundred and fifty tons of rock and earth – according to calculations made by an experienced engineer a short time afterwards – had descended between the river's head and all human interference, so that there was not much fear of any more East Poley manœuvres for turning the stream into their valley.

The inhabitants of the parish, gentle and simple, said that Steve had made ample amends for the harm he had done; and their good-will was further evidenced by his being invited to no less than nineteen Christmas and New Year's parties during the following holidays.

As we left the cave, Steve, Job, Mrs Draycot and I walked behind the Man who had Failed.

'Though this has worked well,' he said to Steve, 'it is by the merest chance in the world. Your courage is praiseworthy, but you see the risks that are incurred when people go out of their way to meddle with what they don't understand. Exceptionally smart actions, such as you delight in, should be carefully weighed with a view to their utility before they are begun. Quiet perseverence in clearly defined courses is, as a rule, better than the erratic exploits that may do much harm.'

Steve listened respectfully enough to this, but he said to his mother afterwards: 'He has failed in life, and how can his opinions be worth anything?'

'For this reason,' said she. 'He is one who has failed, not from want of sense, but from want of energy; and people of that sort, when kindly, are better worth attending to than those successful ones, who have never seen the seamy side of things. I would advise you to listen to him.'

Steve probably did; for he is now the largest gentleman-farmer of those parts, remarkable for his avoidance of anything like speculative exploits.

THE FAMOUS TRAGEDY OF
THE QUEEN OF CORNWALL

Imaginary View of Tintagel Castle.
at the 'time' of the Tragedy.

T. H.
May 1923.

IN AFFECTIONATE REMEMBRANCE
OF THOSE WITH WHOM I FORMERLY SPENT
MANY HOURS AT
THE SCENE OF THE TRADITION,
WHO HAVE NOW ALL PASSED AWAY
SAVE ONE.
E.L.H.
C.H.
H.C.H.
F.E.H.

The Stage is any large room; round or at the end of which the audience sits. It is assumed to be the interior of the Great Hall of Tintagel Castle: that the floor is strewn with rushes: that there is an arch in the back-centre (a doorway or other opening may counterfeit this) through which the Atlantic is visible across an outer ward and over the ramparts of the stronghold: that a door is on the left, and one on the right (curtains, screens or chairs may denote these): that a settle spread with skins is among the moveables: that above at the back is a gallery (which may be represented by any elevated piece of furniture on which two actors can stand, in a corner of the room screened off).

☞ *Should the performance take place in an ordinary theatre, the aforesaid imaginary surroundings may be supplied by imitative scenery.*

The costumes of the players are the conventional ones of bright linen fabrics, trimmed with ribbon, as in the old mumming shows; though on a constructed stage they may be more realistic.

Imaginary Aspect of the Great Hall at the Time of the Tragedy.

CHARACTERS

MARK, KING OF CORNWALL
SIR TRISTRAM
SIR ANDRET
Other Knights
Squires
Messenger
Herald
Watchman
Retainers, Musicians, etc.

ISEULT THE FAIR, QUEEN OF CORNWALL
ISEULT THE WHITEHANDED
DAME BRANGWAIN
Damsel
The Queen's Attendants, Bowerwomen, etc.

SHADES OF DEAD OLD CORNISH MEN⎫ Chanters
SHADES OF DEAD CORNISH WOMEN ⎭

MERLIN

The Time covered by the events is about the Time of representation.

PROLOGUE

Enter MERLIN, *a phantasmal figure with a white wand. The room is darkened: a blue light may be thrown on Merlin.*

MERLIN

I come, at your persuasive call,
To raise up in this modern hall
A tragedy of dire duresse
That vexed the Land of Lyonnesse: –
Scenes, with their passions, hopes, and fears
Sunk into shade these thousand years;
To set, in ghostly grave array,
   Their blitheness, blood, and tears,
Feats, ardours, as if rife to-day
    Before men's eyes and ears.

The tale has travelled far and wide: –
Yea, that King Mark, to fetch his bride,
Sent Tristram; then that he and she
Quaffed a love-potion witlessly
While homeward bound. Hence that the King
   Wedded one heart-aflame
For Tristram! He, in dark despair,
Roved recklessly, and wived elsewhere
   One of his mistress' name.

I saw these times I represent,
Watched, gauged them as they came and went,
Being ageless, deathless! And those two
Fair women – namesakes – well I knew!
Judge them not harshly in a love
   Whose hold on them was strong;
Sorrow therein they tasted of,
   And deeply, and too long!

                                       [*Exit.*

SCENE I

SHADES OF DEAD OLD ⎫
   CORNISH MEN   ⎪   ⎧ *Right and*
                ⎬ CHANTERS ⎨ *left in*
SHADES OF DEAD   ⎪   ⎩ *Front.*
   CORNISH WOMEN ⎭

CHANTERS: MEN (*in recitative*)
Tristram a captive of King Mark,
Racked was the Queen with qualm and cark,
Till reached her hand a written line,
That quickened her to deft design.

CHANTERS: WOMEN
Then, Tristram out, and Mark shut in,
The Queen and Tristram winged to win
Gard Castle, where, without annoy,
Monthswhile they lodged in matchless joy!

CHANTERS: MEN
Anon, when Queen Iseult had homed,
Brittany-wards Sir Tristram roamed
   To greet his waiting wife,
White-handed Iseult, whom the Queen
Had recked not of. But soon, in teen
   And troublous inner strife,
She Tristram of her soul besought
By wringing letters rapid-wrought
(The King gone hunting, knowing nought)
   To come again to her
Even at the cost – such was her whim –
Of bringing Whitehands back with him
   In wifely character.

CHANTERS: WOMEN
There was no answer. Rest she could not;
Then we missed her, days. We would not
   Think where she might have been.

And, having sailed, maybe, twice ten
Long leagues, here came she back again,
And sad and listless – just as when
 She went – abides her mien!

   CHANTERS: M. AND W.
Hist! . . . Lo; there by the nether gate
New comers hail! O who should wait
The postern door to enter by,
 The bridge being clearly seen?
The King returned? – But that way; why?
Would he try trap his Queen?

   WATCHMAN (*crossing without the archway*)
The King's arriving! Ho!

Enter HERALD. *Sounds a trumpet. Enter* BRANGWAIN.

SCENE II

HERALD, BRANGWAIN, AND CHANTERS.

   HERALD
  The King's at hand!

   BRANGWAIN
God's grace, she's home, either from far or near!

   HERALD
Whither plied she? Many would like to hear!

   CHANTERS: M. AND W.
We do not know. We will not know.
She took a ship from the shore below,
 And was gone many days.
By friending winds she's back before him:
Extol God should she and adore Him
 For covering up her ways!

Enter KING MARK *with* SIR ANDRET *and other Knights, Retinue, and rude
 music of ram's-horns, crouds, and humstrums,* BRANGWAIN *standing
 aside.*

SCENE III

KING MARK, KNIGHTS, RETINUE, ETC.,
BRANGWAIN, AND CHANTERS.

KING MARK

Where is the Queen?

Drinks from a gold flagon[1] which has been standing on the hearth on a brandise. Retinue drink after him from the same.

BRANGWAIN (*advancing*)
       Sir King, the Queen attires
To meet your Majesty, and now comes down.
(*Aside.*) Haply he will not know!

Enter QUEEN ISEULT THE FAIR *attended, and followed by the hound* HOUDAIN.

SCENE IV

QUEEN ISEULT, KING MARK, KNIGHTS,
BRANGWAIN, ETC., AND CHANTERS.

(QUEEN ISEULT *has dark hair, and wears a crimson robe, and tiara or circlet.*)
MARK *smacks the* QUEEN *on her shoulders in rough greeting.*

KING MARK
Why is this brachet in the hall again?

QUEEN ISEULT
I know not how she came here.

KING MARK
        Nay, my wife,
Thou dost know well – as I know women well! –
And know her owner more than well, I reckon,
And that he left the beast to your regard.

           He kicks the dog away.

SIR ANDRET (*aside to* KING MARK)
Aye, aye, great King, thou speakest wisely on't
This time as ever. Wives dost thrid all through!

[*Exeunt severally* KNIGHTS, RETINUE, ETC., *and* BRANGWAIN.

---

[1] A vessel of hammered gold, considered to date from Arthurian times, was found in Cornwall in 1837.

SCENE V

King Mark, Queen Iseult,
and Chanters.

QUEEN ISEULT

I've not beheld of late the man you mean;
Maybe, my lord, you have shut him in the dungeon,
As you did formerly!

KING MARK
You spell me better!
And know he has felt full liberty for long,
And that you would have seen him, and much more,
Had not debarred you one o' those crosses which,
Happily, dash unlawful lovers' schemes
No less than sanct intents. If that good knight
Dallies in Brittany with his good wife –
So finger-white – to cheer her as he ought,
'Tis clear he can't be here.

QUEEN ISEULT (*with slight sarcasm*)
'Tis clear. You plead
Somewhat in waste to prove as much. But, faith,
(*petulantly*) 'Twas she, times tireless, quirked and called to him
Or he would not have gone!

KING MARK
Ah, know'st thou that!
Leave her alone, a woman lets all out!
Well, I may know things too. I slipped in sly
When I came home by now, and lit on this:
That while I've sued the chase you followed him,
Vanishing on a voyage of some days,
Which you'd fain cloak from me, and have confessed
To no one, either, of my people here.

QUEEN ISEULT (*evasively*)
I went to take the air, being qualmed to death.
Surely a queen is dowered with such degree

Of queenship, or what is't to be a queen?
No foot, I swear, set I in Brittany,
Or upon soil of any neighbour shore,
'Twixt putting from the cove below these walls
And my return hereto.

        KING MARK
           Protests – no more!
You sailed off somewhere, – (so a sea-nath[1] hints me
That heeds the tidings every troubled billow
Wails to the Beeny-Sisters from Pen-Tyre) –
At risk, too, of your life, the ship being small,
And trickful tempests lurking in the skies.
A woman does not raise a mast for nought
On a cockle-shell, even be the sea-signs fair.
But I have scorned to ask the mariners
The course you bore – or north, or south, or what –
It might have been to Brittany, it might not!

        QUEEN ISEULT
I have not seen him.

        KING MARK
           Well, you might have done't
Each sunrise, noon, or eve, for all the joy
You show in my return, or gladness wont
To a queen shore-reached in safety – so they tell me –
Since you crept cat-like home.

        QUEEN ISEULT (*indignantly*)
             I saw him not!
You stifle speech in me, or I'd have launched,
Ere this, the tidings rife. See him no more
Shall I, or you. He's gone. Death darkens him!

        KING MARK (*starting*)
So much the better, if true – for us and him! (*She weeps.*)
But no. He has died too many, many times

    [1] *nath*, a puffin (Cornish).

For that report to hold! In tilts, in frays,
Through slits and loops, louvres and battlements,
Has he been pierced and arrowed to the heart,
Then risen up again to trouble me!
Sir Andret told, ere Tristram shunned Tintagel,
How he espied you dallying – you and he –
Near the shot-window southward. And I went
With glaive in hand to smite him. Would I had!
Yea, and I should have done it, limbed him sunder,
Had I been boldly backed; but not a knight
Was near to second me. – Where are they now?
Whence comes this quietude? – I'll call a council:
What's best to do with him I'll learn thereat,
And then we'll keep a feast. A council! Ho!

[Exit KING MARK.

SCENE VI

QUEEN ISEULT AND CHANTERS.
The Queen sits in dejection.

CHANTERS: MEN

Why did Heaven warrant, in its whim,
A twain mismated should bedim
The courts of their encompassment
With bleeding loves and discontent!
Who would not feel God favoured them,
Past wish, in throne and diadem?
And that for all His plaisance they would praise
Him upon earth throughout their deeds and days!

CHANTERS: WOMEN

Instead, see King and Queen more curst
Than beggars upon holt or hurst: –
A queen! One who each night and morn
Sighs for Sir Tristram; him, gloom-born
In his mother's death, and reared mid vows
Of poison by a later spouse:

In love Fate-haunted, doomed to drink
Charmed philtres, melting every link
Of purposed faith! Why wedded he
King Howel's lass of Brittany?
Why should the wave have washed him to her shore –
Him, prone to love our Queen here more and more?

CHANTERS: M. AND W.

In last misfortune did he well-nigh slay
Unknowingly in battle Arthur! Ay,
Our stainless Over-king of Counties – he
Made Dux Bellorum for his valiancy! –
If now, indeed, Tristram be chilled in death,
Will she, the Queen, care aught for further breath?

QUEEN ISEULT (*musing*)

How little he knows, does Mark! And yet, how much?
Can there be any groundage for his thought
That Tristram's not a ghost? O, no such hope!
My Tristram, yet not mine! Could it be deemed
Thou shouldst have loved me less in many years
Hadst thou enjoyed them? If in Christland now
Do you look down on *her* most, or on *me*?
Why should the King have grudged so fleet a life
Its pleasure, grinned with gall at its renown,
Yapped you away for too great love of me,
Spied on thee through his myrmidons – aye, encloaked
And peeped to frustrate thee, and sent the word
To kill thee who should meet thee? O sweet Lord,
Thou hast made him hated; yet he still has life;
While Tristram. . . . Why said Mark he doubtless lived?
– But he was ever a mocker, was King Mark,
And not far from a coward.

Enter BRANGWAIN.

SCENE VII

QUEEN ISEULT, BRANGWAIN, AND CHANTERS.

QUEEN ISEULT (*distractedly*)

Brangwain, he hard denies I did not see him!
But he is dead! . . . Perhaps not. . . . Can it be?

BRANGWAIN

Who doth deny, my Queen? Who is not dead?
Your words are blank to me; your manner strange.

QUEEN ISEULT

One bleeds no more on earth for a full-fledged sin
Than for a callow! The King has found out now
My sailing the south water in his absence,
And weens the worst. Forsooth, it's always so!
He will not credit I'd no cause to land
For the black reason – it is no excuse –
That Tristram, knight, had died! – Landed had I,
Aye, fifty times, could he have still been there,
Even there with her. – My Love, my own lost Love!

(*She bends down.*)

BRANGWAIN

You did not land in Brittany, O Queen?

QUEEN ISEULT

I did not land, Brangwain, although so near. (*She pauses.*)
– He had been long with his White-handed one,
And had fallen sick of fever nigh to death;
Till she grew fearful for him; sent for me,
Yea, choicelessly, at his light-headed calls
And midnight repetitions of my name.
Yes, sent for me in a despairing hope
To save him at all cost.

BRANGWAIN
                    She must, methinks,

Have loved him much!

QUEEN ISEULT (*impatiently*)

Don't speak, Brangwain, but hear me.
Yes: women are so. . . . For me, I could not bear
To lose him thus. Love, others' freakful dainty,
Is my starved, all-day meal! And favouring chance,
That of the King's apt absence, tempted me;
And hence I sailed, despite the storm-strid air.
What did I care about myself, or aught?
– She'd told the mariner her messenger
To hoist his canvas white if he bore me
On the backward journey, black if he did not,
That, so, heart-ease should reach the knight full quick –
Even ere I landed – quick as I hove in sight.
Yes, in his peril so profound, she sent
The message, though against her. Women are so!

BRANGWAIN

Some are, my lady Queen: some may not be.

QUEEN ISEULT

Brangwain, I would you did not argue so. –
While we were yet a two-hours' toss from port
I bade them show the sheet, as had been asked,
The which they did. But when we touched the quay
She ran down thither, beating both her hands,
And saying Tristram died an hour before.

BRANGWAIN

But O, dear Queen, didst fully credit her?

QUEEN ISEULT

Aye! Sudden-shaken souls guess not at guile. –
I fell into a faint at the very words. –
Thereon they lifted me into the cabin,
Saying: 'She shall not foot this deadly land!'
When I again knew life I was distraught,
And sick with the rough writhing of the bark. –
They had determined they would steer me home,
Had turned the prow, and toiled a long league back;

Strange that, no sooner had they put about,
The weather worsed, as if they'd angered God
By doing what they had done to sever me
Even from my Love's dead limbs! No gleam glowed more,
And the seas sloped like houseroofs all the way.
We were blown north along the shore to Wales,
Where they made port and nursed me, till, next day,
The blinding gale abated: we returned,
And reached by shifts at last the cove below.
The King, whose queries I had feared so much,
Had not come back; came only at my heels;
Yet he has learnt, somewise, that I've been missed,
And doubtless I shall suffer – he's begun it!
Much I lament I bent astern so soon.
I should have landed, and have gained his corpse.

BRANGWAIN

She is his wife, and you could not have claimed it.

QUEEN ISEULT

But could I not have seen him? How know you?

BRANGWAIN

Nay: she might not have let you even see him:
He is her own, dear Queen, and in her land
You had no sway to make her cede him up.
I doubt his death. You took her word for it,
And she was desperate at the sight of you.
Sick unto death he may have been. But – dead?
(*Shakes her head.*)

Corpses are many: man lives half-amort;
But rumour makes them more when they run short!

QUEEN ISEULT

If he be not! O I would even condone
His bringing her, would he not come without;
I've said it ever since I've known of her.
Could he but live: yes, could he live for me!

QUEEN ISEULT *sings sadly to herself,* BRANGWAIN *having gone to the back of the hall:*

> Could he but live for me
> A day, yea, even an hour,
> Its petty span would be
> Steeped in felicity
> Passing the price of Heaven's held-dearest dower:
> Could he but live, could *he*
>   But live for me!

> Could he but come to me
> Amid these murks that lour,
> My hollow life would be
> So brimmed with ecstasy
> As heart-dry honeysuck by summer shower:
> Could he but come, could he
>   But come to me!

> [*Exit* QUEEN ISEULT, *followed by* BRANGWAIN.

CHANTERS: WOMEN

Maybe, indeed, he did not die!
Our sex, shame on't, is over prone
To ill conceits that amplify.
Maybe he did not die – that one,
The Whitepalmed, may in strategy
Have but avowed it! Weak are we,
And foil and fence have oft to seek,
Aye, even by guile, if fear so speak!

CHANTERS: MEN

Wounded in Ireland, life he fetched,
In charge of the King's daughter there,
Who healed him, loved him, primed him fair
For the great tournament, when he stretched
Sir Palomides low.

CHANTERS: WOMEN

Yet slight
Was King Mark's love for him, despite!

Mark sent him thither as to gain
Iseult, but, truly, to be slain!

CHANTERS: MEN

Quite else her father, who on sight
Was fain for Tristram as his son,
Not Mark. But woe, his word was won!
Alas, should wrong vow stand as right?

CHANTERS: WOMEN

And what Dame Brangwain did to mend,
Enlarged the mischief! Best have penned
That love-drink close, since 'twas to be
Iseult should wed where promised: wretched she!

CHANTERS: M. AND W.

Yet, haply, Tristram lives. Quick heals are his!
He rose revived from that: why not from this?

WATCHMAN (*without*)

One comes with tidings! – (*to the comer*) Bear them to the hall.

*Enter a Messenger (at back), pausing and looking round. QUEEN ISEULT,
attended, re-enters (at front) and seats herself.*

SCENE VIII

QUEEN ISEULT, ATTENDANT-LADIES,
MESSENGER, AND CHANTERS.

MESSENGER (*coming forward*)

Where is Iseult the Queen?

QUEEN ISEULT
                Here, churl. I'm she.

MESSENGER (*abashed*)

I'm sent here to deliver tidings, Queen,
To your high ear alone.

                                [*Exeunt Attendants.*

QUEEN ISEULT (*in strung-up tones*)
            Then voice them forth.
A halter for thee if I find them false!

MESSENGER
Knight Tristram of the sorry birth is yet
Enrolled among the living, having crept
Out of the very vaults of death and doom!
– His heavy ails bedimmed him numb as night,
And men conceived him wrapt in wakeless rest;
But he strove back. Hither, on swifter keel
He has followed you; and even now is nigh.
            (QUEEN ISEULT *leans back and covers her eyes.*)
Iseult the Pale-palmed, in her jealousy,
With false deliverance feigned your sail was black,
And made him pray for death in his extreme,
Till sank he to a drowse: grey death they thought it,
And bells were bidden toll the churches through,
And thereupon you came. Scared at her crime
She deemed that it had dealt him death indeed,
And knew her not at fault till you had gone.
– When he aroused, and learnt she had sent you back,
It angered him to hot extremity,
And brings him here upon my very stern,
If he, forsooth, have haleness for the adventure.
                                    [*Exit Messenger.*

QUEEN ISEULT
O it o'erturns! . . . 'Black' told she! Cheat unmatchable!
TRISTRAM *heard off, singing and harping in the distance.*

Enter BRANGWAIN.

SCENE IX

QUEEN ISEULT, BRANGWAIN, AND CHANTERS.
THEN KING MARK AND SIR ANDRET.

BRANGWAIN
There stands a strange old harper down below,

Who does not look Sir Tristram, yet recalls him.
KING MARK *crosses the ward outside the arch.*

KING MARK
(*speaking off, and shading his eyes*)
What traveller's that, slow mounting to the wall,
Scanning its strength, with curious halting crawl,
As knowing not Tintagel's Towers at all?

WATCHMAN (*crossing without*)
'Tis but a minstrel from afar, Sir King,
Harping for alms, or aught that chance may bring.

QUEEN ISEULT (*starting up*)
It must be he!
SIR TRISTRAM'S *steps heard approaching. He enters, disguised as a harper.*

KING MARK (*glancing back casually at*
SIR TRISTRAM *in going off*)
Dole him his alms in Christ's name, if ye must,
And irk me not while setting to bowse with these.
Exit KING MARK *from the outside to the banqueting-hall, followed across
the back of the arch by Knights, etc., including* SIR ANDRET.

SIR ANDRET (*to himself as he goes*)
That harper struck me oddly! . . . In his gait –
Well: till the beakers have gone round I'll wait.
[*Exit behind the others.*

SCENE X

QUEEN ISEULT, TRISTRAM, BRANGWAIN,
AND CHANTERS.

TRISTRAM
My Queen and best belov'd! At last again!
(*He throws off the cloak that disguises him.*)

– Know I was duped by her who dons your name;
She swore the bellied sheeting of your ship
Blotted the wind-wafts like a sable swan;
And being so weak from my long lying there
I sank to senselessness at the wisht words –
So contrary to hope! Whilst I was thus
She sallied out, and sent you home forthwith!
Anon I poured my anger on her head,
Till, in high fear of me, she quivered white.
– I mended swiftly, stung by circumstance,
And rose and left her there, and followed you.
Sir Kay lent aidance, and has come with me.

BRANGWAIN

I'll out and watch the while Sir Tristram's here.

[*Exit* BRANGWAIN.

SCENE XI

QUEEN ISEULT, TRISTRAM, AND CHANTERS.

QUEEN ISEULT

You've come again, you've come again, dear Love!

TRISTRAM

To be once more with my Iseult the Fair,

(*He embraces the Queen.*)

Though not yet what I was in strength and stay.
Yet told have I been by Sir Launcelot
To ware me of King Mark! King Fox he calls him –
Whom I'd have pitied, though he would not yield thee,
Nor let you loose on learning our dire need
Of freedom for our bliss, which came to us
Not of fore-aim or falseness, but by spell
Of love-drink, ministered by hand unseen!

QUEEN ISEULT

Knowing as much, he swore he would not slay thee,

But Launcelot told him no man could believe him,
Whereat he answered: 'Anyhow she's mine!'

TRISTRAM

It's true, I fear. He cannot be believed.

QUEEN ISEULT

Yet, Tristram, would my husband were but all!
Had you not wedded her my namesake, Oh,
We could have steered around this other rock –
Trust me we could! Why did you do it, why!
Triumph did he when first I learnt of that,
And lewdly laughed to see me shaken so.

TRISTRAM

You have heard the tale of my so mating her
Twice told, and yet anew! Must I again?
It was her sire King Howel brought it round
In brunt of battle, when I saved his lands.
He said to me: 'Thou hast done generously:
I crave to make thee recompense! My daughter,
The last best bloom of Western Monarchy –
Iseult of the White Hand the people call her –
Is thine. I give thee her. O take her then,
The chief of all things priceless unto me!'
Overcome was I by the fiery fray,
Arrested by her name – so kin to yours –
His ardour, zeal. I thought: 'Maybe her spouse,
By now, has haled my Iseult's heart from me,'
And took the other blindly. That is all.

QUEEN ISEULT

A woman's heart has room for one alone;
A man's for two or three!

TRISTRAM
                    Sweet; 'twas but chance!

QUEEN ISEULT (*sighing*)
Yet there may lie our doom! . . . I had nerved myself

To bid you come, and bring your wife with you.
But that I did not mean. It was too much;
And yet I said it! . . .

TRISTRAM
Lean ye down, my Love:
I'll touch to thee my very own old tune.
I came in harper-guise, unweeting what
The hazardry of our divided days
Might have brought forth for us!
He takes the harp. QUEEN ISEULT *reclines.*

TRISTRAM (*singing*)
Let's meet again to-night, my Fair,
    Let's meet unseen of all;
The day-god labours to his lair,
    And then the evenfall!

O living lute, O lily-rose,
    O form of fantasie,
When torches waste and warders doze
    Steal to the stars will we!

While nodding knights carouse at meat
    And shepherds shamble home,
We'll cleave in close embracements – sweet
    As honey in the comb!

Till crawls the dawn from Condol's crown,
    And over Neitan's Kieve,
As grimly ghosts we conjure down
    And hopes still weave and weave!

WATCHMAN (*crossing without*)
A ship sheers round, and brings up in the bay!
Re-enter BRANGWAIN.

SCENE XII

QUEEN ISEULT, TRISTRAM, BRANGWAIN,
AND CHANTERS.

BRANGWAIN

My Queen, the shingle shaves another keel,
And who the comer is we fail to guess.
Its build bespeaks it from the Breton coasts,
And those upon it shape of the Breton sort,
And the figure near the prow is white-attired.

QUEEN ISEULT
What manner of farer does the figure show?

BRANGWAIN

My Lady, when I cast eye waterwards
From the arrow-loop, just as the keel ground in
Against the popplestones, it seemed a woman's;
But she was wimpled close.

QUEEN ISEULT
I'll out and see.

QUEEN ISEULT *opens the door to the banqueting-hall, and stands in the
doorway still visible to the audience. Through the door comes the noise of
trenchers, platters, cups, drunken voices, songs, etc., from the adjoining
apartment, where* KING MARK *is dining with Knights and Retainers.*

VOICE OF KING MARK (*in liquor*)
Queen, whither goest thou? Pray plague me not
While keeping table. Hath the old knave left,
He with his balladry we heard by now
Strum up to thee?

QUEEN ISEULT
I go to the pleasance only,
Across your feasting-hall for shortness' sake,
Returning hither soon.

VOICE OF KING MARK
Yea, have thy way,
As women will!

VOICE OF SIR ANDRET
Aye, hence the need to spy them!
[*Exeunt* QUEEN ISEULT *and* BRANGWAIN *through banqueting-hall to the outside of the Castle.*

VOICE OF KING MARK
Faith, yes. Slip forth and see what may be toward
With her and her lays of love and tinkling strings!

VOICE OF SIR ANDRET
I'll go, Sir King, wilt give me licence first
To see the bottom of another cup.
Noise of cups, trenchers, drunken voices, songs, etc., resumed till the door shuts, when it is heard in subdued tones.

SCENE XIII

TRISTRAM AND CHANTERS.

TRISTRAM (*going and looking seaward through arch*)
A woman's shape in white. . . . Can it be she?
Would she in sooth, then, risk to follow me?

CHANTERS: MEN
O Tristram, thou art not to find
Such solace for a shaken mind
As seemed to wait thee here!

CHANTERS: WOMEN
One seised of right to trace thy track
Hath crossed the sea to win thee back
In love and faith and fear!

CHANTERS: M. AND W.
From this newcomer wis we pain

Ere thou canst know sweet spells again,
    O knight of little cheer!

TRISTRAM

I cannot halt here, nerve-stretched like a lute-string;
I must fain storm the truth!

                              [*Exit* TRISTRAM.
    Enter SIR ANDRET (*looking about him*).

SCENE XIV

SIR ANDRET AND CHANTERS. THEN ISEULT
THE WHITEHANDED.

SIR ANDRET

She's scheming nothing here that I discern,
But things are schemed without a man's discerning!

Enter ISEULT THE WHITEHANDED. *She has corn-brown hair, and wears a white robe. She starts at seeing* SIR ANDRET *and speaks confusedly.*

ISEULT THE WHITE H.

I saw them coming down to learn my errand,
And crept up by the rear-path, to avoid them
Till I'd disclosed to Tristram. . . .

SIR ANDRET

Who may you be, good lady? feather-shaken
Like a far bird stray-blown. And what's your lack?
Why, you are verily—

ISEULT THE WHITE H.

I come to learn if Tristram, that good Knight,
Is held within these bold embastioned walls.
I'm his much sorrowed wife – Iseult of Brittany.

SIR ANDRET

Ah; Tristram, then, is here? I shrewdly guessed it!

ISEULT THE WHITE H.

I deem I scarce should tell. Yet, as I think,
You are his friend?

SIR ANDRET (*drily*)
In a true sense I am;
Friend for his good. I leave you here to wait.
(*Aside*). It *was* he, then! – The King shall be let know
A short while onward, when he's plumply primed!

[*Exit* SIR ANDRET.

SCENE XV

ISEULT THE WHITEHANDED AND CHANTERS.
THEN TRISTRAM.

ISEULT THE WHITE H.

Have I done mischief? Maybe so, alas,
To one I would not harm the littlest jot!

Re-enter TRISTRAM.

I could not help it, O my husband! Yea
I have dogged you close; I could not bear your rage;
And Heaven has favoured me! The sea smiled smooth
The whole way over, and the sun shone kind.
Your sail was eyesome fair in front of me,
And I steered just behind, all stealthfully!
– Forgive me that I spoke untruly to you,
And then to her, in my bruised brain's turmoil.
But, in a way of saying, you were dead;
You seemed so – in a dead drowse when she came.
And I did send for her at your entreaty;
But flesh is frail. Centred is woman's love,
And knows no breadth. I could not let her land,
I could not let her come!

TRISTRAM
Your speech is nought,

O evil woman, who didst nearly witch
The death of this Queen, saying such of me!

ISEULT THE WHITE H.

Forgive me, do forgive, my lord, my husband!
I love, have loved you so imperishably;
Not with fleet flame at times, as some do use!
Had I once been unfaithful, even perverse,
I would have held some coldness fitly won;
But I have ever met your wryest whim
With ready-wrought acceptance, matched your moods,
Clasped hands, touched lips, and smiled devotedly;
So how should this have grown up unaware?

Enter QUEEN ISEULT *and* BRANGWAIN *in the Gallery above, unperceived.*

SCENE XVI

QUEEN ISEULT, BRANGWAIN, ISEULT THE
WHITEHANDED, TRISTRAM, AND CHANTERS.

QUEEN ISEULT

What do they say? And who is she, Brangwain?
Not my suspicion hardened into mould
Of flesh and blood indeed?

BRANGWAIN
I cannot hear.

TRISTRAM

I have no more to say or do with thee;
I'd fade your face to strangeness in mine eyes!
Your father dealt me illest turn in this,
Your name, too, being the match of hers! Yea, thus
I was coerced. I never more can be
Your bed-mate – never again.

ISEULT THE WHITE H.
How, Tristram mine?

What meaning mete you out by that to me?
You only say it, do you? You are not,
Cannot be, in true earnest – that I know!
I hope you are not in earnest? – Surely I,
This time as always, do belong to you,
And you are going to keep me always yours?
I thought you loved my name for me myself,
Not for another; or at the very least
For sake of some dear sister or mother dead,
And not, no—

                    (*She breaks down.*)

TRISTRAM

I spoke too rawly, maybe; mouthed what I
Ought only to have thought. But do you dream
I for a leastness longer could abide
Such dire disastrous lying? – Back to your ship;
Get into it; return by the aptest wind
And mate with another man when thou canst find him,
Never uncovering how you cozened me:
His temper might be tried thereby, as mine!

ISEULT THE WHITE H.

No, no! I won't be any other's wife!
How can a thing so monstrous ever be?

TRISTRAM

If I had battened in Brittany with thee—

ISEULT THE WHITE H.

But you don't *mean* you'll live away from me,
Leave me, and henceforth be unknown to me,
O you don't surely? I could not help coming;
Don't send me away – do not, do not, do so!

            (QUEEN ISEULT *above moves restlessly.*)

Forgive your Iseult for appearing here,
Untoward seem it! For I love you so
Your sudden setting out was death to me
When I discerned the cause. Your sail smalled down:

I should have died had I not followed you.
Only, my Tristram, let me be with thee,
And see thy face. I do not sue for more!

QUEEN ISEULT (*above*)
She has no claim to importune like that,
And gloss her hardihood in tracking him!

TRISTRAM
Thou canst not haunt another woman's house!

ISEULT THE WHITE H.
O yes I can, if there's no other way!
I have heard she does not mind. I'd rather be
Her bondwench, if I am not good enough
To be your wife, than not stay here at all, –
Aye, I, the child of kings and governors,
As luminous in ancestral line as she,
Say this, so utter my abasement now!
– Something will happen if I go away
Of import dark to you (no matter what
To me); and we two should not greet again!
– Could you but be the woman, I the man,
I would not fly from you or banish you
For fault so small as mine. O do not think
It was so vile a thing. I wish – how much! –
You could have told me twenty such untruths,
That I might then have shown you *I* would not
Rate them as faults, but be much joyed to have you
In spite of all. If you but through and through
Could spell me, know how staunch I have stood, and am,
You'd love me just the same. Come, say you do,
And let us not be severed so again.

QUEEN ISEULT (*above*)
I can't bear this!

ISEULT THE WHITE H.
All the long hours and days
And heavy gnawing nights, and you not there,

But gone because you hate me! 'Tis past what
A woman can endure!

> TRISTRAM (*more gently*)
>> Not hate you, Iseult.
But, hate or love, lodge here you cannot now:
It's out of thinking.
>>>> (*Drunken revellers heard.*)
>>> Know you, that in that room
Just joining this, King Mark is holding feast,
And may burst in with all his wassailers,
And that the Queen—

> QUEEN ISEULT (*above*)
>> He's softening to her. Come!
Let us go down, and face this agony!
>> (QUEEN ISEULT *and* BRANGWAIN *descend from the Gallery.*)

> ISEULT THE WHITE H.
O, I suppose I must not! And I am tired,
Tired, tired! And now my once-dear Brittany home
Is but a desert to me.
>>> (QUEEN ISEULT *and* BRANGWAIN *come forward.*)
>>> – Oh, the Queen!
Can I – so weak – encounter—

> QUEEN ISEULT
>> Ah – as I thought,
Quite as I thought. It is my namesake, sure!
(ISEULT THE WHITE H. *faints. Indecision.* BRANGWAIN *goes to her.*)
Take her away. The blow that bruises her
Is her own dealing. Better she had known
The self-sown pangs of prying ere she sailed!

BRANGWAIN *carries her out,* TRISTRAM *suddenly assisting at the last
moment as far as the door.*

> CHANTERS: MEN (*as she is carried*)
>> Fluttering with fear,
>> Out-tasked her strength has she!

Loss of her Dear
Threatening too clear,
Gone to this length has she!
Strain too severe!

SCENE XVII

QUEEN ISEULT, TRISTRAM, AND CHANTERS.

QUEEN ISEULT (*after restlessly watching* TRISTRAM
render aid and return)
So, after all, am I to share you, then,
With another, Tristram? who, I count, comes here
To take the Castle as it were her own!

TRISTRAM
Sweet Queen, you said you'd let her come one day!
However, back she's going to Brittany,
Which she should not have left. Think kindly of her,
A weaker one than you!

QUEEN ISEULT
What, Tristram; what!
O this from you to me, who have sacrificed
Honour and name for you so long, so long!
Why, she and I are oil and water here:
Other than disunite we cannot be.
She weaker? Nay, I stand in jeopardy
This very hour—
(*Noise of* MARK *and revellers.*)
Listen to him within!
His stare will pierce your cloak ere long – or would
Were he but sober – and then where am I?
Better for us that I do yield you to her,
And you depart! Hardly can I do else:
In the eyes of men she has all claim to thee
And I have none. Yes, she possesses you! –
(*Turning and speaking in a murmur.*)
– Th'other Iseult possesses him, indeed;

And it was I who set it in his soul
To seek her out! – my namesake, whom I felt
A kindness for – alas, I know not why!

(*Sobs silently.*)

CHANTERS: WOMEN
White-Hands did this,
Desperate to win again
Back to her kiss
One she would miss! –
Yea, from his sin again
Win, for her bliss!

CHANTERS: M. AND W.
Dreams of the Queen
Always possessing him
Racked her yestreen
Cruelly and keen –
Him, once professing him
Hers through Life's scene!

Re-enter BRANGWAIN.

SCENE XVIII

TRISTRAM, QUEEN ISEULT, BRANGWAIN,
AND CHANTERS.

BRANGWAIN *stands silent a few moments, till* QUEEN ISEULT *turns and looks demandingly at her.*

BRANGWAIN
The lady from the other coast now mends.

QUEEN ISEULT (*haughtily*)
Give her good rest. (*Bitterly*) Yes, yes, in sooth I said
That she might come. Put her in mine own bed:
I'll sleep upon the floor!

[*Exit* BRANGWAIN.

TRISTRAM
'Tis in your bitterness,
My own sweet Queen, that you speak thus and thus!

Enter KING MARK *with* SIR ANDRET *to the Gallery, unperceived.*

SCENE XIX

KING MARK AND SIR ANDRET (*above*):
QUEEN ISEULT, TRISTRAM, AND CHANTERS.

SIR ANDRET (*to* KING MARK)
See, here they are. God's 'ounds, sure, it was he,
That harper I misdoubted once or twice;
But straight forgot again till I beheld
His wife awaiting him below in tears,
Who split the plot against your husbandhood
While you have been at toss-cup with your knights,
No mischief dreaming!

TRISTRAM
But, my best-beloved,
Forgo these frets, and think of Joyous Gard!
(*Approaches her.*)

QUEEN ISEULT (*drawing back*)
Nay, no more claspings! And if it should be
That these new meetings operate on me
(You well know what I am touching on in this)
Mayhap by th'year's end I'll not be alive,
The which I almost pray for—

KING MARK (*above*)
Yea, 'tis so!
Their dalliances are in full gush again,
Though I had deemed them hindered by his stay,
And vastly talked-of ties, in Brittany.

SIR ANDRET

Such is betokened, certes, by their words,
If we but wit them straight.

TRISTRAM

O Queen my Love,
Pray sun away this cloud, and shine again;
Throw into your ripe voice and burning soul
The music that they held in our aforetime:
We shall outweather this!
(*Enter* DAMSEL *with a letter.*)
Who jars us now?

SCENE XX

QUEEN ISEULT, TRISTRAM, DAMSEL, KING
MARK, SIR ANDRET, AND CHANTERS.

DAMSEL (*humbly*)

This letter, brought at peril, noble Knight,
King Mark has writ to our great Over-King –
Aye, Arthur – I the bearer. And I said,
'All that I *can* do for the brave Sir Tristram
That do will I!' So I unscreen this scroll
(A power that chances through a friendly clerk).
In it he pens that as his baneful foe
He holds Sir Tristram, and will wreak revenge
Thrice through his loins and scale his heart from him
As soon as hap may serve.

KING MARK *descends from Gallery and stands in the background,* SIR
ANDRET *remaining above.*

QUEEN ISEULT (*aside to* TRISTRAM *with misgivings*)

These threats of Mark against you quail my heart,
And daunt my sore resentment at your wounds
And slights of late! O Tristram, save thyself,
And think no more of me!

TRISTRAM

Forget you – never!
(*Softly*) Rather the sunflower may forget the sun!

(*To* DAMSEL) Wimple your face anew, wench: go unseen;
Re-seal the sheet, which I care not to con,
And send it on as bid.

> [*Exit* DAMSEL.

SCENE XXI

QUEEN ISEULT, TRISTRAM, KING MARK,
SIR ANDRET, AND CHANTERS.

TRISTRAM
Sure, Mark was drunk
When writing such! Late he fed heavily,
And has, I judge, roved out with his boon knightage
Till evenfall shall bring him in to roost.

QUEEN ISEULT
I wonder! . . . (*nestling closer*) I've forebodings, Tristram dear;
But, your death's mine, Love!

TRISTRAM
And yours mine, Sweet Heart! . . .
– Now that the hall is lulled, and none seems near,
I'll keep up my old minstrel character
And sing to you, ere I by stealth depart
To wait an hour more opportune for love. –
I could, an if I would, sing jeeringly
Of the King; I mean the song Sir Dinadan
Made up about him. He was mighty wroth
To hear it.

QUEEN ISEULT
Nay, Love; sadness suits you best. . . .
Sad, sad are we: we will not jeer at him:
Such darkness overdraws us, it may whelm
Us even with him my master! Sing of love.
(TRISTRAM *harps a prelude.*)
I hope he may not heel back home and hear!

TRISTRAM (*singing and playing*)

I

Yea, Love, true is it sadness suits me best!
Sad, sad we are; sad, sad shall ever be.
What shall deliver us from Love's unrest,
And bonds we did not forecast, did not see!

II

If, Love, the night fall on us, dark of hope,
  Let us be true, whatever else may be;
Let us be strong, and without waver cope
  With heavy dooms, dooms we could not foresee!

QUEEN ISEULT

Yea, who will dole us, in these chains that chafe,
Bare pity! – O were ye my King – not he!
      (*She weeps, and he embraces her awhile. Scene darkens.*)

TRISTRAM (*thoughtfully*)

Where is King Mark? I must be soon away!
                        (*Scene darkens more.*)

KING MARK, *having drawn his dagger, creeps up behind* TRISTRAM.

KING MARK (*in a thick voice*)

He's in his own house, where he ought to be,
Aye, here! where thou'lt be not much longer, man!

He runs TRISTRAM *through the back with his dagger.* QUEEN ISEULT *shrieks*
TRISTRAM *falls,* QUEEN ISEULT *sinking down by him with clasped hands*
SIR ANDRET *descends quickly from the Gallery. Sea heard without. At-*
tendants enter and surround the Queen and TRISTRAM.

TRISTRAM (*weakly*)

From you! – against whom never have I sinned
But under sorcery unwittingly,
By draining deep the love-compelling vial
In my sick thirst, as innocently did she! . . .
          (*Turning to* QUEEN ISEULT)
My one clear light, my lady and my all,
Faithful to death and dim infinity. . . .

                              (*Kisses her.*)

        (Turning again to KING MARK)

This, when of late you sent for me, before
I went to Brittany, to come and help you!
'Fair nephew,' said you, 'here upswarm our foes;
They are stark at hand, and must be strongly met
Sans tarriance, or they'll uproot my realm.'
'My power,' said I, 'is all at your command.'
I came. I neared in night-time to the gate,
Where the hot host of Sessoines clung encamped;
Killed them at th'entrance, and got in to you,
Who welcomed me with joy. I forth'd again,
Again slew more, and saved the stronghold's fame!
Yet you *(weaker)* requite me thus! You might – have fought me!
        (KING MARK *droops his head in silence.*)

SIR ANDRET

O fie upon thee, traitor, pleading thus!
It profits naught. To-day here sees thee die!

TRISTRAM

O Andret, Andret; this from thee to me –
Thee, whom I onetime held my fastest friend;
Wert thou as I, I would not treat thee so!
        (SIR ANDRET *turns aside and looks down.*)
(Weaker.) Fair Knights, bethink ye what I've done for
   Cornwall, –
Its fate was on my shoulder – and I saved it! –
Yea, thick in jeopardies I've thrust myself
To fame your knighthood! – daily stretched my arm
For – the weal – of you – all!
        [TRISTRAM *dies.*

QUEEN ISEULT
    (springing up, the King standing dazed)

O murderer, husband called! – possest of me
Against my nature and my pleading tears,
When all my heart was Tristram's – his past wording,
To your own knowledge. Now this mute red mouth

You've gored in my Belovéd, bids me act:
Act do I then. So out you – follow him!

She snatches KING MARK'S *dagger from his belt and stabs him with it.*
KING MARK *falls and dies.*

QUEEN ISEULT

Thus. Done! My last deed – save my very last –
To null myself, as if I never had been! . . .
O living years, what sharp entrancements, tears,
Are yours – who are yet but Death with Tristram gone.
– I have lived! I have loved! O I have loved indeed:
Not Heaven itself could size my vast of love!

(*She rushes out.*)

SIR ANDRET, *stooping and finding the King dead, follows after the Queen.
A few moments' pause during which the sea and sky darken yet more,
and the wind rises, distant thunder murmuring. Torches are moving
about in the shadows at the back of the scene. Enter* WATCHMAN; *next*
BRANGWAIN.

SCENE XXII

WATCHMAN AND CHANTERS, WITH THE DEAD
KING AND TRISTRAM; THEN BRANGWAIN.

WATCHMAN

She's glode off like a ghost, with deathly mien;
It seems toward the sea, – yes, she – the Queen.

They turn and look. QUEEN ISEULT'S *form is seen in the gloom to be mounting the parapet. Standing on it she turns, and waves her arm towards the
Castle, as though bidding it farewell. She then faces the Atlantic, and
leaps over. A cry of dismay comes from all.*

BRANGWAIN (*entering hurriedly*)

She's swallowed up, and Tristram's brachet with her! . . .
What have we here? . . . Sir Tristram's body? O!

CHANTERS: MEN. (BRANGWAIN *standing
and gradually drooping during their chant*)
Alas, for this wroth day!
She's leapt the ledge and fallen
Into the loud black bay,
Whose waters, loosed and swollen,

Are spirting into spray!
She's vanished from the world,
Over the blind rock hurled;
And the little hound her friend
Has made with her its end!

CHANTERS: WOMEN
Alas, for this wroth day!
Our Tristram, noble knight,
A match for Arthur's might,
Lies here as quaking clay.
This is no falsehood fell,
But very truth indeed
That we too surely read!
Would that we had to tell
But pleasant truth alway!

BRANGWAIN (*arousing and gazing round in
the semi-darkness*)
Here's more of this same stuff of death. Look down –
What see I lying there? King Mark, too, slain?
The sea's dark noise last night, the sky's vast yawn
Of hollow bloodshot cloud, meant murder, then,
As I divined!

Enter ISEULT THE WHITEHANDED, *Queen's Ladies, Retainers, Bower-
women, and others.*

SCENE XXIII

ISEULT THE WHITEHANDED, BRANGWAIN,
QUEEN'S LADIES, ETC., AND CHANTERS.

ISEULT THE WHITE H.
I heard her cry. I saw her leap! How fair
She was! What wonder that my brother Kay
Should pine for love of her. . . . O she should not
Have done it to herself! Nor life nor death
Is worth a special quest.
(*She sees* TRISTRAM'S *body.*)

What's this – my husband?
My Tristram dead likewise? *He* one with *her*?
                    (*She sinks and clasps* TRISTRAM.)

CHANTERS: M. AND W.
Slain by King Mark unseen, in evil vow,
Who never loved him! Pierced in the back – aye, now,
By sleight no codes of chivalry allow!

ISEULT THE WHITE H.
And she beholding! *That* the cause wherefor
She went and took her life? He was not hers. . . .
Yet did she love him true, if wickedly!

Re-enter SIR ANDRET, *with other Knights, Squires, Herald, etc.*

SCENE XXIV

ISEULT THE WHITEHANDED, BRANGWAIN, SIR
ANDRET, ETC., AND CHANTERS.

SIR ANDRET (*saturninely*)
Nor sight nor sound of her! A Queen. 'Od's blood,
Her flaws in life get mended by her death,
And she and Tristram sport re-burnished fames!

ISEULT THE WHITE H.
(*regarding* MARK'S *body*)
And the King also dead. My Tristram's slayer.
Yet strange to me. Then even had I not come
Across the southern water recklessly
This would have shaped the same – the very same.
                    (*Turning again to* TRISTRAM.)
Tristram, dear husband! O! . . .
                    (*She rocks herself over him.*)
What a rare beauteous knight has perished here
By this most cruel craft! Could not King Mark
If wronged, have chid him – minded him of me,
And not done this, done this! Well, well; she's lost him,
Even as have I. This stronghold moans with woes,

And jibbering voices join with winds and waves
To make a dolorous din! . . .

(They lift her.)

Aye, I will rise –
Betake me to my own dear Brittany –
Dearer in that our days there were so sweet,
Before I knew what pended me elsewhere!
These halls are hateful to me! May my eyes
Meet them no more!

(She turns to go.)

BRANGWAIN
I will attend you, Madam.

Exit ISEULT THE WHITEHANDED, *assisted by* BRANGWAIN *and Bower-women. Knights, Retainers, etc., lift the bodies and carry them out. A Dirge by the Chanters.*

EPILOGUE

Re-enter MERLIN

Thus from the past, the throes and themes
Whereof I spake – now dead as dreams –
 Have been re-shaped and drawn
In feinted deed and word, as though
Our shadowy and phantasmal show
Were very movements to and fro
 Of forms so far-off gone.
These warriors and dear women, whom
I've called, as bidden, from the tomb,

May not have failed to raise
An antique spell at moments here?
– They were, in their long-faded sphere,
As you are now who muse thereat;
Their mirth, crimes, fear and love begat
  Your own, though thwart their ways;
And may some pleasant thoughts outshape
From this my conjuring to undrape
  Such ghosts of distant days!

Begun 1916; resumed and finished 1923.

Notes

I

Old Mrs Chundle

Hardy heard the story from the Curator of the Dorset County Museum, Henry J. Moule, with whom acquaintance began in his youth when he became interested in water-colouring. Moule was, in Hardy's words, 'an adept in out-door painting'. (See his recollections of him in *Thomas Hardy's Personal Writings*, ed. Harold Orel (Lawrence, Kan., 1966; London, 1967), pp. 66–72.) Though the story is founded on fact, as Florence Hardy told Professor R. L. Purdy, its most amusing and moving turns are obviously fictional.

He wrote the story 'about 1888–1890', and probably made no attempt to publish it: too many readers would have deemed him guilty of irreverent designs. Florence Hardy thought otherwise, for after his death she made arrangements for its publication in the *Ladies' Home Journal* (Philadelphia), where it appeared in February 1929; the editor, who must have had his information from her, announced that it was 'the only unpublished story by the late Thomas Hardy'. The same year she published it in the limited Crosby Gaige edition (New York), despite the very strong objection of her co-executor Sydney Cockerell, who, when occasion arose, thought it becoming to state his position in a letter to the editor of *The Times Literary Supplement* (14 March 1935). Whatever he thought of its humour (and the story is amusing), there can be no doubt that the story reaches a deeper reverence for humanity than any other by Hardy, and is, all in all, one of his best.

The sketching curate was suggested by Moule, whose father had been vicar of Fordington, Dorchester, for many years. Corvsgate ruin is Corfe Castle; Enckworth (as in *The Hand of Ethelberta*) is Encombe House, in a beautiful valley near the coast to the south; Kingscreech takes its name from Kingston, a village two miles south, and Creech Barrow, a high conical hill to the west, of Corfe Castle; 'plock' is a dialect form of 'block'.

Destiny and a Blue Cloak

Readers with modest expectations may be disappointed with Hardy's first short story, and find it difficult to realize that when he wrote it he was already becoming famous on both sides of the Atlantic as the author of the serialized *Far from the Madding Crowd*. The request for the story had come (through an intermediary) from the editor of *The New York Times*, in which it was published on Sunday, 4 October 1874. The narrative was written hurriedly and dispatched a week before Hardy's marriage. A few months before his death he described it as 'an impromptu of a trivial kind', and refused to have it reprinted (R. L. Purdy, *Thomas Hardy: A Bibliographical Study* (Oxford, 1954), p. 294). In 1921 Florence Hardy thought it 'unsatisfactory'. It certainly gives the impression that Hardy in 1874 did not regard the writing of short stories for newspaper or magazine readers very seriously. It is interesting, nonetheless; the conclusion makes a strong imaginative impact, and reveals an intuitive conception of female rivalry which suggests an unusual writer.

Hardy's refinement of Farmer Lovill in the more ingenious Lord Mountclere, and the adaptation of his ruse for deceiving a heroine intent on escape, in his next novel, *The Hand of Ethelberta*, clearly indicate that he regarded 'Destiny and a Blue Cloak' as nothing more than an expendable story. So too does the common use of actual place-names, since his Wessex background design began with *Far from the Madding Crowd*. Cloton is Netherbury, a small village south of Beaminster with which Hardy became familiar in 1871–2, when he assisted the architect Crickmay with alterations to Slape House (*The Architectural Notebook of Thomas Hardy*, ed. C. J. P. Beatty (Dorchester, 1966), p. 8). The mill may still be seen.

Winwood's examination success and career in India recall those of Hardy's Dorchester friend T. W. Hooper Tolbort, who had been a pupil at the private school kept by the poet William Barnes. He had a great facility in languages, but owed much to Barnes's tuition, and headed the Indian Civil Service examination list by a large margin (F. E. Hardy, *The Life of Thomas Hardy 1840–1928*, (London and New York, 1962), pp. 32, 161–2).

At the end of the first section, there seems to be an obvious mistake: Miss Lovill altered her mind about staying at Maiden-Newton. The 'long hill' from this village in the direction of Beaminster is referred to elsewhere in Hardy as Crimmercrock Lane. The use of 'antique' with reference to Farmer Lovill (VI) recalls Marlowe's lines:

> My men, like satyrs grazing on the lawns,
> Shall with their goat-feet dance the antic hay.

The 'tilt' (VIII) was a fitted canopy.

The Doctor's Legend

The opening and close provide a narrative setting which indicates that this story was written for inclusion in *A Group of Noble Dames*. Six of the stories in this collection were first published in the Christmas Number of *The Graphic*, 1890; 'The Doctor's Legend' appeared in *The Independent* (New York) the following March. Its exclusion from *A Group of Noble Dames* and its publication abroad may have been due to Hardy's reluctance to offend a local family, to the fact that Lady Cecilia's role is a minor one, and to the wormy circumstance and general gloom of the story.

In July 1891 Hardy dined at the Milnes-Gaskells' and, after hearing from Lady Catherine that the Webbs of Newstead Abbey had buried the skulls Byron used to drink from but that the place seemed to throw 'a sort of doom on the family', told her the story of 'the tragic Damers of the last century, who owned Abbey property' (*Life*, p. 237). John Damer of Came House married Caroline, daughter of the Duke of Dorset, bought Milton Abbey, and became the first Earl of Dorchester. He built a mansion by the Abbey church, and removed the village. His son married the sculptress Anne Seymour Conway, and committed suicide in 1776.

Much of the story was traditional in the Dorchester neighbourhood, and Hardy thought it 'extraordinary how firmly it was believed in by the old men' who told him it when he was 'young'. He had visited Milton Abbey in his youth to sketch its architecture, and became very interested in its history and the folk-lore and traditions of the place. In 1882 he was there with the Field Club (a branch of the original Society which provided the fictitious audience for *A Group of Noble Dames*) to hear a paper by William Barnes, the poet and rector of Winterborne Came. The church of the story stands near Came House, where the Damers lived; it was the parish church where Barnes preached, and only a mile from Hardy's home at Max Gate.

The title indicates Hardy's sceptical attitude towards the traditional story which he elaborated. He found much on the Damers in the fourth volume of his John Hutchins, *The History and Antiquities of the County of Dorset*, 3rd ed. (1861–73); more in the letters of Horace Walpole, a cousin of Anne Seymour Conway who married the tragic John Damer in 1744. In the relation of his suicide Walpole repeated a sentence he had written to Horace Mann four years previously: 'I have often said, this world is a comedy to those that think, a tragedy to those that feel.'

II

An Indiscretion in the Life of an Heiress

The story was composed from those portions of 'The Poor Man and the Lady', Hardy's first (unpublished) novel, which remained after he had adapted parts of it for inclusion in the novels which followed: *Desperate Remedies, Under the Greenwood Tree, A Pair of Blue Eyes*, and perhaps the next but one, *The Hand of Ethelberta*.

It is possible to form a general estimate of Hardy's first novel, and of several of its episodes, from a number of sources, though in his later years he could not remember how it ended.[1] Alexander Macmillan's letter to Hardy (10 August 1868), however, refers to the death of the heroine.[2] One episode is preserved in the poem 'A Poor Man and a Lady'. Like the poem, the novel was in the first person. Hardy tells us that he used his

[1] Sir Edmund Gosse, 'Thomas Hardy's Lost Novel', *The Sunday Times*, 22 January 1928.

[2] Charles Morgan, *The House of Macmillan (1843–1943)* (London, 1943), p. 89.

knowledge of Dorset and London primarily with the aim of writing a satirical 'socialistic' novel (*Life*, p. 56). In 1913, after he had decided not to include 'An Indiscretion' in *A Changed Man*, he told his publisher that the 'point and force of the original story was abstracted from this pale shadow of it'. When he prepared it in 1878 he was no longer interested in the satire of his first novel, which was sometimes farcical, generally extreme, and remarkably wide-ranging (*Life*, pp. 61–2). He had just completed the unexpectedly long and complicated task of writing *The Return of the Native* and, with preparations to make for his removal from Sturminster Newton to London, and little time left to comply with the editorial deadline of 10 March, realized that a relatively quick and easy way of producing a romantic story was at hand in giving unity to selected portions from all that remained of 'The Poor Man and the Lady'.

'An Indiscretion in the Life of an Heiress' was first published in July 1878, in *The New Quarterly Magazine* (London) and *Harper's Weekly* (New York); later in the same year it appeared in a Boston magazine. From this one can assume that it was a financial success, and that Hardy thought his adaptation worth while. It did not appear again in his lifetime. When Florence Hardy published an edition of one hundred copies in 1934, her co-executor disapproved, and not merely because she had failed to consult him (see the note to 'Old Mrs Chundle').

Unlike that of *Harper's Weekly*, the romance of *The New Quarterly Magazine* version (which Florence Hardy reproduced) is set in motion, rather abruptly, by the threshing-machine episode. As 'The Poor Man and the Lady' began with Christmas Eve scenes at a tranter's which had been revised for *Under the Greenwood Tree*, one must conclude that this opening was devised rather hastily for the magazine story. How far Hardy's style differs from the original is unknown; it exemplifies his proneness to split infinitives. It does not suffer unduly from 'the affected simplicity of Defoe's' which he found in the text of the novel, and the ending is remarkably effective in its combination of imaginative feeling and restraint. Whatever its inspiration, it would be hard to surpass the exquisite delicacy of 'death felt for her and took her tenderly'. The quotations show Hardy's early attachment to Shelley, Browning, and Shakespeare.

Will Strong, the hero of 'The Poor Man and the Lady', was in some respects like Hardy. To accentuate the class contrast, his father was made a peasant who worked on the squire's estate. Hardy's father was a local building contractor, who worked occasionally at Kingston Maurward, the original of Tollamore in 'An Indiscretion' and Knapwater in *Desperate Remedies*. Strong and Hardy were both architects who worked in London. A resemblance may be seen in their names, but, though Hardy shares Strong's political views, he was far too shy to engage in active politics. In the shorter story the hero is a schoolmaster who, like Hardy, aspired to be a writer and had thought of entering the Church. According to G. W. Sherman (*Notes and Queries*, September 1953), he was named after Sir Richard Mayne, the Police Commissioner who took unusually strong measures to preserve the peace at a working-class rally organized by the Reform League in 1866. The offices of the League were on the ground floor below those of the architect Arthur Blomfield, and Hardy was interested in its activities. As may be deduced from his poem 'Discouragement', his own sentiments are reflected in Egbert Mayne's views on class discrimination.

Hardy's romance originated from his boyhood love of 'the manor-lady' of Kingston Maurward (see *Life*, pp. 19–20, 101–2), and has all the improbability of a youthful dream. Despite realistic assessments which make it seem doomed from the start, it reburgeons rather surprisingly towards the end, nourished by the feeling that, though 'The world and its ways have a certain worth', there is 'a law of nature' which is stronger than convention.

Although Tollamore represents Stinsford and Lower Bockhampton, and Tollamore House is based on Kingston Maurward, little attempt at topographical representation has been made. Melport is Weymouth, but the other places are not identifiable, though Fairland has the hermitage associations which Higher Bockhampton had for Hardy.

Notes on the Text

PART I

Chapter 1. Epigraph: Shakespeare, *Measure for Measure*, Act II, sc. IV, ll. 1–4.
The description of the congregation in the opening paragraph is found elsewhere in Hardy: *Desperate Remedies*, ch. 12, sect. 8, and the poem 'Afternoon Service at Mellstock'. The marble monument with the winged skull and cherubim may be seen in Stinsford Church.

Chapter 2. Epigraph: Browning, 'The Flight of the Duchess', stanza VIII.

Chapter 3. Epigraph: Tennyson, *In Memoriam*, sect. LXVIII.
built by his father's father. Like the house at Higher Bockhampton where Hardy wrote 'The Poor Man and the Lady'.
dropping of lives. The 'livier' system made tenancy dependent on certain lives, generally leading to succession within the family for three generations. When the last of these tenants died, the house 'fell into hand' (became the property of the landowner) and the family tenancy expired, unless an agreement had been reached for its extension.

Chapter 4. Epigraph: Shakespeare, Sonnet 111.
Ulysses before Melanthius. Homer's *Odyssey*, bk XVII.

Chapter 5. Epigraph: Browning, 'Instans Tyrannus'.

Chapter 6. Epigraph: Byron, *The Corsair*, canto III, stanza VIII.
It is sweeter to fancy ... forgiven ... sinned. Repeated in *Desperate Remedies*, ch. 12, sect. 8.

Chapter 7. Epigraph: From the concluding observations in Thackeray's *The Book of Snobs*. The stone-laying episode is founded on that witnessed by Hardy between his master Arthur Blomfield and the Crown Princess of Germany at New Windsor (*Life*, p. 48).

And calumny meanwhile shall feed. . . . Shelley, *The Revolt of Islam*, canto IX, stanza XXXI.
Chapter 8. Epigraph: Browning, 'The Statue and the Bust'.
the law of nature. In principle Hardy was opposed not only to class divisions but also, it seems (like Shelley; see note to *Queen Mab*, canto V, l. 189, and Hardy's poem 'The Christening'), to the constraints of the marriage tie.
first met on the previous Christmas. Perhaps this was left in by oversight; it links up with the opening of 'The Poor Man and the Lady'.
The truly great stand on no middling ledge . . . *unknown*. Repeated in *Desperate Remedies*, ch. 3, sect. 2.

PART II

Chapter 1. Epigraph: From Dryden's translation of Virgil's *Aeneid* (bk v, ll. 439–42), a copy of which Hardy received from his mother in his boyhood (*Life*, p. 16). The quotation occurs in *Desperate Remedies*, ch. 12, sect. 5.
the game of sink or swim. The five-year interim period was filled in succinctly by Hardy when he prepared 'An Indiscretion' in 1878. Though he had himself made a careful study of London picture galleries, he alludes to the kind of life he had chosen *not* to follow. Referring to the period before he left London and began 'The Poor Man and the Lady' at Higher Bockhampton, he wrote: 'He constitutionally shrank from the business of social advancement, caring for life as an emotion rather than for life as a science of climbing, in which respect he was quizzed by his acquaintance for his lack of ambition' (*Life*, p. 53).
the Psalms, "And he shall be like a tree . . . *prosper"*. Repeated in the metrical form in *Desperate Remedies*, ch. 12, sect. 1.
Chapter 2. Epigraph: Shelley, 'Epipsychidion', ll. 219–21; repeated in *The Woodlanders*, ch. 28.
Chevron Square, where their town-house stood. The Swancourts' town-house was 24 Chevron Square, and the chapter which gives this information (*A Pair of Blue Eyes*, ch. 14) contains an adaptation of the Rotten Row scene in 'The Poor Man and the Lady' which Alexander Macmillan praised (*Life*, p. 58). The concert scene appears to be a repetition of that in the novel.
Chapter 3. Epigraph: From Shelley's 'When the lamp is shattered'; repeated in *Desperate Remedies*, ch. 6, sect. 1.
The narrative in this chapter seems to be a substitute for some rather farcical action in the novel (as it was remembered by Sir Edmund Gosse).
Chapter 4. Epigraph: Ecclesiastes, II 15. In London Hardy 'began turning the Book of Ecclesiastes into Spenserian stanzas, but finding the original unmatchable abandoned the task' (*Life*, p. 47).
Chapter 5. Epigraph: Shakespeare, *The Merchant of Venice*, Act III, sc. II, ll. 108–10.

this sacrifice . . . Against her wishes. The same situation is more tragically and convincingly portrayed in *Desperate Remedies*.

'Better . . . shouldst not vow . . . pay.' Ecclesiastes, V 5.

Chapter 6. Epigraph: Shakespeare, *Romeo and Juliet*, end of Act II, sc. II.

Chapter 7. Epigraph: From Edmund Waller's 'Go, lovely Rose'.

A silence which doth follow talk. Shelley, *The Revolt of Islam*, canto VI, stanza XXXI.

weak act of trying to live . . . wrestling . . . powers of the universe. Repeated in the account of Miss Aldclyffe's dying (*Desperate Remedies*, ch. 21, sect. 3).

III

These notes and outlines for short stories were first published by Evelyn Hardy in *The London Magazine*, November 1958. Whether they were preserved by accident or design is not known, and it is surprising to find that one was written on an envelope post-marked 21 March 1916, many years after Hardy had given up prose fiction in favour of verse. The first is dated 1871, and may be the earliest short story he planned. It is rather complicated and contrived, with familiar background interests. His sister had taught in schools for eight years; he himself was a violinist; and he probably imagined Salisbury Cathedral or Sherborne Abbey as the place for the extraordinary proposal. The plan suggests a greater regard for a sensational ending than for an imaginative whole. The second scheme presents a situation rather than a story; perhaps the husband's unpleasant traits were based on the drinking habits of Hardy's friend Horace Moule. How it came about that the third was written or copied long after the expiry of Hardy's interest in the writing of Christmas stories for magazines is puzzling. *A Laodicean* (1881) shows that he had been interested in gambling literature for fictional purposes; the villain William Dare studies 'Moivre's Doctrine of Chances' and tries to make a fortune at Monte Carlo.

The story relating to the violinist and composer Barthélémon clearly excited Hardy's imagination more than any of the preceding. His interest sprang from his love of the familiar setting to Bishop Ken's hymn 'Awake, my soul', which he remembered from his boyhood (*Life*, p. 10), and from the discovery that this uplifting music had been written by one who had been leader of the orchestra at Vauxhall Gardens, the popular haunt of London pleasure-seekers. His notebook and the second and third outlines indicate his interest in Barthélémon's life. Yet, attached as he was to the subject, there is little narrative in it, and it is very doubtful whether Hardy could have done better than he did in the poem 'Barthélémon at Vauxhall' which he subsequently wrote to mark the anniversary of the composer's death in 1808. The rector of St Peter's, Dorchester, knowing how dear it was to Hardy, made arrangements for the hymn to be sung specially for him in July 1921, and the poem soon followed. Hardy 'had often imagined the weary musician, returning from his nightly occupation of making music for a riotous throng, lingering on Westminster Bridge to see the rising sun and being thence inspired to the composition of music to be heard hereafter in places very different from Vauxhall' (*Life*, p. 414). In the first plan of the story the musician sees the sunrise behind St Paul's dome.

Hardy's hesitation about the fifth story is obvious. It turns on one of his typical ironies of circumstance, but he cannot decide to end it happily or unhappily. He is fascinated by the bird's-eye view technique, but this fancy presents obvious difficulties for the reader. If, for example, the sparrow can see into the mind of the bachelor, but does not know how the young lady responds, it suggests that, though not as conducive to 'pretty touches', the alternative narrative viewpoint is more sensible. The church must be St James's, Piccadilly, where Hardy's mother worshipped (*Life*, p. 235). The title 'For Want of a Word' seems to allude to the proverbial

> For want of a nail the shoe was lost,
> For want of a shoe the horse was lost,
> For want of a horse the rider was lost,
> For want of a rider the battle was lost,
> And all for the want of a nail.

This story is followed by a series of sparrow 'glimpses', only the first of which is given at some length. Like the tragic ending of *Two on a Tower*, it appears to be based on the unforgettable shock Hardy experienced in London on discovering that the lady he had loved in his boyhood had become old and grey (see *Life*, pp. 41, 102, and the poem 'Amabel'). The opening of the second recalls the strange marriage of Hardy's cousin Rebecca Sparks, who appears never to have lived with her husband. The note on 'No. 5, etc.', 'Anything suggested by what you read in the newspapers', is a reminder that truth is often stranger than fiction, and that Hardy took the substance of some of his most telling fictional details and events from newspapers, especially of the past. The outline of one of the final grim stories suggests that the author was probably right in his conclusion that 'perhaps it would suit the character of the series better to adhere to natural stories'.

Interesting though some of the above stories might have been, not one of the outlines suggests anything comparable in experimental importance to what might have developed from Hardy's London observations (see *Life*, pp. 204, 206, 210). In their present form, it seems hazardous to conclude that any one of them ranked among those he had intended writing when he decided to abandon prose fiction.

These outlines are printed exactly as they appear in the manuscript in the Dorset County Museum, with the exception that contractions such as 'wd' have been expanded and '&' has been printed as 'and'.

IV

The Thieves Who Couldn't Help Sneezing

Like many old-time tales for children, this will appear incredible to modern adult readers. Nevertheless one can be certain that it is of the type which would appeal to young readers, and prove to be hilariously amusing in its climax. The old Christmas Eve and carol associations would subconsciously reinforce the hope that all will end well. Hardy's story was, in fact, the opening one in *Father Christmas*, published in December 1877 by *The Illustrated London News*. It was therefore one of the earliest short stories Hardy wrote, at a time when his major occupation was *The Return of the Native*, his sixth novel to be published.

Vale of Blackmore. In north Dorset.

spirits from the vasty deep. From Shakespeare's *1 Henry IV*, Act III, sc. 1, l. 53, where Glendower boasts, 'I can call spirits from the vasty deep'.

Our Exploits at West Poley

Hardy's assurance that his story would have 'a healthy tone, suitable to intelligent youth of both sexes', when he agreed in April 1883 to supply it for serial publication in *The Youth's Companion* (Boston, Mass.) suggests that, after *Two on a Tower* (published in Boston the previous year), he was regarded rather apprehensively by editors as a writer of risqué fiction. 'Our Exploits' seems to have been written mainly for boys, however. It is a tale of caving adventures in the Mendip Hills of Somerset, and ingeniously structured in episodes which create surprise, wonder, alarm, the thrill of escape, and heroism. All is carefully calculated to discourage rashness. In a restrained manner the story is explicitly moral, stressing the grave consequences of meddling with what is not understood, and the value of 'perseverance in clearly defined courses' over 'erratic exploits'. Even the final feat of heroism emphasizes the danger which results from initial error.

Aimed at older readers than 'The Thieves Who Couldn't Help Sneezing', 'Our Exploits' suggests that Hardy expected them to be as scholarly as he was when he went to school. There are references to Roman history and *Hamlet*; others indicate that, though he could create the kind of adventure which would appeal to youth, he readily assumed that they could share his more academic interests, appreciating Carlyle on Cromwell, Jeremy Bentham's 'utilitarian philosophy' (on the happiness of the greatest number), and that 'poetico-philosophic strain' in the Man who Failed which might have 'led him on to the intellectual eminence of a Coleridge or an Emerson'. He takes care to explain the function of the 'white' wizard, though most readers would be unaware of the folklore which differentiates between 'black' (evil) witchcraft and 'white' (curative).

The story has a strange history. It was sent to the Boston editor in November 1883. By 1886 it had not appeared, and Hardy suggested it might be suitable for a Christmas number (Steve's reward takes the form of nineteen Christmas and New Year parties). The tale had been filed away with many others and, had the editor's son-in-law not required copy for his 'story-paper', no one knows when it would have been published. The result was its serialization in *The Household*, chapter by chapter from November 1892 to April 1893, the final part appearing ten years after Hardy planned it and accepted the contract. (For further details, see Purdy, pp. 301–3.)

The writing of 'The Romantic Adventures of a Milkmaid' in the winter of 1882–3 and of 'Our Exploits at West Poley' the following summer suggests that, after *Two on a Tower* (1882), Hardy was at a loss for a major fictional subject until he began work on *The Mayor of Casterbridge* in 1884.

V

The Famous Tragedy of the Queen of Cornwall

The play was begun in 1916, after Hardy had visited Cornwall with his wife Florence, partly to ascertain that the tablet he had designed in memory of his first wife had been 'properly carried out and erected' in the church at St Juliot. As he wrote to Sydney Cockerell on his return, Tintagel revived memories of his visit with Emma Gifford in 1872 – 'with an Iseult of my own, and of course she was mixed in the vision of the other'. He did not complete the first draft until April 1923, and yet it had been in his mind since he and Emma first visited Tintagel in the summer of 1870. 'Why he did not do it sooner, while she was still living who knew the scene so well, and had frequently painted it, it is impossible to say' (*Life*, p. 78).

Hardy was not greatly inspired by the subject when at last he attempted it, and his immediate aim in finishing it was its performance by the local Hardy Players. It was published in November 1923, shortly before their production. In the light of this performance, and the rehearsals leading up to it, Hardy made most, if not all, of the revisions and 'enlargements' which appeared in the 1924 edition. In the meantime the play had been produced in London and, with musical arrangements by Rutland Boughton, at Glastonbury. Hardy's 'imaginary view' of Tintagel Castle was drawn in May 1923; the interior sketch was prepared for the local production, and sent with the manuscript to the publishers on the recommendation of Granville Barker, 'who happened to see it' and thought it 'a great help to reading the play' (Purdy, p. 229).

Changes in the 1924 edition affected the stage directions very slightly and the text in a number of places, particularly in Scene XIII, which was divided for the insertion of a new scene in which Sir Andret learns from Iseult the Whitehanded that she has come to Tintagel in search of Tristram. Thus King Mark's suspicions of the 'strange old harper' who has appeared are confirmed. Scene XIII of the first edition becomes Scenes XIII–XV, and the play is extended from twenty-two to twenty-four scenes. Second verses were added to two songs (VII and XIX/XXI). Further additions were made to Scene XIX/XXI to strengthen the emotional climax, and the stage directions here and in the following scene were extended to create a stronger sense of growing darkness in harmony with the tragic conclusion.

Although Iseult of Cornwall has dark hair, according to tradition ('Fair' in the Prologue with reference to both Iseults means 'beautiful'), there can be no doubt that, as his letter to Sydney Cockerell indicates, Hardy associated her with the Emma Gifford of his own Cornish romance, and that memories of her (his 'lily-rose') are woven into Tristram's song at the end of Scene XI. They visited Nietan's Kieve in 1871, and it can be assumed that 'Condol's crown', a familiar landmark, had equally happy associations. In the verse added to the song sung by Tristram to Queen Iseult in Scene XIX/XXI Hardy recalls a severe crisis in their married life when he wrote 'Sept. 1896 – T.H./E.L.H.' against lines in Arnold's 'Dover Beach' which begin, 'Ah, love, let us be true to one another'. His self-condemnation is felt even more in his sympathetic portrayal of the neglected Iseult of Brittany. The link with Emma is very clear in her first appearance: 'She has corn-brown hair, and wears a white robe.' This is how Hardy remembered her from her portrait; he refers to her 'corn-coloured hair abundant in its coils' (*Life*, p. 73). His contrition may be felt in Iseult the Whitehanded's final words, with their overtones of Cornwall:

> Dearer in that our days there were so sweet,
> Before I knew what pended me elsewhere!

The play is dedicated to those most intimately connected with Hardy's visits to Cornwall and Tintagel: Emma Lavinia Hardy (*née* Gifford), the Rev. Caddell Holder, Mrs Helen Catherine Holder (Emma's sister), and Florence Emily Hardy.

Hardy's stage recommendations show that his theatrically progressive ideas are founded on the practice of the Greeks and Romans. One alternative he suggests recalls the seating in their amphitheatres. His main criticism of the English stage resembles that of Addison at the beginning of the eighteenth century: the presentation of the human passions was regarded as less important than magnificent settings, robes, and other 'real and sham-real appurtenances'. Hardy believed that 'the material stage should be a conventional or figurative arena, in which accessories are kept down to the plane of mere suggestions of place and time, so as not to interfere with the required high-relief of the action and emotions' (*Thomas Hardy's Personal Writings*, p. 139).

He had long thought that 'the rule for staging nowadays should be to have no scene which would not be physically possible in the time of acting' (*Life*, p. 234); and within a continuous action of about an hour (the scene-divisions merely demarcating changes in *dramatis personae*) he has concentrated a succession of events leading to the catastrophe. The relevant past is sketched in with an amazing economy, which seems admirable to a reader after the rather dazzling and bewildering fluencies of Swinburne. The action is simplified by Hardy's observance of the Greek unities of time and place. No messenger is employed to report the catastrophe, however; it is presented directly, and is original as far as it relates to Queen Iseult. The Chanters play the role of the Greek Chorus. If one may judge by the ending of his preface to *The Dynasts*, Hardy, in styling his tragedy 'a play for mummers', implied that it was best acted in a subdued, rather 'monotonic' manner, especially by the Chanters (shades of Cornish men and women long since dead), to suggest a kind of dream re-enactment conjured up by the magician Merlin.

There is a quaint ruggedness about much of the verse, which varies from the more flaccid to the clipped and dramatically vigorous. At times its texture is remarkably reinforced with alliteration. Generally it is workmanlike rather than inspired. In the cause of economy, Hardy is partial to archaisms and monosyllabic verb coinages (such as 'home', 'small', 'forth', 'size'). The love of alliteration and archaism can produce verbiage, as in 'What meaning mete you out by that to me ?' Lyricism in the songs is brief, and Hardy's decline in poetic vitality (he was in his eighty-fourth year when he completed the play) has been highlighted by the remarkable discovery of Richard Snell ('A Self-Plagiarism by Thomas Hardy', *Essays in Criticism*, January 1952). The scene in which Iseult the Whitehanded pleads with Tristram reminded Hardy of Elfride and Knight, first when he leaves her in Cornwall and secondly when she follows him to his chambers in Bede's Inn, London. In paraphrasing several passages of these scenes (*A Pair of Blue Eyes*, chs 34–5) for transfer to Scene xiv/xvi of the play, Hardy may have reasoned that what was convenient was justified because he was using as far as he could the most moving language appropriate to the occasion in accordance with the belief he voiced in the Epilogue. How closely he copied may be seen in the sample comparison which follows:

> – Could you but be the woman, I the man,
> I would not fly from you or banish you
> For fault so small of mine. O do not think
> It was so vile a thing. I wish – how much! –
> You could have told me twenty such untruths,
> That I might then have shown you *I* would not
> Rate them as faults, but be much joyed to have you
> In spite of all. If you but through and through
> Could spell me, know how staunch I've stood, and am,
> You'd love me just the same. Come, say you do,
> And let us not be severed so again.

'O, could *I* but be the man and *you* the woman, I would not leave you for such a little fault as mine! Do not think it was so vile a thing in me to run away with him. Ah, how I wish you could have run away with twenty women before you knew me, that I might show you I would think it no fault, but be glad to get you after them all. . . ! If you only knew me through and through, how true I am. . . . Say you love me just the same, and don't let me be separated from you again. . . . I cannot bear it. . . .' [*A Pair of Blue Eyes*, ch. 35]

> All the long hours and days
> And heavy gnawing nights, and you not there,
> And gone because you hate me! 'Tis past what
> A woman can endure!
>
> TRISTRAM (*more gently*)
> Not hate you, Iseult.
> But, hate or love, lodge here you cannot now:
> It's out of thinking.

'. . . all the long hours and days and nights going on, and you not there, but away because you hate me!'

'Not hate you, Elfride,' he said gently. . . . 'But you cannot stay here now – just at present, I mean.' [*A Pair of Blue Eyes*, ch. 35]

Glossary of Place-Names and Rare Words

Beeny-Sisters, small islands off Beeny Cliff, to the north-east of Boscastle and Tintagel.

Pen-Tyre, a headland south-west of Tintagel.

Condol's crown, the highest point (1000 feet, crowned with a prehistoric barrow) three miles east-south-east of Tintagel.

Nietan's Kieve, a striking waterfall in a wooded valley two miles east of Tintagel.

an if if	*popplestones* shingle
brachet small hound	*quirked* followed sudden inclinations
cark heavy anxiety	*recked not of* not considered
con examine	*seised of* possessing
conceits fancies	*sooth* truth
cozened deceived	*spell* understand, interpret
fetched recovered	*thrid* understand the deviousness of
God's 'ounds God's wounds	*unweeting* unaware of
(cf. 'Od's blood)	*weens* surmises, imagines
haply perchance	*wis, wit* know
holt copse	*wisht* melancholy
hurst wooded hill	*witlessly* unknowingly
mete measure	*wont* customary

KING ALFRED'S COLLEGE
LIBRARY

BIBLIOGRAPHICAL NOTES

The text of 'Old Mrs Chundle' is reproduced from Hardy's manuscript in the Dorset County Museum; that of 'Destiny and a Blue Cloak' from *The New York Times* (4 October 1874); and that of 'The Doctor's Legend' from the manuscript in the Berg Collection, New York Public Library.

'An Indiscretion in the Life of an Heiress' follows the version of the story published in *The New Quarterly Magazine* (July 1878).

'Outlines for Stories' reproduces a collection of manuscript notes in the Dorset County Museum.

The text of 'The Thieves Who Couldn't Help Sneezing' is that of the Christmas annual, *Father Christmas*, published by *The Illustrated London News* in 1877, and reprinted by the Colby College Press in 1942. 'Our Exploits at West Poley' is based on the text of *The Household* (Boston) from November 1892 to April 1893 (vol. xxv, no. 11–vol. xxvi, no. 4).

The Famous Tragedy of the Queen of Cornwall appears in its revised and enlarged form, that of the second edition of 1924.